Solving for Nic

SOUTHERN STYLE

LEXXI
CALLAHAN

Solving for Nic

This is a work of fiction. All the characters and events portrayed in this book are either products of the author's imagination or are used fictitiously.

For my husband who never thought twice about me taking this detour

and

For Sarah Frantz who showed me the way.

ACKN⊚WLEDGEMENTS

This book may be self-published but I certainly did not do it by myself.

I would never have finished without the support, hand holding, butt kicking, critiquing and generosity of Penny Watson. (@pennyromance) Thanks, Penny!

I also want to thank my beta readers. Michele, Dabney, Eagle, Sharon, and Teri-Beth. You guys, rock! Thank you so much!

Thank you to Silva Ami for the Italian translations.

And my editors, Kim, Rahab and Lynda. Your input was invaluable.

A NOTE FROM LEXXI

Solving for Nic is book two in the Southern Style series. It is not meant to stand alone. If you have not read *Sweetened with a Kiss* you may want to read it first or check out the cast of characters at the end of this book.

CHAPTER ONE

A date?

He'd brought a date?

Lizzie Sellers closed her eyes as shock and disappointment slammed into her. She took a deep breath and steadied herself. Tripping was not an option, so she stepped carefully into the sanctuary and started down the aisle.

Parts of her chipped off and died with each step. By the time she reached the dais and took three careful steps, she was light-headed and her chest throbbed from the crazed racing of what was left of her heart.

She turned, hit her mark, and found Nic Maretti in her line of sight. She couldn't look away from him, or the arm he'd casually draped behind the stunning redhead seated next to him.

He was so beautiful; his lean face a collection of hollows and angles. His sculpted mouth was at odds with his hard jawline. The combination of perfect features, tobacco brown hair and warm brown eyes was fascinating, but it was his confidence that drew her. He was always so sure of himself. The world couldn't touch him and he owned any room he occupied.

Now, his slow appraisal burned a trail along her skin until the redhead spoke to him. He glanced away from Lizzie and smiled at his date. Nic was damned dangerous when he smiled. His whole face creased and relaxed into an unearthly beauty.

She shuddered in relief when the music changed. Everyone stood and turned as Jen appeared in the doorway on Jared Marshall's arm. She was breathtaking in the sheath dress they had poured her into earlier. It had taken Lizzie fifteen minutes to fasten the covered buttons that ran the full length of the gown. Stefan was going to have a meltdown when he discovered there wasn't a zipper on Jen's dress. Lizzie couldn't help but smile. She almost forgot about Nic for a whole second.

Jen met her eyes and her expression dimmed. Lizzie straightened and pasted a bright smile on her face. It hurt but it worked. Jen smiled back and turned to Stefan. They really loved each other and Lizzie loved them. She refused to let the melodrama of her persistent, childish crush on Nic Maretti ruin this day.

It was time to grow up.

She wasn't his type. He liked to dance with her, tease her, but he wasn't interested. They had nothing in common. The pretty bridesmaid dress and killer shoes did not change who she was. She was not Nic's type.

The ceremony didn't take long. Stefan had refused a full Catholic Mass because he wasn't going to "stand up in a tux that long." He'd won the battle but lost the war when it came to the receiving line. When the ceremony was over the entire wedding party was trapped in the vestibule shaking hands with an endless line of guests since no one had sent their regrets.

Lizzie gritted her teeth again, smiled and shook hands with yet another well-meaning aunt who asked when she planned on settling down and getting married.

"You're not getting any younger, dear."

"Yes, ma'am." Lizzie wanted to point out that she was only twenty-one. She was also in a five-year graduate program and didn't have time to date. Of course, then she'd have to explain she was in the theoretical mathematics program at Princeton and no she wasn't going to teach math in high school. If she did try to explain what it meant, her great aunt's eyes would glaze over. Everyone's eyes always glazed over. She had stopped trying a long time ago. People preferred her when she was cute and ditzy.

Her aunt moved on. She was shaking hands with one of her mother's cousins when Nic stepped into her peripheral vision. She didn't know what she said or what her cousin said, because Nic and the redhead were speaking to the Bride and Groom.

As Nic and his date approached, it was impossible to keep him out of her periphery. Before long he was all she could see. Her heart stopped for a second then snapped back at triple speed. Nic Maretti should be illegal. He wasn't as tall as her father or brother, but he'd always seemed larger than life to Lizzie. He was six feet of European elegance in a custom-made Italian suit with a date who would be home on any red carpet. They matched in height and sleek perfection. There was an unspoken intimacy between them, knowing looks and half smiles exchanged, charming everyone they met.

Then he focused on her, as a mild smile tugged at his sculpted mouth, finishing off what was left of her. Without realizing what she was doing, she turned and walked away. She was almost to the reception hall before she fully grasped what she had done. Now she registered his faint surprise and the frown creasing his forehead when she was about to turn away from him. She ducked into the nearest ladies room grateful to be alone for a minute.

This was her fault. She'd addressed the wedding invitations. She addressed his to Nicolas Maretti and guest. She should have been prepared for this. No one went to weddings alone. Of course he would bring a date. Of course his date would be gorgeous. It was Nic. He was only seen with stunningly beautiful women. They probably wouldn't stay long. He'd have other plans. Plans she refused to contemplate, otherwise her skin might peel off.

It was stupid. She had no right to feel this way.

The first time she saw Nic was at her brother's best friend's wedding. Rogan had married Nic's sister, Angie. Lizzie had refused to be a bridesmaid so she was sitting with her parents when Nic Maretti walked down the aisle to sit in the reserved seating on the bride's side. From the second he'd passed by wearing a gunmetal grey English-cut suit, Lizzie had lost her mind. She'd never seen anyone like Nic before. She didn't think men like that existed in real life. And when he asked her to dance later that evening, she'd been so shocked she forgot to decline and suddenly found herself on the dance floor.

It was devastating being so close to him. Every second of that dance was tattooed on her soul. She could still remember how spicy he'd smelled, the feel of the expensive suit under her fingertips, the heat of his fingers curled around hers and the way his other hand didn't stay at her waist. He'd curved it around her rib cage and his fingers had burned across the skin the back of her dress left bare.

In the space of one song, with a simple box step and kiss on the cheek, Nic had wiped away every other man on the planet. They were all shadows. He'd walked away and Lizzie had spent the rest of the night trying to sort out what had happened. He'd pulled her out of her safe little world, into a reality she hadn't expected existed. She hadn't quite recovered her footing when she saw him again, less than a year later at his nephew's christening.

He'd asked her to dance again and had kept her on the dance floor for another song. She'd been sure she'd hear from him. She'd let herself hope. He hadn't so much as emailed her. Instead, three days later, she'd seen him plastered all over a gossip blog with Miss Texas. Then a few weeks later with Miss Arizona. Then a few weeks later with some Senator's daughter. Then the daughter of a Texas oil family.

She'd been crushed. Then furious at herself for being crushed. It wasn't like she didn't know his reputation for breaking debutante hearts while making obscene amounts of money without appearing to do any work. He was no Prince Charming and while she didn't necessarily want Prince Charming, she didn't want Casanova either.

She didn't want anyone. She didn't have time. Her course load was bad enough, but they also expected her to teach next year. This crush slash obsession whatever-it-was thing she'd had for Nic had to go. She couldn't let some overblown girlish fantasy continue to eat away at her like this. Because that's all it was.

A fantasy.

Time to put away childish things.

Besides, there was no way the real Nic would ever measure up to the ideal she'd built in her head.

Maybe she'd ask him to dance this time. Prove to herself that he was nothing special once and for all. He'd brought a date. She couldn't ask him to dance but she could find Adam and stay close to him. His band, Sugar Coma, was playing at the reception. He and Jared would switch up singing and playing lead guitar so they could take breaks. She'd dance with both of them.

Who needed some too old, too slick, drop-dead gorgeous playboy, when she could have a scorching hot rock musician who did want her? Girls lined up for blocks to get into Trick's when Adam played. They went to great lengths to get a glimpse of blue-tipped black hair and dark blue eyes. Adam had been asking her out for months. Well she was going. Starting tonight, Nic no longer existed.

He was a cloudy childhood memory.

"What was that about?" It was a minute before his PA's question penetrated Nic's brain as he stared at the space Lizzie no longer occupied.

"I have no idea." He no more understood Lizzie's reaction than he did his own feelings of guilt and worse, disappointment. He was also annoyed, because he didn't do guilt or disappointment, or anger. Except he was angry. How the hell had she tied him in such a complicated knot of emotions by walking away?

"Nic." Pam nudged him and he shook hands with the groom's parents without missing a beat.

"Glad you came, Nic." Mac Sellers shook his hand, his grip too hard before giving him a huge grin with lots of warning behind it. "My daughter's dance card is full tonight."

Nic didn't flinch. "I'll keep that in mind."

"Good to have you with us."

"Okay," Pam said, as they cleared the line. "Now what was that about?"

Nic shrugged. "He warned me off her four years ago."

"You're kidding?"

"She was seventeen, it wasn't necessary."

Pam laughed, grabbing two glasses of wine from a passing server and handed him one. Nic accepted the glass reluctantly.

"Relax. All the wine tonight is from De Santis Farms, compliments of you."

He relaxed and sipped the wine. "Thoughtful of me."

He spotted Angie across the reception hall, standing next to her husband, Ben Rogan. Their son, Zachary had been the ring bearer. Rogan had Zachary on his shoulders and Angie was talking to a bridesmaid. They were trying to reconcile and it appeared to be working. Nic hoped it lasted this time.

A flash of pale green caught the corner of his eye. Lizzie was standing near the bandstand talking to a musician. Nic stiffened when the boy with blue-tipped hair pushed one of her gold curls behind her ear. She smiled at the boy, laughing at something he said, then she leaned in and patted him on the chest.

"Nic." Pam dragged his attention back. It took longer to uncurl his fingers from the fist they were clenched in. "You okay?"

"Of course." He kept the irritation out of his voice. Of course he was okay.

Except he wasn't.

Worse, he wasn't sure why. He had no claim on her and she'd made it pretty clear a few minutes ago she wanted nothing to do with him.

Nic had never understood his reaction to her. He preferred tall women, with dark hair and long legs. Lizzie was the polar opposite of the women he usually dated. She was small, perfectly shaped for her size, with a crazy waterfall of blond curls spilling down her shoulders and ocean blue eyes...Nic had drowned in them the first time he'd met her. He'd asked her to dance, she glanced up at him and for a moment his heart had stopped.

She'd been seventeen. Her age had saved her, not the warning Mac Sellers had wasted no time in delivering when he noticed Nic's interest in his daughter. Startled she was so young, Nic hadn't danced with her again, but he spent the evening watching her pretend not to watch him. He'd left early, before he did something stupid.

Less than a year later, he'd seen her again at his nephew's christening. He danced with her again, then leaned down to whisper in her ear.

"When you grow up, *bella*, come and see me."

She'd trembled and swayed, instead of running away like he'd expected. Like he'd counted on. She hadn't wanted him to let go. He hadn't wanted to let her go. She made him feel things he'd buried a long time ago and want things he knew better than to want. He'd left the party early before what was left of his resolve melted from the warmth he found in her arms.

Their paths continued to cross at random parties and family functions. He always asked her to dance, she always said yes. She always made it clear she didn't want him to let her go and Nic always left before the night was over. It should have gotten easier each time. He should have gotten good at it.

She was so sweet. So...innocent. So not for him.

Across the reception hall, she laughed at something the boy said. Curls escaped the complicated hairstyle she'd tamed them into and the boy pushed another one back, stroking his fingers across her cheek as he pulled his hand back.

Nic almost snapped his wine glass stem in half.

He wasn't walking away tonight.

"Nic." Pam took the glass away from him and lowered her voice. "You're enjoying this, aren't you?"

"What? The infamous Nic Maretti tied up in knots?" She shrugged her elegant shoulders and signaled another server for more wine. "You have no idea."

He watched Lizzie reluctantly leave the musician and make her way to the huge display of berries. It took her a minute to get there because she had to stop and speak to so many people. Nic glanced back at the blue-haired musician who was watching Lizzie closely. He frowned, feeling like he'd been punched in the gut. Maybe she wasn't that innocent anymore.

"I can fire you, you know," Nic said, his attention never leaving Lizzie.

Pam coughed back a laugh. "You won't last forty-eight hours. You'll beg me to come back and I'll make you double my salary. You're better off just putting up with my mouth. Besides, right now, you should probably go get some strawberries."

He smiled. She was always right. He did need some strawberries.

When he joined Lizzie at the strawberry display, the berry she held under the chocolate fountain tumbled into the basin.

"Here." He grabbed another stick, speared the strawberry then set it on her plate. He speared a second strawberry, swirled it under the chocolate before placing it next to the other. "Save me a dance later?"

Her breathy reply caught him off guard. "I'm with someone."

"Who?" The word ripped out of him before he could help it. "The musician?"

She continued to ignore him as she scooped blueberries onto her plate.

Annoyed, he leaned in. "You always dance with me."

She stepped away, the blueberries trembling on the plate. He took the plate and set it down before she dropped it. Catching her hand before she could pull away, he stroked his thumb across the backs of her fingers. Her breath hitched and he swallowed back a satisfied smirk. So she wasn't oblivious to him. Good.

"Unless you really don't want to dance with me."

"Won't your date mind?"

"Not if she wants to keep her job."

"What?" She breathed out the words, her voice lower than it should be, stirring up things better left alone.

Nic smiled slowly. She was jealous. "She works for me, *bella.*"

"You hired a date? Like an escort?"

Nic's smile died. Did she think he would have to hire a date? "No." The denial was harsher than he meant it. "She's my assistant. I don't take dates to weddings. It sends the wrong message."

The tiny smile tugging at her mouth told him she knew she'd gotten to him and she'd done it on purpose. Her mischievous smile was infectious and the anger and indignation melted away. It was replaced by the overwhelming urge to taste and touch. His mouth burned. His fingertips tingled. Nic had never been ruled by his baser instincts, no matter how much he wanted something, so he didn't reach out and push the escaping curls back. He didn't tug her closer and pull her into him so he could feel her body tremble. He didn't let his fingers curve around the pale skin of her neck, or taste her lush bottom lip, but he wanted to.

He had to clear his throat to continue. "Who are you with?"

"No one."

He should not be so relieved. "I'll find you later. We'll dance."

"Okay."

He let her go, but made sure he did not lose sight of her. He didn't try to follow the conversation around his table although Pam tried to keep him clued in a few times.

Instead, he watched Lizzie move from table to table, talking to elderly relatives, covering strawberries in chocolate for a growing line of children. She laughed, held the berries under the chocolate fountain little hands couldn't reach. One child tried to grab a strawberry too quickly and it splattered chocolate across the front of her dress. Nic held his breath, waiting for her smile to give away to exasperation or worse, anger. A second later he was holding his breath as she laughed, raked a finger across the stain and tasted it. He wasn't close enough to hear what she said to him, but Nic could hear the young boy laughing.

Lizzie dropped down to the kid's level and hugged him tight. When she straightened a caterer had arrived and put someone else in charge of the strawberries. The caterer handed her a damp cloth and she dabbed at the stain, but her expression never flickered. The women he knew would have gone nuts if chocolate had been smeared across their dress. His stepmother or sister would already be halfway back to their hotel in a panic. Nic couldn't believe she genuinely wasn't upset.

She was smiling when she snagged a wine bottle on the way to the bride and groom's table. She filled everyone's wine glass before sitting down. They were ribbing her about the chocolate but her smiles got brighter.

She was too good to be true. No one was that sweet. Or cute. Nic didn't do cute.

"She's not your type." Pam distracted him.

Startled, he realized they were alone at the table. Couples had started dancing, including Angie and Rogan with Zachary perched on Rogan's shoulders. His nephew was oblivious to his parents' on-again-off-again separation.

Nic knew what it was like to be a child caught up in an adult dispute. He refused to let Zachary endure the same helpless fear when everyone fought for control of your life without thinking twice about what was good for you. No, the moment his nephew was affected by his parents' inability to grow up, Nic planned to step in.

"Have you decided what you're going to do?" Pam asked, pulling his attention back to her. "I'm asking because I've gotten another text from your father's PA."

"I'm not giving them an answer until Monday," Nic reminded her. "If he texts again, the answer is no."

"You're going to give the old man a heart attack."

Nic sipped his wine and swallowed down the bitter anger he'd been trying to ignore for the last two weeks. He'd known Andreas Maretti had no head for business. He'd recently lost a huge deal with a Russian oil company to Mac Sellers and now Maretti Oil was on the verge of bankruptcy. Nic couldn't understand how Andreas had squandered the fortune his second wife brought to their marriage, but now that it had happened, he couldn't say he was surprised.

Andreas Maretti loved money. He loved to spend it, but had no idea how to make it.

Nic accepted he was partially to blame for Andreas losing the deal, but that deal had never been Andreas' to lose. Now, as much as he despised the idea of giving the old man one red cent, he couldn't watch his sister and her son lose their inheritance. He watched Angie and Rogan dance. Their son's cheek rested on Rogan's head as the little boy tried not to fall asleep. No, he couldn't let Maretti Oil fail.

"Wait." Nic set his wine glass down and Pam paused typing on her phone. "Tell him I'll be there Monday morning. We'll sort it out."

Pam made no effort to conceal her shock. "You are supposed to be on a flight to Hong Kong Monday morning."

"Delay it for a few days."

"I can't believe you are going to bail him out."

"I can't either…" Distracted by a familiar flash of green, Nic turned and Lizzie was all he could see. She was dancing with her father, who for such a big man was light on his feet.

Nothing had changed over the years. She looked innocent and untouchable. He couldn't help remembering how sweet she'd been the first time they'd danced. When he'd pulled her into his arms she fit like she'd been made for him.

"She's very young," Pam said before he could take a step.

He hesitated. "Yes."

"She has worked this entire room without once glancing at this table." Pam traded her phone for her wineglass. "She's too sweet for you, Nic."

He nodded again. She'd get no argument from him.

"You're not going to do the smart thing, are you?" She sighed, shaking her head when he said,

"No."

She pushed away from the table and held her hand out for him. "Dance with me first before you jump off that cliff."

Pam was right. He should leave her alone.

He wasn't going to.

CHAPTER TWO

"Nic Maretti has been watching you all evening. You want to tell me what that's about?"

"Your imagination." Lizzie evaded as she danced with her father.

"He's not for you. You have a brilliant career ahead of you and do not need the distraction. He's too old and too much of a player."

"He's not that much older."

Mac huffed. "He's a decade older, but, Lizzie love, it wouldn't matter if you were the same age. He won't like it when he finds out how smart you are. I know I didn't like it when I found out you're smarter than me."

"I'm not smarter than you. You always beat me at chess."

"You let me win." Mac's voice gentled, making the conversation harder to bear. "He's looking for an ornament. An undemanding girl who spends most of her time getting ready for him. Not researching millennium problems and trying to solve the secrets of the universe. His ego won't take it."

She tried to laugh, but it was a forced, choked noise. Because she knew her dad was right. Nic would never be interested in someone like her. "You know—" she cleared her throat, "—if he'd ever asked me out I might pay attention to what you're saying."

Mac laughed. "Stubborn little cuss, aren't you?"

"You've obviously confused me with Stefan."

"Stefan wishes he was as stubborn as you. Maretti has not asked you out because I made it clear at Rogan's wedding that you were too young and off-limits."

"You did not," Lizzie cried. "Tell me you didn't."

She tried to stop moving but Mac kept them going on the dance floor. "Damn sure did and again at Zachary's christening. He was smart enough to walk away then too. You're twenty-one now. I'm staying out of it, but, sweetheart, he's all wrong for you. I'm asking you to tell him no."

"You're worried about nothing." Lizzie tried to lighten her voice but her throat was too tight.

"I don't think so." The music started to slow down. "One more thing, baby girl, I'm asking you politely to say no for his sake too. Because when he hurts you, I will tear him limb from limb and you don't want his blood on my hands, do you, sweetie?"

"Okay," she agreed, needing the embarrassing conversation to end.

"Good." The music slowed to a stop and Mac glanced past her. "Maretti."

"Sellers," Nic rumbled from behind her, sending the hairs on the back of her neck to attention.

"Hmm." Mac gave Nic a look that sent most men running. Lizzie swallowed hard, surprised when Nic held his ground. Mac turned to her. "Remember what we talked about."

As soon as Mac was out of earshot, Nic held out his hand for her. "Let me guess, I'm too old for you?"

Caught off guard, she laughed. "Maybe."

Nic eased her into his arms before she could protest. Not that she wanted to protest. The world faded to a distant memory. The heat of his body and his spicy lime scent had the same effect as a bunch of tequila shots.

"Did he really warn you off me?" Lizzie cringed.

Nic shrugged. "He did. It was refreshing. I'm used to society parents shoving their daughters at me, not trying to keep me away."

"We're not exactly society, are we?"

He tightened his arm around her. "I think the four hundred-odd people attending this wedding would disagree with you."

The hand at the small of her back pressed against her before she could move away. She melted into him and tried not to think about the four hundred people she wished weren't in the room with them.

"Lizzie, relax." The gentleness in his voice made it worse.

"How?"

He leaned down, brushing his mouth across her forehead and setting off a chain reaction inside her. She would've jerked back if he hadn't tightened his hold on her again.

The hand at her back stroked her lightly. "It's okay, dance with me."

This wasn't a simple dance. Nothing was simple about being in Nic's arms. She forgot reality. The connection between them felt so real it was easy to forget it was an illusion.

"I'm in town for a few days." The music slowed. "Let me take you out to dinner."

Her forehead hit his chest as every cell in her body screamed yes. YES! Then she remembered what her father had said. "My life's kind of complicated right now."

Nic flinched. "That's my line. It's a good one too but it won't work this time." His mouth brushed the top of her head. "You know as well as I do it's only a matter of time."

"Can I think about it?"

He nodded with a wry smile. "Yes. Think about where you'd like to go to dinner."

She glanced sideways as Jen and Stefan moved past. They both had their eyes closed and were lost in each other. Her chest tightened, and she blinked back tears. She loved them both and she was happy for them, but things would be different now.

"They seem happy." Nic's hand stroked up her spine, soothing her into him again.

"They are," Lizzie agreed. "Finally."

"Finally?" He sounded surprised.

She took a deep breath, not wanting to think about how Judge Robicheaux and his granddaughter Madlyn had tried to break up Stefan and Jen. Anyone could see they were made for each other.

"Jen's been through a lot. Her entire family was killed when we were kids."

"I know about the accident. Madlyn was engaged to Robert Taylor when he was killed."

"Madlyn?" Lizzie missed a step and he paused. "You know Madlyn Robicheaux?"

Nic's smile was bland, but his eyes narrowed on her. "Yes, for a long time. She introduced me to your brother and Rogan when I first invested in their company."

All the magic around her started to die. She hadn't known Stefan and Rogan had met Nic through Madlyn. "You're friends with her?" Lizzie choked the words out. "Do you know what she did to Jen? She lied to her, tried to convince her Stefan didn't love her. She and her grandfather have been conspiring to take over Jen's Trust. How can you be friends with—"

His mouth touched hers, cutting her off with an electric shock.

Lizzie tried to push back from him, unable to believe anyone would want anything to do with Madlyn Robicheaux after the things she had done. "They tried to have her committed," Lizzie hissed, lowering her voice as her anger rose. "I can't believe you're friends with the Red Queen."

Nic's hold tightened. A tiny chill licked up her spine, sparking off a strange heat that streamed through her. He could be dangerous, she realized. Excited when she really shouldn't be.

"She knows you call her that but I've never understood why." He said it like they were discussing the weather. "I know she can be intimidating but I don't think she's ever decapitated anyone."

"Not the Queen of Hearts." Lizzie tried one last time to pull back.

"Not going to happen, *bella*," he said softly, ramping her up from turned-on to nuclear meltdown.

What the hell was wrong with her? He was scaring her and she liked it? Maybe she had walked through the looking glass.

His smile told her he knew everything she was feeling. He opened his mouth but Lizzie beat him to it. "Don't you dare tell me to relax."

He leaned down until all she could see were his eyes. "*Bella*, the only thing you should be afraid of is getting blood on your dress if your father slips the short leash your mother currently has him on."

She bit back a smile. "That's not funny." It might not be funny, but it was ridiculous.

"Don't worry." His smile turned gentle. "We're all mad here."

Lizzie caught her breath and couldn't help returning his smile as he quoted the Cheshire cat, one of Lizzie's favorite characters from Alice in Wonderland. "You know the difference?"

"Yes, but I don't see how Madlyn compares to the Red Queen. Is it because she always wears red?"

"The Red Queen is the chess queen not the card queen. She may appear to be helping you but she has her own agenda. She's cold and calculating and will make any move she wants to."

"Ah." Nic's smile widened in appreciation. "True. You have to watch yourself around Madlyn. You might lose more than your head."

"Exactly," Lizzie whispered, not used to anyone catching on to her strange logic.

"You should tell Madlyn. She'll love it. We can discuss it more at dinner, but right now I want to hold you a little longer."

She made the mistake of looking up. He smiled that slow, sexy smile and Lizzie was lost. Why did he have to be so heartbreakingly beautiful? Why did she have to be such a sucker for gorgeous fallen angels with dangerous smiles?

"Okay."

He brushed his mouth across hers. "Any more and I won't stop, *bella*."

She nodded and melted into him, knowing there was no way she would ever get him out of her system. She floated in his arms, drinking him in and enjoying a temporary slice of heaven. This tiny moment of perfection was all she would allow herself. She couldn't go to dinner with Nic. Walking away from him when the song ended would be hard enough. Dinner wouldn't stop at dinner. How would she be able to walk away then?

Nic watched Lizzie work the room. He couldn't seem to stop. He was fascinated by the way she interacted with her family and friends. She was all smiles and laughter but her demeanor changed depending on which generation she talked to. With her elderly relatives she asked questions, nodded and listened to their answers as if she hung on every word. With her parents' contemporaries she answered their questions politely and smiled while they hung on her every word, laughing as she floated to the next group.

With her friends she let down her guard. Laughing, kidding around, and making everyone laugh, she was a human ray of sunshine who somehow escaped being annoying. There was a kindness in Lizzie, a sweetness. He'd let himself taste it in the past. Now he wasn't sure a taste would be enough.

"I kind of love her, Nic." Pam nodded toward Lizzie and her father.

Lizzie was pointing out two men sitting at the Bride and Groom's table to her father. They'd danced with other people all night, but not with each other when it was obvious to everyone they were together. Mac listened to Lizzie, shook his head in exasperation and stalked across the ballroom. He barked something at the couple and they knocked over their chairs trying to get to the dance floor fast enough to satisfy him. Lizzie hugged her dad, who brushed the whole thing off.

"You should marry her," Pam announced. Nic choked on his wine.

She patted him on the back. "Not today, Maretti, but don't wait too long."

"Do you want me to fire you?"

She grinned.

Then everyone was getting ready for the bride and groom's big exit. Lizzie appeared with a large basket full of bird seed tulle pouches and handed them out to a line of children. Even his nephew, who never stood still for any reason was listening to her as she warned them with adorable fierceness to wait for her signal before they pelted anyone with the contents of their patches. They followed her out like little soldiers.

Pam was laughing and shaking her head in disbelief. "She's good with kids."

He sighed and tried to shake off the pesky warm feeling turning him soft. Pam was right. She was too sweet for him but when they danced, the heaviness of his world fell away. Lizzie was different. That difference drew him like nothing ever had. He wasn't sure what it meant, but she was twenty-one now. No reason he couldn't find out this time.

He followed the others outside, watching as Jen stood in the back of the red convertible and threw her bouquet straight at Lizzie with such precision it was impossible for Lizzie not to catch it. Although, to her credit, Lizzie did try to sidestep but the bouquet hit her square in the chest then fell down in her arms.

The crowd roared their approval and clapped. Lizzie covered her initial horrified reaction with a bright smile. Then pulled the bouquet apart and gave all the little girls around her flowers.

Pam nudged him with her shoulder. "Seriously, I like her."

"Seriously, you can be replaced," he shot back, but there was no heat in his words.

He liked her too. She was a breath of fresh air and so lovely it made his chest hurt. Coming to this wedding had been a huge mistake. Dancing with her had been a critical error. Because for those few short minutes he held her, there'd been nothing but the music, how good she smelled, how soft her skin was and how peaceful and beautiful everything had seemed. It was a seductive illusion. Nic wasn't easily seduced, but for some reason, this time he had no desire to put up a fight.

Lizzie watched the red convertible slide away in a hail of birdseed and confetti. She swallowed back a strange sinking feeling. Everything had changed without her noticing it. She wrapped the tulle bow around her wrist and decided she was going to get Jen back the first chance she got but not tonight. Not when her friend was swept away on the fairytale she'd almost given up on.

"You need a ride?" Rogan asked as he stepped up behind her. She was turning to say yes but stopped. He wasn't alone. Angie glared at her with more open animosity than Lizzie was ready for. Nic and his assistant were standing next to her.

Outnumbered, Lizzie smiled. "No, I'm riding with Jared and Adam."

Nic's eyes narrowed on her. "Ride to where?"

"There's an after-party at Stefan and Jen's. You guys should come," Rogan said.

"They aren't leaving on their honeymoon?" Nic asked.

"Not until next month." Rogan winked at her and Lizzie couldn't help but smile. He and Jen were up to something. They had a big surprise planned for Stefan. She suspected it had to do with the Iron Man World Championship. Stefan hadn't been able to run in the New Orleans Iron Man to qualify and he was refusing to try another race. He claimed to be over it but they all knew better.

"Nic can drop me and Zachary home on his way back to the hotel," Angie said to Rogan. "You go ahead."

Lizzie flinched as Rogan's smile died a quick death. "You're coming too."

Angie shook her head, glaring flaming daggers at Lizzie. "I'm tired and I —"

"You should go, *cara*." Nic's arm curved around his sister's waist. "We can take Zachary back to the hotel."

"Yes," Pam said, looking up. "Stacey and I are taking our kids to the zoo tomorrow. Zachary can go with us. Kevin and Rosy would love to see him."

Angie's resolve weakened and Rogan moved quickly. "Sounds like a plan." He shook the little boy still sleeping on his shoulders. "Hey, buddy, you awake? Zio Nic wants you to go with him."

Zachary straightened up with a big yawn. Nic stepped up and Lizzie's heart missed a beat as he held up his hands for Zachary.

"Come on, *mio tigre*."

Zachary shifted his weight and rolled over into Nic's arms. "Not tiger. Am boy, Zio Nic."

"Yes, and a big boy," Nic agreed.

Lizzie couldn't breathe. She'd never imagined he would be good with kids, or like them. Now, watching as he cuddled the boy and whispered things in Italian that made the sleepy boy laugh, Lizzie felt her insides melt.

Adam and Jared arrived in time to distract her ovaries from exploding. They'd changed into street clothes and had their guitars over their shoulders. They were scorching hot and should've shut down her ridiculous response to Nic holding Zachary. No such luck.

Adam slid his arm around her in an uncharacteristic possessive manner. She leaned into him and pretended not to notice Nic's reaction. Damn peripheral vision. Her skin felt funny and her heart was ready to break free. Was he angry? She tried to shake it off, then Adam's arm tightened around her and Angie suddenly became the life of the party.

"Okay, baby, you have a good time with Zio Nic," she crooned, reaching up to ruffle her son's hair. "Mind Aunt Pam and Aunt Stacey."

"You ready?" Adam rumbled, distracting her from watching Nic walking away.

"She can't ride with you, freak." Jared laughed. "Not in those shoes. They're smoking hot, Lizzie, you should change them. We're playing at Trick's later and I'm not sure you'll want to dance in those."

"Are you crazy?" Lizzie ignored the burning sensation sliding all over her. "These are my dancing shoes."

"Come on, runt." Jared twirled her around. "The night is young and music's high —"

Adam groaned. "We are not singing that song tonight."

Lizzie let them sweep her along to Jared's SUV, while Jared sang "Dancing Queen" and Adam sang "Enter Sandman" back. Their banter didn't distract her from remembering how Nic had backed his sister up and how gentle he was with his nephew. The memories burned themselves into her brain right along with the dance they'd shared tonight, the almost kiss and the other times they'd met. Pretty memories, she told herself. She didn't have time for anything else.

CHAPTER THREE

The after-party at the house on St. Charles should've been more fun than the reception. There were no elderly relatives to worry about. No children tugging on her dress, begging for strawberries or asking her to add huge random numbers in her head. She glanced around the backyard where Stefan and Jen swayed under the colored lanterns she'd made Jared and Adam string into the pergola that morning. Jared and Adam sat in the corner remaking tired old 90s songs into acoustic romance. The music blended perfectly with the sounds of street cars and the city.

It was a beautiful, perfect night. There was more food, more wine, cold beer and warm brownies. Everyone grabbed a stick when she produced giant marshmallows to roast over the copper fire pit blazing on the patio. Lizzie tried to pretend she didn't feel like the marshmallow she held over the fire. Burnt around the edges and starting to dissolve.

"It might be a little too crispy." Adam nudged her shoulder with his and the marshmallow fell into the flames.

"Hey." She forced a laugh, then handed him her empty stick.

"It deserved a proper Viking funeral." He grinned, his dark blue eyes at odds with the exotic features he'd inherited from his Japanese grandmother. Adam was all kinds of beautiful and there were girls in the city who would give up years of their life to have him smile at them the way he did at her. That she could smile straight into those beautiful eyes without her heart so much as hesitating proved there was something wrong with her.

It wasn't fair.

He pulled her to her feet. "Dance with me, Lizzie."

She let him tug her under the soft-colored lights and hold her close. She loved dancing with Adam. His natural rhythm was easy to follow. The lean body under the faded black T-shirt and threadbare jeans was hard but comfortable at the same time. His arms were reassuring and warm but it wasn't the same.

Dancing under those colored lanterns with possibly the nicest guy in the world, Lizzie hated Nic. Hated herself for not being able to shake him off and get on with her life. Nic had ruined her for all other men.

"We're playing at Trick's at midnight." Adam's breath was warm against her ear. Her forehead pressed against his chest. He rested his cheek on the top her head. Why couldn't there at least be a spark? It was a crime Adam wasn't the one. She backed up, blinking back tears and trying to move away from him before he noticed.

He noticed.

"You're killing me, Lizzie."

It would be easy to be with Adam. There was no way it wouldn't be amazing. But she would always compare him to Nic and she cared about him too much. Because she would never inflict the flaying sensation she couldn't shake on anyone else.

She had the sudden urge to go home. The bleakness ached inside her. The home she wanted didn't exist anymore; the flood waters had washed it away years ago.

"Come to Trick's tonight. I'll buy you breakfast when the sun comes up." He kept hold of her hand as they walked off the patio and into the house.

"I don't know, Lizzie," Jared chimed in from behind them, popping Adam on the shoulder and spoiling the serious expression on Adam's face. "Be careful with this guy. He has a thing for knots."

Adam's arms went out, as he spun around and pushed Jared hard. "Shut the fuck up, Marshall."

"Are you blushing?" Jared crowed with laughter as he stumbled back. "He's blushing, Lizzie. He's cute when he blushes."

"Fuck you." Adam tried to sound fierce as he caught the motorcycle jacket Jared tossed at him but Lizzie had known them too long to believe their posturing.

At least she was laughing now and it definitely felt better.

"You wish, Granger. I don't like knots. Now can we get the hell out of here before Sellers explodes? There're like a gazillion buttons on Jen's dress. Really don't want to be here when he goes all Neanderthal and starts bodice ripping."

Lizzie smirked. "She will skin him if he rips her dress."

"Come to Trick's, we'll dance." Jared twirled her in his arms.

"She's coming." Adam tried to catch Lizzie back but Jared was too fast for him and dipped Lizzie low on his arm.

When they straightened, Lizzie was officially in a better mood.

"Yeah—" Jared threw one arm over Adam's shoulder and the other over Lizzie's, "—but she's riding with me. No way is she getting on your bike in those shoes. Those shoes are hot, Lizzie. Have I told you they're hot?"

"Are you drunk?" She slid out from under his arm and turned to face him. He was talking too fast and his eyes were wild. She put her hands on his chest when he tried to brush past her. She saw a brief flash of pain before he covered it.

"Oh." She breathed out the word.

"Oh, nothing." He laughed. Because Jared always laughed. He was never serious, until he was. Then he was a tiny bit dangerous. "It's not what you think, now less talking more dancing. Let's go."

The line at Trick's was down the block and around the corner. They parked in Elliot's restaurant's parking lot, one of the few actual parking lots on the edge of the French Quarter. They walked the two blocks to the back entrance and downstairs. The walls and ceiling were vibrating from the other band. Sugar Coma had an hour before they were due on stage. They headed straight into the crush of bodies writhing on the dance floor.

She danced with them until a girl with white blond hair dragged Adam away. Jared took the opening, grabbed Lizzie and dove into a sea of people. Jared was lethal on the dance floor. Dancing with Adam was fun. Dancing with Jared was the equivalent of a spin class combined with an MMA session on steroids. Actually, it was better. Within minutes Lizzie lost herself in the rhythm and the energy sizzling through the crowd. She was burning up, but she didn't stop. Couldn't stop. Jared moved her so deep into the music she forgot where she was.

It was nothing like when Nic held her. There was no electricity, no breathless excitement, no aching longing. This was muscle and sweat and music and heat and Lizzie loved it, but it wasn't the same.

Sugar Coma took the stage but Jared stayed with her.

"You're not going to play?"

He shook his head, leaning into her. "They'll be okay for the first set."

"Are you okay?" she asked between songs.

He nodded. "I will be."

She didn't believe him. "Does Jen know?"

"No!" He jumped back from her. "No." His voice was calmer but he didn't meet her eyes. "It got real with the priest and all. They're really married." Jared exhaled a painful breath. "It's cool."

It wasn't cool. He was hurting. Lizzie couldn't believe she'd never noticed his feelings for Jen might be stronger than friendship. Jen hadn't either. She would never have asked him to walk her down the aisle if she suspected. "Jared…"

He shook his head again, as if shaking off the pain. "He loves her."

The music was building again. Lizzie had to shout. "He always has."

"It's a pain being nice to him." Then a wicked grin broke out across his devilishly handsome face. "Screw him, he has to be nice first. Now dance."

She had no idea how much time passed before Jared leaned down and whispered in her ear, "Brace yourself. Incoming."

Hard hands closed around her waist. Jared made no attempt to stop the force of nature who jerked her away from him. Instead, he laughed. "Have fun, brat, I'm going to play." He dropped a kiss on her cheek and escaped toward the stage.

The hands spun her around and she collided with a heat her body instantly recognized. She lost her breath as hungry eyes narrowed on her. There was no mistaking Nic, but it was a Nic she didn't recognize. All his smooth, detached calm was gone, replaced by a raw edginess that lent an air of danger to him.

Jared plugged his guitar in and blew the dance floor wide open. The frenetic energy cresting across the dance floor turned more sensual as Sugar Coma launched into their cover of "Little Wing."

Nic's arm went around her waist and she melted into him, losing herself in the heat of his body and the rhythm he set. Chills danced across her skin and she let the music take over. She had no idea how long they danced. Nothing else existed except the wild pulse of music and Nic. He was here. With her. Like they'd been together forever.

Her arms wound around him and held on tight. She refused to let go of him. She wanted to hide in his arms as long as possible and maybe, she'd get lucky and the sun wouldn't rise.

She lost all track of time. Forgot where they were. She sighed in protest when he led her off the dance floor toward the bar. Despite the crowd, he procured a bottled water for her and long neck beer for himself. There was something so wrong about Nic drinking a beer but he wasn't that elegant man tonight. He'd changed into jeans and a black button down shirt, his hair was a rumpled mess and he hadn't shaved either.

"How did you find me?"

"Rogan told me when I dropped by Jen and Stefan's." He finished the beer.

"Were you looking for me?" The idea made her breathless.

"What if I was?"

She opened her mouth, then realized she didn't know how to answer. She settled for a smile and hoped it was mysterious.

"You waiting for them to finish their set?" He nodded toward the stage where Jared and Adam had the crowd under their spell.

Lizzie smiled as she watched Jared crouch down and sing to a couple of girls standing by the stage. One almost fainted. Adam shook his head in disgust and played his guitar. He was as serious as Jared was crazy.

Then fingers had hold of her chin bringing her attention back to the man holding her. Jared and Adam were boys compared to Nic. Lizzie was way out of her league with him.

"The musicians. Are you waiting for them to finish?"

She tilted her head and slicked her tongue across her dry bottom lip. She loved the way he honed in on the small movement. It made all the liquid in her body start to simmer.

"What if I was?" she taunted, knowing she was poking a real live tiger. She couldn't stop herself.

Her breath caught as he moved in, backing her up against a wall vibrating with bass. He crowded straight into her personal space until nothing else existed but him. His dangerous edge was back and once again her response was seriously inappropriate. Instead of trying to get away from him, she lit up like a Roman candle.

"Tell me about blue-haired boy."

She tried to smile but she was trembling too hard. This was definitely not the elegant man she'd danced with at the wedding. This guy was ruthless and…hungry?

"He's a friend."

He relaxed but didn't move away from her. Instead his head came down, but he didn't kiss her. His mouth opened against her throat and

Lizzie's water bottle crashed to the floor, water going everywhere.

"Are you really this sweet?" The words wisped against her ear, making the tiny hairs on her body decide to tango. "You are, aren't you? Are you going to let me find out?"

"Yes." The word trembled out despite her mouth and throat feeling as dry as the Sahara.

"Then come with me, Lizzie."

"Okay." Her eyelids were starting to lose the war. The muscles in her neck were protesting and she wanted to lean into him until she was no longer in the world. Her body was going to burn to a crisp if she didn't get next to him soon.

"Don't you want to know where?"

"Doesn't matter."

His smile was strange. "Then let's go."

Her lips parted to speak as she stared up at him again. Time froze around them while they continued to move. Or they had slipped into imaginary time. Lizzie wasn't sure.

She was standing at one of the crazy crossroads life liked to throw at you. She saw her life down one road, all planned out and ready to go. Graduate School. Full Professorship. Tenure. Field medals. Finding a real unicorn or a nontrivial zero that wasn't on the half line of the critical strip. Her odds were on the unicorn.

There was another, darker road, but Nic blocked the entrance. He held out his hand, ready to drag her away from both paths. His way was the most dangerous. The devil had nothing on Nic Maretti. The devil, like the unicorn, was the safer bet. He only wanted her soul. Nic would take everything.

There was no way she could go back the way she came. If she did, she'd lie awake every night for the rest of her life regretting it. She had to go with him or she'd never get him out of her system.

Staring at him too long was like staring into the sun. Her eyelashes flickered and she smiled. Alarm bells went wild in her head, but she ignored them. "Okay."

A smile curved his sensual mouth ripping through her like shrapnel. She had been gloriously and deliciously wrong. The fantasy she'd built around him wasn't even the tip of the iceberg. Nothing about Nic was ordinary. He was pure, dark, dangerous magic, and the rest of her life could hold on because Lizzie was going. Anywhere Nic wanted to take her was fine with her.

He slid his arm around her waist then they stepped outside. The

French Quarter was in full swing. People were milling everywhere as they walked to his SUV. He'd also parked at Elliot's which surprised her. He opened the car with his remote and Lizzie reached for the passenger door at the same time he did but his hand flattened on the window before she could pull the door open.

Confused, she turned about to ask what was wrong when his mouth crashed into hers, his tongue stabbing deep as his arm curled around her, keeping her upright. She'd wanted him to kiss her for so long. She'd lost count of the nights she'd sat up in bed sweating and gasping from vivid dreams that left her tingling and disoriented.

None of it had prepared her for the reality of Nic.

Nic broke her wide open, one hand holding the back of her head, the other at her waist urging her hips forward as he pressed her back against the warm metal car door. Shock and panic warred with excitement and an unexpected rush of intense heat streamed through her body full force.

He devoured her, right there in the parking lot. There was nothing else but the taste of him, his mouth raging on hers and the hands holding her where he wanted her.

When he lifted his head, it took her a minute for her eyes to open. He didn't release her, which was good since she would've slid to the gravel-covered ground if he let go.

He lowered his head again and she instinctively pulled back. Her mouth was already starting to swell and while the ache was delicious the onslaught had made her gun-shy. His slightly crooked smile slid under her defenses, but this time when those warm, dangerous lips touched her, they were gentle. Whisper soft, as they moved over hers, in the kind of first kiss she'd dreamed of with him.

His lips tasted and searched, teasing her until she was drowning in something sweet. He tilted his head, taking the kiss deeper, invading every part of her. Reaching out to stop from falling, her hands flattened against the soft shirt covering a granite hard chest. Long fingers, twined in her hair, pulling back to give him better access and he did things to her with his mouth she hadn't thought possible. He broke the kiss and they both dragged in air.

Then he kissed her again, like he was taking his last breath. Lizzie fell…no…jumped into the kiss. Base jumped. Without a parachute. The free fall was unbelievable as she opened up and let him take everything.

Lizzie spent an eternity watching him start the car, reverse out of the parking spot and drive through the busy streets of New Orleans. She kept trying to think of something to say but all she could do was drink in his fierce expression as he drove. Silent too, he darted quick glances at her when he thought she wasn't looking. Then a valet was opening her door under the bright lights of the entrance to The Maretti Riverwalk and Casino.

Nic walked her through the lobby straight to an elevator. She leaned into him, refusing to think about what they were doing. When they walked into what had to be one of the largest suites she'd ever seen, she stopped short. The dining room table had been set for two, complete with white tablecloth, candles and delicate pink roses in a low vase.

It was lovely and romantic and everything she would have wanted on a first date. She swallowed hard when she felt his hand touch her waist.

"Breakfast?" His words brushed across the delicate skin of her ears, lifting all the tiny hairs on her body at once.

She shook her head, turning to face him as she did. "I'm not hungry."

Wildfire blew up between them. "Good." The word ground out of him and he was kissing her again. Backing her farther into the suite until she felt the edge of the bed behind her legs. Panic teased at her. This was very real. Not another dream at all.

Shock tingled along her nerve endings when he dropped to his knees in front of her and started undoing the fine leather straps of her heels. He traced the indentations left by the straps.

"Why do women insist on wearing such uncomfortable shoes?"

"They make our legs look sexy?" All the air fled her lungs, along with the last of her survival instincts.

"Your legs don't need any help."

He took her foot in both hands and kneaded away a soreness she'd forgotten was there. His hands slid up her calves, then back down again, his thumbs pushing deep into the sole of her foot until she flinched at the sudden sharp pain, then groaned at the pleasure that followed it. By the time he moved to the other foot, Lizzie was pretty sure her spine had dissolved. She couldn't sit still, and squirmed, trying to press her legs back together.

One warm hand slid all the way up her leg, and pressed against the inside of her knee. Heat flooded through her. "Stay like this." There was something low and warm in his voice that made her keep her legs still despite the overwhelming vulnerability consuming her.

His fingers continued up her legs. "You're so soft, Lizzie, but there's muscle underneath."

"My spin instructor is a sadist." She could die from this. The way his hands moved on her was electric. Darts of pain followed by pleasure sent pulses straight to her core.

Nic straightened and pulled her to her feet. "Is all of you this soft?" He turned her away from him and pressed his mouth against the sensitive place where her neck curved into her shoulder.

She felt the zipper ease down and she tried not to gasp too loudly when his fingers skimmed along her bare back. His hands moved up, curving around her rib cage. His breath caught when the edge of his fingers brushed the underside of her bare breasts. She couldn't wear a bra under the dress, not that she needed one. Now the backs of his fingers teased along the ultra-sensitive skin, causing her stomach to contract painfully. Heat flared deep inside her. His fingers continued to scorch along her skin until they reached her shoulders and tipped the straps off. The dress slithered down her body, pooling at her ankles in a soft rasp of sequins and chiffon.

He caught her forearms before she could cover herself. "Keep them there."

His palms skimmed up her rib cage again, before long fingers teased the soft swell of her breasts. A strangled breath escaped him as her whole body shuddered from the sparks shooting through her. His hands molded around the sensitive flesh, his thumbs flicking over her nipples, making them tighten and sting. Heat spiraled through her and her whole body jerked as she struggled to breathe when he rolled the hard tips between his fingers. Pain spiked sharp and sweet, shredding through her, and Lizzie shuddered, crying out before she could stop herself.

He spun her around, pulling her hard against his chest. "You should be locked up," he bit the words out before crushing her mouth. She kissed him back, running her fingers through his hair and leaning into him. He tasted too good. There was no way to get enough.

He lifted her again. "Too fast?" he rasped against her mouth, but he wasn't stopping.

She bit his lower lip. "Not for me."

He tumbled her back onto a bed and came down over her, his knee between her legs. "Last chance to say no, beautiful."

"Okay." She focused on undoing the buttons of his shirt. She couldn't wait to get her hands on all the bronzed skin. Lizzie knew his father was from Italy, but Nic had grown up in Houston. He had the slightest Texas drawl that didn't match his European style. "Do you make love in Italian?" She pushed his shirt off his shoulders, her fingers aching to rub all over the fine smattering of dark hairs covering his chest.

He caught her hand and kissed her wrist. "Let's find out."

The moment his mouth touched her, Nic knew he'd made a serious error in judgment. Not that he'd been thinking clearly all night. Lizzie had gone straight to his head, chasing away all rational thought and he'd been functioning on instinct since she'd walked away from him on the dance floor.

Now he had her here, in his bed, and kissing her was about as close to perfect as he'd ever gotten. He groaned at the simple pleasure of having her fingers sinking into his hair. All that soft skin teasing against his chest was making him crazy. He had to touch her everywhere. His hands couldn't get enough of the feel of her. He dragged away from her plush mouth, licking across the slight pout of her bottom lip, to trail kisses down her throat.

She was soft and sweet and everything he'd never thought he wanted. The small cries and moans that escaped her as he tasted sensitive flesh and traced his tongue across the indentations on her midriff were driving him over the edge much faster than he wanted to go.

He was buying her health club because her spin class instructor needed a raise.

He moved back up, catching one small perfect bud in his mouth, trailing his tongue in a hot circle and tightening his hold on her as she bowed off the bed. One hand tightened on her rib cage to hold her still as his other moved to shape the small swell. Her hand tightened in his hair and she gasped as he sucked hard and deep. His name was a breathless plea on her lips. It scorched him beyond reason.

He slid one hand down her body and between her legs. Her body arched up against his as he pushed into all the slick wet heat. He caught her surprised cry with another deep kiss while his whole body shook with some primitive pleasure he'd give some thought to in about fifty or sixty years when he refused to regret this night. She was tight, too tight, but the flames in his mind burned away a flicker of his seldom used conscience.

He caressed and worked her responsive flesh. Her soft mews of pleasure and fleeting gasps weren't enough. He wanted more. He wanted all of her. He wanted her to scream his name. She whimpered when he pulled his hand back, her hips following him until he broke the connection.

He caught her hand when she reached for him, and laced his fingers with hers with one hand while his other hand pushed her legs farther apart.

He parted the silken flesh and kissed her. He could feel her body coiling tighter and tighter. As far gone as he was, he knew he'd never get enough of her but he didn't stop. When the storm was ready to break free, her hand gripped his until he almost couldn't feel his fingers. She arched as he forced her higher. A cry flew out of her, sending heat rippling all through him.

Nic was nowhere near done. He had to see how many different ways he could break her apart and put her back together. He found himself cataloging the details and trying to remember what flick of his tongue caused which reaction or where to apply more pressure. Her response captivated him. He forgot there was more to it than her cry of pleasure when she came apart for him again and again.

As he built the next orgasm in her, he knew he was stoking a dangerous fire. This one would be spectacular and he wanted to see her face. Catch her cry with his mouth. He needed to see her eyes. He replaced his mouth with his hand, his fingers sinking deep inside her. She trembled as she moaned. He kissed his way up her body, pausing to tease tight nipples as his thumb pushed her closer to the brink.

All the oxygen fled Nic's system. Her face was damp, wrecked with tears and too many emotions to count. He kissed her again, wondering if he'd ever get enough of the taste of her. "Hold on, beautiful."

She nodded and almost smiled but took a deep breath instead. He rolled on the condom with unusually shaky hands, then moved over her. He kissed her again, fighting to hold back when every one of his instincts screamed to go deep.

He paused when he felt her stiffen at his first nudge against her.

He slid his fingers in again, teasing at her clit until she was gasping and tilting her hips up for him. When his name escaped on her next breath, Nic eased inside. "You're so tight," he whispered against her ear. "Relax, Lizzie."

"Please don't stop." The soft words broke something deep inside him. She rocked against him and Nic hissed as her body pulled him in. Air stalled in his throat and he drowned in the beautiful perfection of her flesh making way for his. He had to pause for a moment, and not to give her time to adjust to him. No, Nic paused because he never wanted to forget what it felt like being inside Lizzie for the first time. Her sweetness washed over him, stripping away years of jaded disbelief.

As it consumed him, he knew he didn't deserve this. She deserved better. Because he was taking every bit of her. He couldn't help himself. He was like an opium addict in a field of poppies. He could appreciate their beauty but he would destroy them all to feel like this.

Her arms tightened around him and he dropped his mouth to hers. "You feel like heaven."

Lizzie wasn't sure how she'd gone from the most intense orgasm of her life to having Nic so deep inside her that her body vibrated with his pulse. Relieved it hadn't hurt and he hadn't seemed to notice, she tightened her arms around his neck. She didn't want to ever let him go. "We're really going to do this?" she whispered.

He braced himself on his forearms, teasing her mouth with his. "We're already doing this."

She dragged in another ragged breath, sighing as his mouth slid across her jaw. "Good."

She tried not to tense up, expecting it to hurt or burn or worse when he pulled back. Her heart stopped when he sank back into her. Relief had her tearing up because it didn't hurt. The last thing she'd wanted him to know was that it was her first time.

He moved again and another moan escaped her. It definitely didn't hurt.

"Lizzie."

Hearing her name dragged her back into real time. She relaxed into it, opening up for him and he slid deeper. The intensity caught her off guard. She couldn't breathe, couldn't think. All she could do was feel him. He was inside her, a part of her and he was perfect.

"Beautiful." The gentle word started everything inside her spinning. The muscles in his back flexed under her fingers. He was strong but the long, powerful strokes were controlled. She wasn't sure she'd survive if he let loose. All she could do was hold on as he drove harder and deeper and changed everything she'd imagined about being with him.

Then he was reaching down between them teasing her back to the edge, whispering things that made her burn hotter. He slid his hands beneath her, lifting her up, changing the angle and Lizzie lost the battle with the emotions building in her chest. Tears choked her as she came apart. She almost missed that he was falling apart with her.

She couldn't stop shaking as he rolled them to their sides. She hoped he hadn't been disappointed or noticed she hadn't been sure what to do. She smiled when she felt his mouth press against her neck as he whispered her name again. His chest heaved and his hands didn't feel quite steady.

Not disappointed. She decided. Relief warmed through her, then he eased away from her, his body sliding free of hers and she tried not to yelp at the sharp feeling of loss and unexpected burn of raw, over sensitized flesh. He swung off the bed. She curled onto her side and watched him disappear into the bathroom. A light switched on and she blinked back the intrusion of reality.

Her body was still vibrating from his touch when she sat up, pulling the sheet with her. She drew her knees to her chin and refused to regret this. The emotions churning inside her were hard to ignore. She hadn't expected her first time to be a religious experience, but she hadn't expected it to be so intense.

This was what she had wanted. Why in the hell was she on the verge of tears?

When he slid back into bed a few minutes later and pulled her tight into the warmth of his body, Lizzie felt cold. She forced her breathing to calm. She couldn't face him yet. She was afraid he'd see the shock crawling through her like acid.

She'd wanted Nic to be her first. It had been impossible to be with anyone else because she had only wanted Nic.

Careful what you wish for?

She swallowed hard on a hysterical laugh. It had all been too much. She'd miscalculated in a big way. She'd wanted him out of her system and all she'd done was make things worse.

He rolled her to her back then, his gaze skimming over her in the low light. She forced a smile. Then the Rolling Stones started singing "Angie."

Nic groaned. "She wouldn't be calling this late if it wasn't important. I'll be right back."

He slid out of bed and a few minutes later she could hear him speaking in low tones to his sister. He was speaking in Italian, which Lizzie found oddly endearing. When he ended the call, he didn't come straight back to bed. She listened to him pour himself a drink in the quiet suite.

She feigned sleep when he returned and slid back into bed. She tried to stay relaxed as he pulled her into him. The warmth from his body and the strange safety she felt with him curved around her lulled her into a strange place between dreaming and consciousness.

Later, when she was sure he was asleep, she eased away from him, flinching as the slightest sound echoed through the quiet room.

Reality hit her as soon as her feet touched the floor. She'd had sex with Nic Maretti. In real life. Not a dream.

She'd expected to be elated, but she wasn't sure how she felt.

Now what?

Panic?

He was asleep now, but what about when he woke? What would she say? She didn't know how to handle the morning-after part.

Panic was the correct answer and it clawed deep when it hit.

What if it hadn't been great for him? She couldn't face finding out something so important to her was an ordinary hook up for him. She couldn't stay. She needed to be anywhere else in the world. Her heart and her pride wouldn't survive an awkward scene.

She eased out of bed and into her clothes. She could leave a note, but she had no idea what to say. She'd text him later, tell him what a great time she'd had. She fastened the straps on her heels in the elevator on the way down. It wasn't morning yet. Maybe her bridesmaid dress wouldn't be too out of place when she walked through the lobby.

He'd be relieved, she assured herself when a valet put her in a taxi. She was saving him the awkward morning-after scene where they pretended it meant more than it did. He'd want to see her again and she'd say absolutely. Then he wouldn't call and she would pretend it wasn't eating her alive. No, she couldn't. She had school to think about. She had her life all planned. Nic didn't fit anywhere in her plans. Not that he would want to. She wasn't his type.

No. She refused to be sorry about any of this. Now if she could stop crying, things would be perfect.

Dawn crept through the windows of the hotel suite and his cell phone was buzzing somewhere in the room. Nic didn't move. He'd been awake for a while, lying in bed with his eyes closed. He couldn't bring himself to look at the empty pillow next to him. The idea made his stomach clench and all of him ache.

He wasn't sure when she'd left. He remembered pulling her tight into his body as she'd gone to sleep safely wrapped in his arms, her even breathing lulling him into an uncharacteristically deep sleep.

The anger and emptiness churning in his stomach was real. He didn't like the unfamiliar hollowness slowly expanding in his chest.

He straightened, swinging his legs around until his feet touched the floor. This was why he had rules. He did not spend the night with his lovers. It gave them the wrong idea.

But he hadn't wanted to let Lizzie go. The sex had been amazing. Her lack of experience had been refreshing. He'd wanted to hold her and feel her heart beat while she slept.

The irony was not lost on him. The girl who made him forget all his rules had walked out on him. It made him feel...foolish and that other thing he refused to deal with. *Abandoned.*

No. He pushed out of bed and headed for the shower, anger churning away the other feelings he'd spent his whole life avoiding.

She'd done him a favor. She saved them a big uncomfortable scene. His anger was misplaced, and by the time he walked out of the suite dressed and ready to leave, he was himself again. Everything was calm and under control.

As long as he didn't close his eyes, because the minute he did the night played out again for him in full Technicolor and the hollowness threatened to consume him.

CHAPTER FOUR

"You're sure about this?" Pam repeated the question for the millionth time before they stepped into the executive elevator.

"Yes." Nic shoved his hands in his pockets, hiding his clenched fists.

"It's a lot of money." Pam's attention was fixed on the screen of her tablet as she swiped through the pages of the agreement Nic was on his way to sign. "You'll never see it again."

Nic nodded. He didn't care about the money. Money had never been an issue for Nic. He had way more than his fair share and no matter how much of it he gave away or loaned, he seemed to make more. It wasn't the money that had his stomach churning in protest. It was the hour he was going to have to sit across a conference table from the pompous bastard who took the money as his due.

Nic conceded Andreas Maretti might not be wrong but he was tired of being constantly reminded of the sacrifices Andreas had made. Nic hoped the obscene amount of money he was handing the old man would shut him up once and for all.

"Have you decided who you're going to appoint to the board?" Pam glanced at him when he didn't answer. "They are going to ask."

"I have sixty days to decide. I'll let you know."

"Make sure it's not me," she warned him. "I will quit if you make me work with your father. It's bad enough being in the same building with him but I'm not cleaning up his mess."

Nic nodded. He hadn't planned to saddle Pam with trying to put Maretti Oil back together. Andreas had done a spectacular job of running it into the ground. Whoever Nic put in charge of damage control would have a full time job. He couldn't spare Pam. "I was thinking about Madlyn Robicheaux," he admitted.

"She won't leave New Orleans," Pam dismissed. "You should appoint Mac Sellers. Can you imagine the look on Andreas' face?"

Nic choked back an unexpected laugh as the elevator doors slid open on the top floor. He braced himself then stepped into the ostentatious outer office of Maretti Oil. When Andreas had taken over his second wife's family company, he'd had the unmitigated gall to rename the company and redecorated the office in what could only be called vintage Euro-trash.

Nic and Pam were shown to a conference room. The lawyers from both sides were already seated at the table. Andreas Maretti was not. Nic had purposely been ten minutes late for the meeting and had expected to find the old man signing his part of the paperwork. He should have known better.

He slid Pam's chair out for her and waited for her to be seated before he took the seat next to her. He waved away the hovering secretary who wanted to bring him coffee or something more personal if he wanted, if the look she gave him was anything to go by.

Five minutes later, Pam covered his hand and Nic realized he'd started tapping his fingers on the conference table.

"We'll take that coffee." She broke the tense silenced in the conference room as the attorneys seated across the table pretended to be paying attention to what they were saying to each other. When everyone knew they were just waiting for Nic to lose his cool.

Except Nic never lost his cool. This power play of Andreas' was almost pathetic. A smart man wouldn't have left Nic cooling his heels in a conference room full of junior lawyers and assistants. A smarter man would've already signed the loan paperwork before he arrived. A smarter man would have known Nic would rather walk back out the door than hand over the amount of money he was about to give to his worst enemy.

Andreas' PA swept into the room, breaking the tense silence. "Mr. Maretti, I'm very sorry. He's been delayed by an international conference call."

Nic did not acknowledge the younger man, but Pam did. "Steven, please make sure your boss understands he has two minutes before Mr. Maretti leaves this horror of an office, then walks out of this building while Maretti Oil goes under."

Steven nodded as he hurried out of the room.

"Amateur," Pam hissed under her breath. "Why are we here again?"

"Zachary," Nic said and Pam nodded.

"You could take this money and start a new company for Zachary. This is crazy, Nic."

"Maybe you're right."

"I'm always right." Pam pushed back in her seat and prepared to stand.

Nic waved her back down. Zachary was only one of the reasons for the loan. Guilt was the other one. Gnawing, soul-sucking guilt Nic hadn't been unable to shake for over twelve years.

The smoked glass doors pushed open and the pompous peacock strode in wearing a new custom suit and enough Botox on his face to paralyze an army. He was every bit the gracefully aging Italian aristocrat. He should have been standing on the deck of his yacht or gambling at a casino on the French Riviera. Andreas was pushing sixty-five but didn't appear a day over fifty. Preservation didn't come cheap. Nothing about him suggested he was drowning in debt and Nic was throwing him a life preserver.

Nic regretted not insisting on signing the paperwork separately. Arrogant as usual, Andreas had demanded they sign the paperwork at the same time. Nic hadn't been surprised Andreas had the nerve to try and dictate terms.

He should've refused. Agreeing to meet in person had given Andreas the wrong impression. Nic hadn't been the eager-to-please son for a long time. Andreas' ego would be his downfall.

"Nicolas." Andreas was all delighted charm and winning smiles with his arm extended as if they were a loving father and son.

Nic had no choice but to stand and shake hands. He reminded himself this man had no power over him. He swallowed down his bitterness as Andreas clasped his hand in a too-tight grip. The same grip that had dragged a six year old Nic away from his mother's graveside and away from the only home he'd ever known.

"Son, it's good to see you."

Nic's molars ground together as he forced out a semi-polite response.

"How long are you in town? You should come out to the ranch. Claudia would love to see you."

"Nic has a flight leaving in two hours," Pam answered for him. "We're on a tight schedule. Let's get started."

Unruffled, Andreas took the seat at the head of the table and made a big show of putting on his reading glasses and looking the paperwork over. He asked some questions he already knew the answers to and expressed concerns over details teams of lawyers had worked out weeks ago.

Nic let Pam answer the questions while he took a deep, calming breath and tried to picture the waters off his place in the Keys. He did have a flight but it was to Miami, then he was driving to his house in Key Largo and spending some time shaking off the anger that always followed his meetings with Andreas. Except this time, the marine blue waters off his home weren't what came to mind. No, it was a pair of blue eyes widening in shock as he took possession of her for the first time.

Nic's whole body tightened as the night with Lizzie replayed itself. She had been sweeter than she looked. His fingers clenched into fists but there was nothing he could do now but let the memory wash over him. He could still taste her, hear the tiny cries of surprise, and still feel the hard bud of her nipple on his tongue. The whimpers that had given way to delicate growls of pleasure had pushed his control to the limit as the heat of her body took him deep, shredding away all his expectations of sex and showing him how jaded he had become.

He'd forgotten the excitement of it until her eyes flew wide and she wound her arms around him and pressed so hard against him she penetrated the layers of distance he kept between him and the rest of the world. It was as if she'd pulled him out of a cave despite his protests then flung him into the sun.

It had rocked Nic to his foundation. He hadn't known sex could be like that. She'd been inexperienced but it hadn't mattered. Her response, the total surrender in her eyes—all of it had been more than Nic had ever dreamed possible. He'd found something precious with Lizzie. He'd fallen asleep with her in his arms planning breakfast and thinking the world might not be such a bad place after all.

Then she'd taken it away. Done what everyone else he let himself care for did. She'd left.

She'd walked out of his hotel room and disappeared, leaving him empty except for the raging hunger he'd been unable to slake with anyone else. Last night he'd tried but had ended up leaving a beautiful girl in tears when he told her it wasn't working.

Pam's hand on his forearm under the table kept Nic from clawing the table in half. She handed him a pen. He didn't read the paperwork. He signed it, handing over almost two billion dollars he'd never see again. A family debt paid.

Family? The word was laughable. He shared the Maretti name but they were not his family. Not that he needed one, Nic reminded himself. He didn't need anyone, other than the woman sitting next to him in this farce of a meeting, and the large man standing by the door, who never left Nic's side. Both Pam and Tag, the head of his security team, had enormous salaries in return for keeping the world away from him. Nic didn't need anyone else.

"Miss Sellers, are we boring you?"

Lizzie's chin slipped off her palm as she straightened in the uncomfortable desk. Cringing, she ignored the snickers and took a deep breath. "No, sorry."

"Maybe you aren't interested in Riemann surfaces."

Heat crawled up the back of her neck and she wiped her hand across her face, hoping to stop the angry color burning under her skin. Hatton wasn't the most fascinating lecturer in the department. Normally she fooled him into thinking she was paying attention, but today she was off her game.

She wasn't back in the real world yet. Everything was slightly out of sync. Sleeping with Nic had been a huge mistake. She was haunted by the glide of his hands over her, the way his legs felt tangled with hers. She could still feel him and taste him. She couldn't close her eyes without the night replaying itself for her. Had he been disappointed? Had he not called because their night hadn't been anything special?

Lizzie swallowed hard and tried not to fall apart.

He hadn't called because she'd walked out on him.

"Sellers!"

Her attention snapped back to him again. He was staring up at her from his podium, eyebrows raised. Had he asked her a question? Lizzie wasn't sure. She searched the last few minutes but there was nothing. And there was never nothing. Tears burned her throat and panic started to set in. She'd never felt so out of control before.

"We're waiting—" Hatton leaned against the podium.

This confrontation had been brewing all semester. It had started when she'd asked him a question he couldn't answer the first week of classes. She hadn't meant to embarrass him, but she'd ended up making a serious enemy. She'd promised herself she wouldn't let him get to her and she managed to ignore him. Now, on the last day of class, she bit down hard on the inside of her lip and tried not to say something she couldn't come back from.

"Or are you all out of your famous questions?"

She was on her feet before she realized what she was doing.

"You take one step and you're out. The rest of you get out, class dismissed."

The room quickly emptied out, but he took his time packing his messenger bag with his laptop and papers. "I told Dr. Pak it was a mistake to let you into our program," he said without looking up. "Would you like to know why?"

"I can't wait," she muttered under her breath.

He glanced up at her, gray eyes frosted over. Hatton wasn't completely horrible-looking but the post-grunge look was dead as far as Lizzie was concerned.

"You're too smart, Miss Sellers." He started up the steps. "It's too easy for you. You spend most of your time daydreaming and trying not to nap when there is a waiting list of students who would work their asses off to be in your place."

She started to protest but he stopped right in front of her.

"There are men who spend their entire careers trying to work through equations you can do in your head but what do you do? You yawn. You doodle. You daydream. You make it clear to everyone around you that you think you're slumming."

Lizzie shook her head. "No."

"And then you take off for a week—"

"I had a family thing."

"Family thing?" He smirked and pushed his rectangle glasses up. "A wedding you mean? Tell me, did you catch the bouquet? Is that why you're even more distracted than usual? At least before your week back to the swamp you made the attempt to look as though you were interested but since you've been back…well, you didn't come back. Did you leave your brain at home dreaming of wedding dresses and flowers?"

She flinched because he wasn't completely wrong. It wasn't the wedding that had her distracted. It was Nic.

"Maybe I'm right and math isn't your thing. You should consider fashion merchandising or journalism? Maybe you'd—"

"I get it," she snapped.

Lizzie's arms tightened around the notebook and computer she clamped to her chest. She blinked back tears refusing to cry.

"You're a cruel joke on the entire mathematics community. How is anyone supposed to take you seriously when you look like you just walked off the *Good Ship Lollipop?*" He waved his hand at her hair.

Lizzie's jaw dropped at his verbal attack. She'd never had anyone be so openly vicious to her face.

"Are you going to cry?" He raised his eyebrows at her.

She shook her head. Her skin burned with humiliation and something else she hadn't expected. *A cruel joke on the entire mathematics community?*

Who did he think he was?

"Is that what you want? To make me cry?"

He laughed, turning away from her. "Oh, no. I want to make you leave. In fact, I have an opening for TA next year. I think I'll put in a request for you."

"What?" She gasped, anger getting the best of her. "There's no way. Dr. Pak—"

"Dr. Pak, what? Promised you a position on his team? That's too bad."

Anger sputtered out of her without warning. "Why would you even want me on your team when you think I'm such a joke?"

His smile was cruel. "Because you'll need my approval to make it through your second year, and if you continue like this you're never going to get it."

Lizzie opened her mouth to tell him exactly where he could go, but he shook his head.

"Grow up, Miss Sellers. And if you show up this fall, be ready to work your ass off."

She nodded, unable to even come up with a defense. "Okay."

His head snapped back when she didn't argue.

"You're right," she said. "I'm sorry."

His body language completely changed and she had the distinct impression she'd surprised him. "You have a gift, Sellers," he spoke in a much more reasonable tone. "Whatever has you so distracted has got to go. You have more important things to do."

She nodded again, because he might have the facts wrong, but he was absolutely right.

Sunshine blinded her when she stepped outside, but she kept walking until she found an empty bench. She sucked in a breath, blinking back burning tears. She covered her face with her hands. This was not who she was.

This was not how things were supposed to be. She'd dreamed about Princeton for longer than she dreamed about Nic. Now Nic hadn't just ruined her for other men, he'd put her future in jeopardy. She couldn't let that happen. She had plans, goals, and problems to solve. She didn't have time to be distracted by schoolgirl crushes.

She sucked in another breath and swallowed everything down. Hatton was right. She'd been coasting. It wasn't because she was bored. New Jersey was a world away from New Orleans. At home people were at least polite to your face. Here, they were cold and rude. The other students in the department had dismissed her on the first day as one step down from Elle Woods.

She'd spent the first twenty years of her life not talking about math and making people forget she was a mathematical genius so they didn't treat her like a freak. Now she was surrounded by people who loved the same things she did and she had no idea how to talk to them. She was a freak. She didn't fit anywhere.

The first day of class she'd discovered she didn't know how to approach people. She'd never realized it before because she was always surrounded by people she knew. In high school and college, she'd always had Jen and Jen never met a stranger. Lizzie hadn't realized she'd been floating in Jen's wake all these years. When faced with so many strangers and Jen nowhere in sight to break the ice, Lizzie hadn't known where to start. It was easier to keep to herself. Easier to go to class then back to her apartment.

Now, the last place she wanted to go was that empty apartment. She wanted to be as far away from this place as possible. But she also wasn't ready to go home either. She wanted hot sunshine and warm sand. The beach. She wanted to go to the beach. Maybe she could get in the ocean and scrub her skin clean. She would call Rogan. He wouldn't ask a lot of questions and he'd let her have a condo for a few days. She could watch a bunch of chick flicks, eat way too much ice cream and get this nagging pain out of her system once and for all. She would regroup.

She dug her cell phone out of her shoulder bag and flipped it on. She ignored the twinge in her stomach. There were no missed calls or text messages. Had she honestly expected to hear from Nic after she'd crept out of the hotel suite while he was asleep?

Had she really thought having sex with Nic Maretti would help get him out of her system? Talk about epic fail.

The memories washed over her again. His hand moving over her, the crisp hairs on his legs and chest tickling her skin. She could feel him moving inside of her, turning her into someone she didn't recognize anymore. She'd lost herself with Nic. She didn't think her skin would ever feel normal again. Her lungs didn't work right. She ached everywhere for something she couldn't let herself have again.

Being with Nic had been too intense. The sounds he made and things he said to her. It had all been too much. She couldn't feel the ground under her feet.

There were dozens of half-started e-mails in her Drafts folder, text drafts on her phone but she hadn't known what to say. Sorry for running away from the best night of my life. She'd stared at her phone for days, trying to think of something clever to say and to apologize for leaving the way she did. At some point she'd realized the phone went both ways. He had her number but he hadn't sent her a clever e-mail or text message either.

She'd done something stupid then. She Googled him and found photographs of him all over a southern bachelor gossip blog with a beautiful brunette who'd been Miss Austin. Sometime later, with her face pressed against the cold tile floor of the bathroom while the contents of her stomach flushed away, Lizzie decided it was for the best. That night had meant nothing to him. He'd probably been disappointed. He hadn't been interested in a repeat performance.

No, he'd been at a loose end. She'd been a bridesmaid. One of her favorite movies claimed bridesmaids always got sex.

It was casual, post-wedding bridesmaid sex, or worse, forgettable sex for him while she couldn't think of anything else. Until now, because she was officially over him. She intended to power watch Richard Curtis rom coms until she didn't cry when Mathew gave Gareth's eulogy or when Anna asked William to love her.

Done.

Rogan answered on the first ring.

"I need a favor," she said without any sort of preamble. "Can I borrow your condo for a few days and could you not tell anyone?"

"Why? Did—"

"Or ask any questions."

He was quiet for a minute. "You're welcome to the condo but I have a better idea."

"Doubtful." Because nothing sounded better than a few days alone at the beach with DVDs and magic cookie dough ice cream. Well, maybe if Jen came but she couldn't ask her.

"The Miami Maretti Resort's grand opening is this weekend. Nic's out of the country so I have to do the final walk-through with the contractors and inspectors. The party will be huge, kiddo. There'll be dancing."

A huge dance party? In Miami? And no danger of running into Nic. Sold.

"I'm in." Then reality tapped her on the shoulder. "Wait. What about Angie?"

"She's already in Miami."

A chill danced across her shoulders. "Rogan, did something happen? You guys seemed to be getting along at the wedding."

"Yeah, well…" He cleared his throat. "I thought so too until she went back to Miami and took Zachary with her."

"If you show up with me in Miami, it's not going to help things. She hates me."

"She doesn't hate you."

"Are you crazy? She totally hates me and she's going to freak out if I walk in with you."

"Maybe I want her to freak out."

"Yeah, but—"

"Lizzie, I don't want to walk into that party by myself but I can't take a date, now can I? Come with me. You'll have fun and I'll get a shot at bringing her back home without having to crawl on my knees. Which is what she fucking wants."

He sounded desperate which surprised her but she couldn't imagine her big Cajun begging for anything on his knees. Angie needed to wake up and realize she was going to push Rogan too far.

"Okay," Lizzie agreed, ignoring the warning pinging along her nerve endings. She would go and dance and have a great time and it might be good if Angie got jealous for a change. Maybe she'd appreciate Rogan more. Fight for him.

Lizzie smiled for the first time in days. She was definitely going to need a great dress.

The cell phone buzzed again, and Nic's heart skipped a beat although he knew there was no way it was the call he wouldn't admit he wanted to receive.

He took his time setting the fishing rod in the holder and pulled the phone out of his pocket. The sun was high and bright today. Blue skies, fluffy clouds, and the water was so still it mirrored the sky. It was a perfect day to be on his boat, but he'd stayed in his pier. He'd been too restless to take his boat out.

"Your sister called," Pam announced without any sort of preamble when Nic called her back.

"This is news?" The ice chest creaked as he opened the lid and grabbed a bottled water. "She's been calling me too, but I'm in Hong Kong, remember?"

He shut the lid then sat down on the ice chest as Pam snorted her disapproval. He scanned the empty horizon, refusing to notice the water was the same color as Lizzie's eyes. "I'll call her," he relented.

"And Marcy?"

He flinched at the name. Not one of his finer moments. "Yeah, that's done too."

"I know, I've been on the phone with her all morning too. I think you hurt her, Nic."

He shuddered at the memory. He didn't like crying women. He also didn't like feeling like a total bastard, the way he always did when they realized he'd been serious when he'd said he wasn't looking for the future Mrs. Maretti.

Marcy had been the full package of everything he didn't want in a relationship. He should have seen it sooner and left her alone. He'd been off his game. Still angry about waking up alone in his hotel suite and angrier about bailing out Maretti Oil. He'd delayed his trip to Hong Kong and gone to the Keys instead. He'd wanted to get his head straight first, but he was surrounded by water that had once soothed him for the same reason he now wanted to drain the Gulf of Mexico dry.

"Aren't you tired of all this serial monogamy? It's not like you don't know who you want, Nic. You've known for the last four years. Now that I've seen her I get—"

"Two words. Severance. Package."

"Oh, good," Pam shot back. "I've been meaning to ask for a raise."

He covered his eyes with his hand and pressed his fingers and thumb into his temples. He would never fire her. They both knew it. She ran his companies like a well-oiled machine and she was one of the few people in the world Nic trusted. They'd met each other in the principal's office in seventh grade. Nic for beating up the school bully and Pam for making her English teacher cry. They'd been friends ever since. Now she made sure he could avoid Houston and people as much as possible. No one got to him without going through Pam.

But Lizzie was not something Nic was prepared to discuss with Pam. He wasn't ready to discuss Lizzie with anyone. He wouldn't know where to start.

Pam broke the brief silence first. "No more beauty queens, Nic. They don't take rejection well."

"Fine, send her something pretty. A bracelet."

Pam sighed. "That's been taken care of. I had a bracelet and tangerine roses on standby after your second dinner date."

"Tangerine is pretty specific."

"She'd already started pinning wedding place settings and bridesmaids' dresses."

Nic's brain shut off at bridesmaids. "If you're going to stalk my girlfriends' social media, you could at least give me a heads-up before they flake out on me."

She laughed. "You don't need a heads-up. Your anti-commitment radar works fine on its own and honestly, your heart wasn't in it this time."

"My heart is never in it. That's the point."

"I'll take care of Marcy but you need to call Angie. Her last phone call was hysterical. Apparently, Rogan is going to Miami and he's not alone this time."

"What?" Nic choked on the word. "Not alone? What the hell does that mean?"

"I'm not sure. She was crying. None of it made sense. Maybe you should go to the grand opening after all."

Nic groaned and wiped his hand across his face. "Fine, I'll drive in tomorrow."

"You need to call her," Pam insisted. "This was not her usual melodrama. Something is wrong."

He ended the call only to have the Rolling Stones start singing "Angie" on his phone. He'd forgotten to change the ringtone again. His sister had programmed it in months ago as a joke. She thought it was funny, but it was getting old. He was always so relieved when their conversations ended he forgot to change the ringtone back.

As soon as the call connected, there was a gulp, a sniff and a ragged intake of air.

"Don't cry, I'm coming to Miami. Now, tell me what's going on."

She choked on a sob. "We got into a huge fight and I…"

Angie lost the battle with her tears. They were authentic sinus-blocking tears of a devastated woman with a broken heart.

Nic closed his eyes, wishing he could make all this go away. "Do you want to tell me what the fight was about?"

"It's always the same thing. He spends all his time with his friends. If it's not Stefan and Jen, it's Lizzie…"

"Lizzie?" he echoed, his mental clamp creaking as he refused to let images of long lustrous curls form in his mind. "For the last time, Rogan is not cheating on you with Lizzie. She's like his sister."

"She's here in Miami with him and trust me, I know you think I'm crazy but there's something going on between them."

Nic froze, the hairs on his arms and neck standing up without warning. Lizzie was in Miami? He stared out to sea, not seeing anything but he could feel her. Taste her skin. The sound of his name on her breath. A low ache started deep inside him and the craving fired up again as his body flat refused to care that she'd walked out on him. No, it wanted who it wanted and she was in Miami.

Less than an hour and a half away.

"I'll be there tonight. Stop worrying. If there is something going on, I'll deal with it."

"Okay, Nic, thank you." Then she added, *"Ti voglio bene."*

Nic was on his feet, reeling in the line and tossing the custom-made rod and reel onto the deck of his boat without thinking. He didn't believe for a second anything was going on between Rogan and Lizzie. They'd known each other all their lives. It made no sense.

As hot water rushed over him in the shower, he couldn't wait to see her. Would she try to explain why she left? Would he care?

CHAPTER FIVE

Lizzie did another sweep of the crowded ballroom, before turning back to Rogan. "Did you see her? She's over by the bar."

She'd caught a glimpse of Angie earlier, but it was hard to see anything in the throng of people.

"Do you think she saw us?"

Rogan shook his head in indulgent disbelief. "Lizzie, everyone saw us."

She sipped her champagne, her eyes wandering across the room full of glittering people, and gold, aqua and pink lanterns gave the whole atmosphere an early sixties vibe. She had to hand it to Angie. The other girl might be a total bitch but she knew how to throw a party. Beautiful people lounged on low leather sofas and sipped martinis. Lizzie expected Don Draper and Roger Sterling to walk in at any time. The entire hotel was a midcentury modern dream come true.

"Where did you say you got that dress again?" Rogan asked.

"Don't you like it?" she asked, twisting so the sequins danced.

"Too much." Rogan shook his head again.

It was a scandalous dress. It had taken her two glasses of champagne to stop feeling so exposed in it. It wasn't too short but the red dress slithered down her body like liquid fire and the sunburst pattern of gold sequins flared whenever she moved. She'd found it in one of the resort's outrageous boutiques. It was the first time she'd ever used her Amex. Her father was going to choke when he got the statement. He'd given it to her five years ago and she'd made up for five years with one dress and a pair of wicked shoes. The shoes were totally worth it.

She sipped more champagne and did her best Scarlett O'Hara impersonation. She was good at worrying about things tomorrow. Living in the now. And right now, she was determined to make Angie Rogan fight for her husband. Maybe she'd finally appreciate what a great guy Rogan was if she had some competition. Angie believed Lizzie harbored a secret love for Rogan and any day Lizzie would snap her fingers and Rogan would come crawling to her.

She dragged Rogan back onto the dance floor and put the red dress to work. Rogan was a better dancer than he thought, but even he couldn't keep up with Lizzie tonight. He caught her around the waist and pulled her up against his side. "Are you having fun yet?" He grinned. The devil knew exactly what she was doing and had decided to play along.

Rogan was spinning her again when she stumbled then leaned into him for real.

Nic.

Nic was not supposed to be here.

She swallowed hard and glanced back around again to make sure she hadn't imagined him.

No. There he was. In the flesh.

And pretty spectacular flesh.

Lizzie's whole body reacted at once. Chaos zinged through her as memories of him crashed back down on her without warning. She'd had too much champagne but she couldn't wait to get another glass.

"There she is. In the red dress."

Nic turned in the direction his sister indicated and scanned the crowd. It took less than half a second for him to spot the girl clinging to his brother-in-law's arm. Nic struggled for a second to keep his breathing easy. Her burnt red dress skimmed every curve of her small but perfect shape. The dress was covered in gold sequins that caught the light as she moved. Long loose curls spilled all around her shoulders and down her back. Her hair should have clashed with the slinky dress. Instead, she was a smoldering red coal reaching its peak temperature. His eyes narrowed on the slim fingers clinging to Rogan's arm as Rogan swung her around.

There was something off in the way Rogan was smiling at her while they danced much too close together. He didn't believe Rogan would get involved with Lizzie but he didn't like the way she leaned into him. They were too close. Rogan's knee went between Lizzie's legs and Nic's central nervous system went haywire. A long dormant hunting instinct stirred inside him as he watched the two dance. Nic was putting a stop to their little show. Right now.

"Nic, are you listening to me?" Angie's voice rose in alarm, he stepped forward.

"No." The word seethed from between his teeth. Every muscle in his body was poised to spring. He turned back to his sister and tried to keep his voice calm. "Will it help if I distract her from your husband?"

Angie's brittle smile wavered. "What are you thinking?"

Evisceration was what Nic was thinking. He grabbed two glasses of champagne instead and handed one to his sister.

"You let me worry about that. I'll get her out of the way."

"How?" Concern laced her words. "You can't run off with her."

Watch me. Nic thought, sipping his champagne. His hinges were coming loose but he didn't care. Lizzie leaned into Rogan and his hand slipped too low on her hip. Evisceration might not be enough.

"I don't know what Ben is thinking."

Nic turned, blocking Angie's view. "You need to decide what you want. If you want him back, I'll remove her from the equation but if you do want a divorce, I'd rather not chew up and spit out such a pretty young thing for no good reason." Well, at least not in front of everyone. One way or another, he was going to separate her from Rogan. What he did afterwards was up in the air. He knew what he wanted to do but the civilized part of his brain seemed to have rebooted and was now running on a backup generator.

"Ask her to dance so I can talk to him?"

"He's your husband. You should walk down there and talk to him anyway."

She sighed. "It's not that simple."

"It's exactly that simple. Come on, I'll show you."

He slid his arm around her waist and started across the ballroom.

Lizzie watched Nic move through the crowd toward them. She eased into Rogan, no longer pretending to hang on him. "Nic's here."

Rogan spotted his wife. Lizzie felt his body grow tight as he held on to her. She didn't mind, she needed the support. Nic was staring straight at her and a laser beam cutting her in half would have been less painful.

Okay, it was possible her plan had backfired.

It was like being circled by a shark. A hot shark and a dangerous predator Lizzie had no defense against. In fact, she wouldn't mind being lunch or dinner. She wanted to fling herself at him and let him devour her. It was the reason she existed. Who was she to fight the universe?

Except as he approached, something cold trickled down her spine. He was all cool, elegance again. Not an emotion in sight.

She'd expected him to be angry. She couldn't have been more wrong. Ice rained over her, freezing all her crazy emotions in place. An unexpected calm settled over her as bored brown eyes swept over her.

She hadn't been a blip on his radar. He hadn't tried to get in touch with her because he hadn't thought twice about her. Her vertebrae froze solid and without warning, instead of bursting into tears she lit up like Christmas morning. Throwing her arms around Angie, she hugged the startled girl like a long lost best friend.

"Angie!" She gushed and bounced on her tip toes. Screw Nic and the horse he rode in on. Now she was so over him. He was history. "Rogan, here she is. He's been trying to find you all night." She hugged Angie again and pretended she didn't notice the other girl pulled away from her. Lizzie continued her chatter, anger pumping adrenalin through her veins. "This party is fabulous and the hotel is amazing. I adore midcentury modern and I swear Roger Sterling is going to walk in any minute. Not Don Draper because he's an ass. Nic, ask me to dance, it's been ages."

She purposely switched gears in mid-breath but she didn't catch him off guard. His smile was slow and dead sexy as it spread across his gorgeous face.

"Great idea."

Lizzie met his gaze head-on and set her party girl persona to stun. She held out her hand for him and went for it. She'd finally asked him to dance first. It would be the last time she indulged herself. She was not a damned blip on anyone's radar, but after tonight, he would be one on hers.

The second his fingers curled around hers, she wavered. Electric shock sizzled down her hand to her arm and right straight through her. Panic slicked along her nerve endings and she hoped her vacant smile was in place. She couldn't feel her skin so she wasn't sure.

This might not have been the best idea.

Warmth radiated off him. Her bones softened as she leaned into him, letting him control their movements. The rest of the dancers faded away. A familiar lethargy pulled her into a strange slow motion. He smelled so good. Felt so familiar. An ache started deep inside her.

Definitely a mistake but how could anything that felt so wonderful be a mistake?

The slow song ended and the band broke into a much faster more modern song. He didn't release her. Relieved, she let go and lost herself in the music, the beat, and the proximity to him. Now, as Nic's fingers slid over her, scorching her through the dress and keeping her in a constant state of motion, Lizzie forgot she had a plan. Everything slid right out of her mind. He spread through her system like pure alcohol. He spun her around and pulled her back. His hands flattened against her stomach tightening her hips against his. Lizzie stretched and swayed to the music. When his mouth brushed against her shoulder, tasting her, she nearly went supernova right in the middle of the dance floor.

They lasted two more songs before he clamped his hand around hers and walked her out of the crowd. He didn't speak. Neither did she. There was nothing to say. He didn't lead her to the open bar. Instead they walked straight out of the ballroom and down a few steps to a lounge where some grand opening guests had gathered for a more subdued atmosphere.

The cooler air in the lounge helped clear her head but she was floating from dancing, the loud music and being so close to him. The contact between their hands kept the combustion going and Lizzie was pretty sure she would have followed him straight into a volcano just to cool off. He found an empty booth in the back, ordered a bottle of wine, then turned his full attention back to her.

"What have you been up to lately?"

He was too close to her in the booth, making it difficult to breathe. She managed not to jump out of her skin when his arm went around her, resting against the back of the booth, but she couldn't look at him, not unless she wanted to asphyxiate. She laughed to cover her breathlessness. "Really?"

His eyebrows lifted. "You didn't answer my question."

Did he ask a question? She blinked, the weight of her head becoming harder and harder to sustain. There was something she was supposed to be doing, but she couldn't remember what it was. Kissing him, maybe? No. It sounded like a great idea but she was pretty sure that wasn't her plan. "This and that."

Nic had the most beautiful mouth she'd ever seen. Lizzie blinked and pretended she hadn't been staring. His thigh brushed against her as he eased around until he was almost in front of her. Her weight sank back against the booth and her bones started to melt again. He blocked out the rest of the world as she could barely keep her head up.

She forced herself to face him, then wished she hadn't. The apex predator staring back at her wasn't hungry. He was furious.

"Oh." She swallowed hard. If he was a predator, she was prey. She was not as upset as she should've been. A wildly inappropriate sizzle started deep inside her.

"Yeah. Oh." His smile was not nice. "You owe me breakfast."

The tone of his voice didn't reflect the anger rolling off him. He had it under control. She shivered, wondering how she would survive the anger she could feel rushing out of him. She was in way over her head. When the backs of his fingers stroked slowly down the inside of her arm, she didn't care anymore. It was such a simple touch, a light caress, but it felt like electricity scalding down her arm.

"Your skin is so soft." The words were low and smoky, and sending her deeper into a drugged state she had no idea how to deal with. Not that she wanted to deal with it.

"Nic, I…"

Their wine arrived. He released her and waved off the server. He poured two glasses and handed her one. Cold and crisp, the wine was delicious.

"Not too sweet?" He set his glass aside, turning toward her in the booth.

"Perfect." She sounded breathless and she couldn't take her eyes off him. She drank the wine too quickly and almost dropped the wine glass when he tried to refill it.

"Relax." His voice was husky and warm and tingling over her skin like static electricity.

"How?" She whimpered, wondering if she was going to come right out of her skin.

He was too close. She couldn't think.

"Close your eyes," he suggested.

"Not a chance." She gasped out the last word when his hand moved over her knee and between her legs. His fingers burned the sensitive skin of her inner thighs as they pressed in, easing her legs apart.

His smile turned devastating then. "You're burning up, aren't you?"

She scooted back in the booth, making it easier for his palm to press against her inner thigh. His thumb teased over the damp lace. "Nic…wait…"

"Don't move," he whispered against her mouth before claiming it with his own.

Her head fell back as the kiss deepened. His taste rushed through her system, imprinting itself on every part of her. She couldn't get enough. Never wanted it to end.

"You left me." The words grazed across her lips, as his teeth nipped and pulled her bottom lip. "I should punish you."

If what his fingers were doing was his idea of punishment, Lizzie decided she would be bad for the rest of her life. She gasped, no longer caring they were in a public place.

"I panicked." She whimpered when his fingers pushed the lace aside and there was nothing stopping him from sliding deep inside her. He stopped when her words sank in. "I woke up and panicked. Kind of like I'm about to do right now."

Something strange flickered in his eyes and his face softened into a more familiar version of him. He eased his hand back, his palm soothing down her thighs until her legs stopped shaking.

"I'm sorry." She traced her fingers along his shadowed jawline. He leaned into the caress, his eyes fluttering shut as he ducked his chin. She felt him shudder, but he was covering her hand with his. "I didn't know what to do."

He cleared his throat, his voice raspy and not unaffected by what had almost happened. "I should have called you." The words were low and filled with self-recriminations, not criticism for her.

She nodded. "I wanted you to call."

She'd been devastated when he hadn't and furious with herself for being devastated. That was not who Lizzie thought she was. She was logical not irrational. That night with Nic had been more than her first time, it had made her question everything about herself and all the things she told herself she wanted but for once logic and numbers were no help in understanding what was happening to her.

He topped off their wine glasses, emptying the bottle. "We can make it up to each other. I have a place in the Keys. Spend the week with me."

"Seriously?" The invitation was the last thing she'd expected.

"There's a boat and a pool and if it gets too quiet, I'll take you shopping."

Take her shopping? Who did Nic think she was?

He kissed her again. His mouth moved slowly over hers, grazing tender flesh with his teeth then soothing her with his tongue. Long fingers wrapped around the back of her head and held her there. He lifted those golden, jungle animal eyes. "Spend a week with me and let Rogan and Angie have some time alone." His hand stroked down her cheek until his thumb pressed along her bottom lip.

Oh, that's who he thought she was. Maybe her performance had been too good. Now she was Angie's problem and Nic wanted to get her out of the way. It stung, but she couldn't blame him. Nic had never seen her in the real world. They'd met at parties and family functions.

She relaxed back in the booth, her eyes closing as he tasted the soft skin below her ear. Hot chills slid over her, shutting down her brain. Not thinking was perfect. Everything fell away. Hatton. School. Angie and Rogan.

She wanted to go with him. Wanted to spend more time with him. Wanted to forget all the pressure and problems and live in the now. What would a few days hurt?

"Will there be more kissing?" She flicked the tip of her tongue against his thumb.

He raised his head, eyes meeting hers. "Definitely. Lots of kissing."

"And you have a boat?"

"Fishing trawler but plenty of places for you to tan. My house sits right out on the water. You'll love it. Take a chance, *bella*. It's paradise, I promise you."

Paradise? Perfect. "Sounds like fun. Give me fifteen minutes to grab my stuff."

"As long as you don't change your mind."

He was surprised when she met him downstairs. He took her carryall bag in one hand and her arm in his other. She let him lead her outside to the rental waiting in valet parking and within minutes they were headed south.

She was so quiet Nic expected to see her sleeping when he darted a quick glance at her. She surprised him when she smiled. What was it about her that set his blood on fire? He'd dated some of the most beautiful women in the world but none had had him in a state of constant frustration. His whole body ached. His fingers tightened around the steering wheel again and he tried to focus on driving.

She wasn't his type. Nic preferred tall, elegant women who knew the score. Despite the streaks of mascara at the end, he'd done no real damage to them. They recovered. They all did.

Would Lizzie recover if he let himself get too close to her? Would he break her if he took what he wanted until he didn't want it anymore?

Yes. He knew it as sure as he was breathing. There was a vulnerability there she went to great lengths to hide. He suspected most people never spotted it but he could see it clearly. It sang to him like a damned siren, firing up some primitive protective instinct in him. He hated to admit it but he understood why she'd taken off.

He groaned in protest as the source of his anger melted away along with his excuse to do what he wanted next. He should have called her. No, he should have gone after her instead of letting jaded assumptions ruin one of the best experiences of his life. Now he had a second chance to get this clawing hunger out of his system. He'd take things slower this time. No need to rush. This time he wouldn't scare her away.

CHAPTER SIX

Lizzie opened her eyes, unsure where she was at first. She was lying on her stomach against incredibly soft sheets that smelled like the ocean. She could hear the ocean too, and the air smelled like salt. There was a bell sounding in the distance.

The Keys.

She was in the Florida Keys. With Nic.

Lizzie straightened and pushed her hair off her face. She vaguely remembered arriving last night. He'd carried her inside, unzipped her dress and pulled it over her head. When she'd expected him to kiss her, he'd put her in bed, the soft sheets seductively cool against her hot skin. She didn't remember much after that.

Paper fluttered behind a glass of orange juice on the bedside table. *Welcome to Paradise* was scrawled carelessly across it in sharp black strokes. She dragged her hand down her face. What the hell had she been thinking? Or drinking?

Sheer white curtains billowed in the warm breeze let in by the open doors. She took a deep breath, knowing there wasn't an escape route this time. She swallowed down the panic. The curtains danced. Seagulls echoed in the distance.

Maybe it was paradise.

Lizzie grabbed the orange juice and the two painkillers sitting next to the glass. He thought of everything.

She found her dress draped over a chair, with her shoes and carry all next to it. She stared at it for a minute, a tendril of concern floating through her murky brain. Something was missing. She sipped the juice and sighed. She'd figure it out later. She finished the juice as she walked into an open kitchen that would make Jen sob.

When he'd said he had a house in the Keys, she'd pictured a

charming cottage painted bright yellow with a thatched roof. She glanced around the open floor plan. The furniture could have been recovered from a British Colonial tree house. She stepped towards the long bank of glass doors along the back wall. Outside, a swimming pool masqueraded as a rain forest lake with a waterfall splashing at one end.

Beyond the pool, a long pier stretched out into the blue-green water. Nic jumped down from the huge fishing boat floating at the end of the pier. Dressed in a faded pair of cargo shorts that rode dangerously low on lean hips, he had a handful of fishing rods. She couldn't decide which was more scandalous. Nic fishing or Nic in shorts and a faded denim button-up shirt that he hadn't bothered to button up. She forgot the question when he stripped off his shirt and she got a good look at all those long lean muscles. The dark hair covering his spectacular chest made Lizzie's palms itch.

He was, in a word, perfect.

Fascinated, she watched him bait the hooks and cast lines out into the water. He dropped down to sit on an ice chest. Lizzie's head tilted to the side as she watched him. He didn't move other than to make small adjustments on the fishing line.

Nic Maretti.

Fishing?

Not what she expected at all.

She turned away from the window and headed back to the lavish master bedroom. She quickly made up the bed then walked through to the bathroom. The huge whirlpool tub beckoned but she pushed away the urge for a long hot bubble bath. Maybe later.

She dropped her carryall on the vanity and dug out her tooth brush and lime green bikini. While brushing her teeth, she spotted a stack of beach towels with another bathing suit on top. Holding the toothbrush in her mouth with her teeth, she moved across the room to examine the suit. The black suit was her size and looked vaguely familiar. It wouldn't hurt to try it on.

The bikini fit perfectly. Déjà vu teased at the corners of her mind as she picked up the matching sarong and scarf. She loved the tiny shells and charms dangling from the gauzy fabric. She knotted the sarong around her waist. The shells and metal charms jingled as she moved.

She'd seen this bathing suit before. She'd pinned it on one of her Pinterest boards when she'd been snowed in last winter and dreaming of the beach. She went to get her phone to check her Pinterest app then realized what was missing. The beaded bag that had her cell phone, her ID, ATM card and pretty much her whole life in it was not there.

The jingle of metal alerted Nic to Lizzie's approach. Relief swept over him as he realized he'd been holding his breath to see if she'd wear the bikini Pam had had delivered to the house. If she put it on, it meant she wasn't regretting coming with him.

He turned when she called his name and tried to keep his jaw from slamming into the dock. The cute was all gone, replaced by a siren with creamy skin shimmering with sunscreen. The sarong revealed one shapely leg. Her toenails were painted a cherry red and Nic loved cherries. His mouth went dry and his hand clenched the fishing rod so he wouldn't throw it down, then throw her down on the dock and see if she tasted as good as she looked.

Her tentative expression stopped him. She wasn't blushing but she was definitely not meeting his eyes. He could tell she had about a million things she wanted to say but didn't know where to start. A shy siren? That made Nic burn hotter.

"Good morning."

Her tentative smile brightened. "Hey."

"You ready for some breakfast?"

She shrugged. "You mean lunch?"

"Brunch. Do you like eggs?" He pushed to his feet and set the rod and reel aside.

"Yeah." Her answer was too breathy and her eyes still dazed. "But there's something you should know."

He stopped in front of her, having every intention of walking her back up to the house. "Sounds dire?"

Color brushed her cheek. "I'm hopeless in the kitchen. I burn water."

A curl broke loose from the scarf she'd wrapped around her hair. Nic pushed the curl back without thinking. She stretched on her tiptoes, her hands pressing into his chest. The skin at the small of her back was like satin, still slick from the sunscreen. He kissed her without thinking. She tasted faintly of cinnamon and he couldn't get enough.

When he could drag his mouth away, her eyes flickered open. "Good morning."

He fought another smile, but slowly lost the battle. "I did promise you kissing," he reminded her, pleased as her face dissolved into laughter at his mock-serious tone.

"You always keep your promises?"

"I'm terrible at promises, Lizzie, but I'm not expecting any trouble keeping this one."

His hand curved around her waist, turning her to walk back up the pier. She leaned into him but he resisted the urge to sweep her off her feet and carry her back to bed. Instead, he stopped at the pool knowing if she went inside with him, he'd never get brunch started.

"Get some sun. I'll make breakfast." He steered her toward the lounge chairs.

"Oh, but you said I owed you breakfast."

"I meant staying for breakfast," he amended. Proving again his lizard brain was in full command, Nic turned her away from him and untied the string bow at the back of her neck.

"Nic." His name trembled in protest on her breath as she covered herself to stop the bikini top from falling away.

"The patio is protected." His fingers slid down the soft sides of her breasts left exposed by her hands, down her rib cage then back up. She swayed in his arms and he felt her tremble again. Her response was more intoxicating than his favorite scotch. "No one can see."

He held his breath as he untied the string across her back. "Can I have this?" He whispered against her neck, pressing his mouth to the hot skin below her ear. Her head tilted slightly to the side, giving him better access to the vulnerable curve of her neck.

"Please?" His throat tightened as her hands fell away taking the bikini top with them.

For a moment, he couldn't move. Her breath caught and it was the only sound he could hear as they dipped into the place where the world couldn't touch them. He eased her back, his hands going around her sides, sliding under and up her breasts. She leaned into his touch. His thumbs brushed across the stiff peaks and fire raced through him, burning away what little sense he had left. She was so soft. How was he supposed to resist?

Her head fell forward, sighing in pleasure as he shaped the silky flesh. It wasn't enough. He wanted more. He wanted her under him, quivering and crying again. He wanted his name on her last breath before she went over the edge. This time with him so deep inside her he would never find his way back and she wouldn't be able to leave.

Her arms came back up, her hand moving over his. His body turned to steel when he realized she wasn't trying to stop him. She wanted him to touch her but she also needed to hang on before her legs gave way. It wasn't a conscious thought that had him leaning down to slide his arm under her knees. He lifted her easily, then took three steps toward the lounge chair and laid her down against the blue-and-white striped pillows.

Shock sent hot color racing all over her and her jaw gave way so she could drag in more air. Her lungs stopped working altogether when he sat down next to her on the lounge chair. Her eyes never left him as he undid the scarf and her hair spiraled down around her shoulders. She watched, fascinated as he let her curls loop around his fingers as he arranged them. The half-smile was deceptive because the concentration on his face was intense. He eased back, gold eyes burning into her skin. Dizzy and exposed, her eyes started to water because she couldn't seem to blink.

Her hands eased up of their own accord. Instinct told her to cover herself.

"Keep them down." Her eyes widened at the gentle but firm request. There was an edge to his voice that set off a different kind of fire inside her and the ache between her legs deepened into a painful throb.

Her breath caught, her eyes riveted to his but her arms went down. He smiled but didn't break eye contact with her. That smile of pleasure increased the heat moving through her. Then his eyes flicked down. Her blood dissolved into molten lava and her heart pumped it twice as fast through her as the throb radiated out.

His expression turned dark with hunger and... longing? One finger touched her chin as his eyes lifted to hers again. "You're so lovely."

There was no mockery in those gentle words, no arrogance, nothing to make her cringe. She hadn't expected him to be so...serious or sincere.

"My ancestors would've built temples in your honor, *bella*."

His gaze had her trapped. She couldn't look away from the gold lights flickering in them as his hand moved up to cup the side of her face.

"Would you like that, Lizzie?" The words were so quiet she could easily have dreamed them. "Being worshipped?"

She shook her head slightly. "I don't think so."

His mouth brushed against hers and her eyes fluttered closed. It was a slow, light kiss that teased the storm raging inside her. He raised his head, reluctantly pushing to his feet. Her eyes followed the movement but her body was in thrall, unable to move a muscle. She was frozen in time, unable to even breathe, and it was okay because she didn't want the second to end.

"I'll bring breakfast outside. You have time to swim if you want." He broke the spell with those ridiculously normal words. He was so calm she wondered if his heart had missed a beat while she was losing her mind.

She watched him disappear inside. Shaken, confused and incredibly turned on she sat there for a long time, trying to remember how her lungs were supposed to work.

Movement in the sky distracted her and she looked up as a formation of pelicans flew overhead in a loose V, flying so low she was amazed at how large they were.

She dove into the icy water before she could think too hard about it. When she surfaced, it was like swimming up into a new world. The sun was high in the impossibly blue sky. Maybe this was paradise. She'd better keep an eye out for snakes. Nothing this beautiful came without a price. She would pay for all of it eventually, but it would be worth it.

Then she groaned. She'd forgotten the very reason she'd gone outside. Her cell phone. She needed her phone. She levered out of the pool and grabbed one of the white fluffy towels waiting in a teak shelf between the lounge chairs. She dried off quickly then wrapped the towel around herself instead of the sarong. She needed the coverage when she confronted Nic again.

She found him in the kitchen, scrambling eggs. His dangerous smile stopped her in her tracks. "You don't want to eat outside?"

She opened her mouth to say no then saw the tray he'd been loading with toast, butter, strawberry jam and fresh fruit. Her stomach growled a warning at her and Nic laughed. She dropped down on a barstool and grabbed the toast before he could offer it.

"The jam's homemade."

Her knife paused as she scraped butter over the toast triangle.

"You make jam?" she asked, not looking up to see what he thought of her snarky tone.

"I like to cook," he said. "But my talents don't stretch to jam making. I buy it at the local farmers market."

She slathered jam on top of the butter and promised herself she'd do laps in the pool. "You don't have a chef?" She bit into the toast and chewed with relish. She definitely needed to make a side trip to the farmers market.

"I'm not in one place long enough to have a chef. Do you want cheese in your eggs? I can add it if you want, but I don't like anything in my eggs so…"

"No, No," she said, shaking her head trying not to grin like an idiot. "I like plain eggs. Jen is always putting vegetables and stuff in her omelets and I don't like the crunch."

"Eggs shouldn't be crunchy." He pushed a fluffy pile of perfectly scrambled eggs on her plate. "Reminds me of shells."

"Yes." She grinned, relieved he didn't think she was crazy. She tasted her eggs and tried not to moan in pleasure. "Delicious." They were so good it was hard not to scarf them down.

He took her plate when she was finished and set it in the sink. She watched him rinse the dishes and stack them in the dishwasher. She should take a picture because no one would believe Nic knew how to do dishes.

Her phone! She'd forgotten to ask him about her phone. "Nic," she started as he closed the dishwasher. She kept the light airy tone in her voice. "Any idea where I dropped my purse last night? I need to call Rogan and let him know where I am."

"Rogan knows where you are." He turned, leaning back against the counter, his expression unreadable. She was starting to recognize it for a false calm. A mask he slid on when he didn't want to answer the next question. "I talked to him last night." He crossed his arms. His expression didn't flicker. "I thought we agreed we'd give them some time alone."

Okay, why had the temperature in the kitchen dropped thirty degrees?

"Time alone?" she repeated and realized time alone translated to time away from her which was crazy since…

Oops. Warm color singed her ears as she realized Angie wasn't the only one who'd caught their show on the dance floor. "We were just dancing…"

His eyebrows lifted.

"Oh, I can't believe she fell for it," Lizzie rushed on, her stomach flipping over when he didn't react. "Rogan and I..." She stumbled over words that should have been easy.

He shifted his weight, his eyes narrowing. "You were what? Trying to make her jealous?"

"Maybe?" She cringed as she said the word. Maybe running wasn't a bad idea after all. Except she was sitting down.

"I believed my sister was imagining things until I watched you and Rogan last night. You deliberately set out to make her think something was going on, didn't you?"

Storm clouds built in his eyes, turning them scary and sexy. She was in over her head. Every cell in her body wanted to run but sizzled with too much excitement to flee.

"Do you have any idea what you've put my sister through?"

"Your sister?" OKAY, now Lizzie knew how to feel. Angry. She loved Rogan the same way she loved her family. "What about Rogan? He worships your sister and she treats him like dirt under her feet."

"Are you calling my sister a snob?"

"Yes, that's exactly what I'm saying."

Everything about him was calm and casual. Except his eyes. There were hurricanes roaring up and Lizzie hated hurricanes. "You're wrong. Angie might be spoiled but she's not a snob."

"Rogan loves her," she shot back. "He's been miserable this past year. He's hardly seen Zachary and..." She trailed off, blinking back sudden tears and glancing away so he wouldn't see them. "She's going to keep on until she loses him."

"You want them to get back together?" He was genuinely surprised.

"Yes." She choked. Did he really think she would go after a married man? It felt like falling through the ice of a frozen lake. The burn scraped a layer of her skin off and left her raw and bleeding. He should know better.

"You tried to provoke her into fighting for him?"

This trip had been a mistake. How could she expect him to know her better? She was emotionally out of her depth with Nic. She couldn't handle him. She might be emotionally invested in him, but she was a passing blip on his radar. It was ridiculous to expect him to know her better. "I know, it was stupid..."

"No." He turned to wash his hands. "No, it worked."

Her eyes widened as he rounded the bar. The predator was coming for her. The man who stopped in front of her wasn't angry but he was dangerous. She had no defense. He made her hope. He made her want more.

"Lizzie?"

She turned her head until their eyes met.

"Can I borrow your towel?" The low words took a moment to sink in but he was already tugging on the beach towel.

"What? No. Wait…" she yelped, grabbing at the towel to stop him. Caught between outrage and excitement, she lost the battle and the towel.

He tossed the towel aside, then turned the barstool until she faced him. His hands caged her in but his focus was on her lips, which immediately went dry. She swept her tongue across her bottom lip and her heart raced triple time when he leaned into her.

"I don't want to talk about Angie and Rogan anymore." His voice was low and husky. It made her shiver again.

She leaned back on the stool as he moved over her. Her arms wound around his neck and she smiled when he shivered in pleasure this time. "Talking is overrated."

"Agreed," he snapped and then he was kissing her. Her lips parted and she was ready for him this time. She forgot who Angie and Rogan were. She forgot who she was. She forgot everything but his mouth shaping hers. The world fell away again as he deepened the kiss.

Reality was overrated too.

Alarm bells went off in her head but she ignored them. She couldn't let him go. A moment longer wouldn't hurt. There was something she was supposed to ask him but it didn't seem to matter anymore. He broke the kiss without warning, breathing heavily and trying to rein himself in. Giving up contact with him was painful.

"Nic," she whispered, reaching for him. Despite the inherent danger, she wanted him to kiss her again. She needed him to kiss her.

Instead, his hand curved around the back of her head. He pressed her forehead to his chest. His heart was racing and thumping so hard she thought she could feel it against her cheek. He wasn't as calm as he appeared. She liked the way he clamped her against his chest while he fought to regain control. She liked that his heart wasn't slowing down any faster than hers was. The moment was too perfect to do anything but savor it.

"Let's get out of here for a while."

"Sure." She pressed against him, loving the slight roughness of him against her bare skin. She tingled everywhere and his slightest movement sent currents all through her. "What should I wear? My bathing suit, my cocktail dress or the towel?" Humor and disappointment laced the words together. "I didn't bring a lot of clothes."

His hands soothed up and down her bare back, electricity sparking along the contact. "Check the master bedroom closet. Then we'll head over to the resort. You can shop."

"Shop?"

"You try on dresses, pick one out and wear it to dinner."

"At your resort?"

"Resort and Golf club," he corrected lightly. He was teasing her but it had the opposite effect.

The real world intruded and she remembered who he was and who she was. They did not live in the same reality. She might let herself play in his for a while, but getting attached would be stupid. "I have no idea how to be in your world, Nic."

He kissed her nose before stepping back from her. "You just be you, Lizzie."

Her smile faltered. She definitely couldn't be herself.

It took him another few minutes and when he finally eased her away from him, Lizzie held her breath as the ache threatened to consume her. She was definitely in over her head. No matter how careful she was this week, when they parted it was going to leave a scar.

She found a sundress hanging in the master closet. The designer tag confirmed it was a dress she'd pinned a few weeks ago. She wanted to be the girl who hung it back in the closet and refused to wear it. She held it up against herself, admiring the retro fabric.

She should hang it back in the closet. She didn't. She slipped it off the hanger and over her head before she could change her mind. It was perfect. The tight bodice gave her cleavage and the circle skirt was made for twirling. She slipped on the lemon yellow kitten heels and tried not to swoon.

She pulled her hair into a high ponytail and wished again for straight hair with bangs. Otherwise the outfit was perfect. The cute party girl she'd wanted stared back at her from the full length mirror. Mischief lurked in her eyes and her smile wouldn't go away. That girl was up to no good.

She was perfect.

When she stepped back into the living room, Nic was waiting for her. He'd showered and was dressed in khakis and a white button down with the sleeves cuffed below his elbows. She had no idea why it made his arms so sexy, but it absolutely did. Her heart skipped a beat when he smiled at her. He had the most dangerous smile in the world. He'd shaved, which made his face harder than usual. Nic could shave twice a day. The stubble usually shadowing his face made him more approachable. He was much more intimidating with a smooth jawline.

"You keep looking at me like that and we won't be going anywhere."

She shrugged. "You're the one who wants to leave. I was perfectly happy."

He held out his hand and she took it without thinking. "Ever been to the Keys before?"

"No."

"The diving is excellent."

"I'm not sporty. I'm decorative." She flinched. The words had sounded much better in her head.

"Decorative?" he echoed, laughing under his breath when he opened the passenger side door of the convertible Aston Martin parked next to the SUV in his garage. "Aren't you in graduate school?"

She slid into the seat, keeping her voice casual as she tried to think fast. What if he asked what she was majoring in? She could say math. When he asked if she was going to teach, she'd say yes. "I am."

"Lizzie," he said, his voice lower than it should be. "There's something you should know."

"What?"

"Decorative and smart is better."

She went warm in places she didn't know could get warm and she couldn't help the smile that split across her face. Smart she could do. Smart wasn't threatening. He liked smart? Perfect. She could definitely be that girl.

She couldn't lose sight of the fact that when he said smart, he didn't mean academic discussions about gap fluctuations or why P could never equal NP.

CHAPTER SEVEN

The Maretti Key Resort was much larger than the hotel in Miami. Nic gave the keys to valet parking then led her into the open air lobby. A huge fountain dominated the space. Water splashed against mermaids carved into the stone and fresh flowers were everywhere.

Lizzie had forgotten he owned the resort until a young man dressed in khakis and an understated island shirt, came hurrying toward.

"Mr. Maretti." He fell in step with them. "We weren't expecting you today."

"David, I'm not here." He sounded different. Business voice, she guessed, trying not to be impressed. "We're here to shop and maybe have dinner. It's not a surprise inspection. Tell everyone to relax."

"I'm sure you would find everything in order if it was."

"I have no doubt."

David gave them both a polite smile then headed back to the registration area.

"He seems nervous."

Nic shrugged. "Not everyone thinks I'm as nice as you do."

David had apparently set off some type of silent alert to the hotel staff that Nic was in the house. Everyone all but curtsied when he walked by. The manager of the ladies boutique was waiting for them when they arrived.

"Mr. Maretti, so good of you to visit us today."

"Anna." Nic smiled at the older lady and shook hands with her. Did he know everyone or was he reading their discreet name tags? Lizzie couldn't tell and she doubted neither David nor Anna knew either. "This is Lizzie. Let her have whatever she wants."

He turned to Lizzie, his hands on her shoulders. "There's a day spa. I'm sure Anna can take you."

She brightened. A spa sounded wonderful.

He kissed her cheek, then whispered in her ear, "I had better come back and find lots of shopping bags."

"I need some shorts, maybe a pair of jeans."

"Dresses."

She leaned into him. "I can't let you buy me clothes."

Nic blinked. This wasn't a false protest. She really didn't want him to spend money on her. He'd never met anyone like Lizzie before. His former girlfriends, his stepmother and even his sister walked into his resorts and charged whatever they wanted to him. He never saw the bills. Pam took care of those details. It had never occurred to him she wouldn't expect him to pay the bill. Most people in his life treated him like an open line of credit.

Fascinated by her concern, he leaned down, rubbing his face along her cheek until his mouth was close to her ear. "I kidnapped you remember? You have to do what I say until I let you go."

Her face dissolved into laughter. The sound filled his chest until he couldn't breathe. Radiant now, she smiled from ear to ear as she…blushed. He wasn't used to the soft sweep of color or the way it made his lower body turn to stone while the rest of him felt so light he might float away.

He felt her breath on his cheek. "My dad will kill me."

"Then we won't tell him."

"Is this what you do with your women, Nic? Bring them for facials, buy them expensive clothes and—"

"I've never brought a woman here." It was out of his mouth before he could stop it. Something about her disconnected his brain from his common sense. "Key Largo is my sanctuary. I don't even let Pam come down here."

Her lips parted again and she gave a smile of surrender. "Since I have no choice…"

"Lizzie, you always have a choice, but it's okay to choose to have fun occasionally. So, shop." He squeezed her hand before letting it go. "Enjoy yourself. If you want to pay me back you can write me a check later."

Her expression narrowed on him as she tilted her face. "Will you cash the check?"

"No." He choked on laughter then turned her toward the large display across the room. "Did I mention the shoes?"

It was like a choir of angels sang ahhh and a light shone straight down onto a pair of crystal encrusted Jimmy Choos. "You're cheating." She pouted.

"Pick some things out and you can donate them when you're done with them."

"I will never be done with those shoes." She sighed. "If they fit, I don't think I'll ever take them off."

"Take a chance, Cinderella."

She glanced back at him, kissing him lightly on the cheek. "You're a bad influence, Nic Maretti."

"Good. Now have fun, I'll be in the executive office if you need me. Have someone call me when you're finished."

Nic kissed her again. So sweet. He would never get enough. Reluctantly, he raised his head. "Bad, Nic," she whispered and kissed him before he could step back.

When he did step back, he couldn't breathe. He was drunk on the way she smelled, how soft her skin was, and the way her hair felt in his hands. He ached to sink himself into all that softness again and see her expression when he did. He couldn't remember ever wanting anything so much.

On the way to his office, he caught himself before he started whistling. Hell, he didn't know how to whistle and he wasn't about to learn. All these emotions ping ponging inside him were starting to take their toll. He reminded himself why she was here in the first place. He wanted another night with her, wanted her out of the way to give his sister a chance at saving her marriage. It was a bonus she was enjoying herself. It made things easier.

He passed the lounge and decided there was no rush to inspect the offices he knew would be perfect. This resort was one of his top three. The bar was mostly empty and the bartender straightened from watching a rugby game on the widescreen mounted above the bar.

"Mr. Maretti."

Nic held up his hand before sliding onto a barstool. "You get straight A's for watching a real ball game."

The younger man relaxed and started mixing a rum and coke before Nic could ask for it. David had been busy since they'd walked into the hotel. The drink was perfect, the day was gorgeous, and the game was good. He couldn't focus on any of it. He groaned in relief when his cell phone started playing "Lady in Red."

Angie had programmed the ringtone in too, one last feeble attempt to match-make the unmatchable. He'd known Madlyn Robicheaux longer than he'd known Pam. They'd been thrown together a lot as kids by their families hoping to encourage a bond between them that would be a consolidation of power between their two families. They'd bonded all right. Their mutual hatred for the men who raised them and tried to manipulate them had made them close friends very quickly.

"Madlyn, did you find a new office yet or are you ready to come work with me?"

"We swore never to do anything that would make your father or my grandfather happy. At least not on purpose."

"True." Nic sighed. "They get in enough trouble on their own."

"Your amazon gets territorial when I'm around."

"Pam? Territorial?"

Madlyn sounded bored. "I guess I threaten her."

"You threaten everyone."

"What can I say? I'm the Red Queen. Besides, I'm not leaving New Orleans until I get custody of Robbie."

"That shouldn't be a problem with your grandfather in jail."

"Oh." She laughed bitterly. "Haven't you seen the news? Andreas Maretti posted bond for him. How thoughtful, but really, he shouldn't have. The networks are having a field day."

Nic swallowed down the sudden rush of anger. Madlyn had been trying for eight years to get custody of her son from her grandfather. Winston Robicheaux was one of the most corrupt judges in Louisiana. He had powerful friends who owed him lots of favors and it was next to impossible to get the old man to do anything unless he wanted to. Now, since he'd been arrested on corruption charges, Madlyn had her first real chance of getting custody back.

Nic hadn't given Andreas the money so he could let a rabid dog out of jail. "Are you sure you don't want the seat on the board?"

"Not yet." She sighed. "It's not your fault, Nic. You couldn't let all those people lose their jobs. I get it."

"I should have seen it coming and made it a condition of the deal."

"You and I both know my grandfather would have found a way to get the money from your father. Besides, you've been distracted. Or is Lizzie Sellers not in Key Largo with you?"

Nic almost spit out a mouthful of rum and coke. "Excuse me?"

"Is she down there or not?"

"How do you know she's with me?"

"Doesn't matter. She's supposed to be in school. As soon as Mac Sellers realizes where she is, he'll be down there with a shotgun and a priest."

"Don't be ridiculous."

"Think about who you're dealing with. Do you think logic applies?"

He'd known Mac Sellers a long time. He could be a scary bastard, but Nic wasn't worried. "I'm the last person he wants for a son-in-law, Madlyn. Especially when he finds out Andreas bailed out Judge Robicheaux. Sellers is still furious with him about the Volikovneft deal."

"Yes, but you saved the deal from falling apart, didn't you?"

"I might have tipped them off, but Stefan did all the saving."

"Yes, Stefan has the whole white knight thing down to a science. You'll find out first hand when he decides he needs to save his sister from you."

"Stefan owes me and besides, Lizzie is having fun. Tanning, shopping, the spa thing…"

"She's too young for you, Nic. She's way too sheltered and won't understand how things work with you. You sleep with her and she'll think there's a future involved."

There was a weird warm spark somewhere in his chest and for a moment Nic couldn't breathe. He downed the rest of his drink, the ice chinking against the glass. He waved his glass at the bartender, ignoring the younger man's surprise. "Less soda this time."

"Nic, do yourself a favor and put her on the next flight out."

"This is the part where you butt out."

"Fine, be an idiot. You could do worse than Lizzie."

"You have no idea what you're talking about."

"What? Are you saying Lizzie is different?"

Nic opened his mouth to deny it but nothing happened.

Madlyn sighed. "You'll break her heart, Nic, then you'll beat yourself up for it. I know you, remember? Put her on a plane."

"Maybe she'll break my heart," he suggested, sipping the fresh drink.

"Do you still have one?"

"Do you?"

"No. I had it removed years ago."

She was lying. Her heart had been ripped out when her fiancé had been killed in a car accident about ten years ago leaving her alone, pregnant and at the mercy of her narcissistic grandfather.

"Did Angie tell you Lizzie was with me?" he asked, changing the subject. "And don't start with that privilege excuse. You're my attorney."

"Yes, she called this morning. Apparently the divorce is off again."

Relief swept over him. The last thing he wanted was Angie getting divorced because then she would run back to Daddy. Nic didn't want Andreas Maretti having any more influence over his nephew than he did now. Whatever other problems they were having, Rogan was a good father and adored his son. Zachary was a beautiful, thriving little boy. Andreas could end that with a few cutting words. Nic wasn't going to let that happen. "I hope it sticks this time."

"Be careful, Nic. Lizzie isn't what—"

"Why do you care, Madlyn? After what the Sellers family has put you through, you should be encouraging me to break her heart."

It was silent on the other end. He was afraid he'd dropped the call. "Maddie?"

"Forget I said anything. I called you because I need you to stop your father from bankrolling my grandfather. In all the years I've known you, I've never asked you for anything, but I need you to do this."

"I'll make a call."

"Thank you."

"If you need—"

"I don't."

She ended the call before he could. He stared at his phone for a long time before sending Pam a text asking her to check on the money Andreas was sending to Winston Robicheaux. If the old man was sending company money, Nic was not going to be responsible for what happened next. He'd had enough of Andreas Maretti.

His team scored and the roar of the crowd on the television distracted him. He stared at the game but couldn't focus. Madlyn was right. He should put Lizzie on a plane before this got out of control.

He wasn't sure how when all he could think about was how sweet Lizzie tasted. He stared at his drink and contemplated the ice cubes as they chinked against the sides of the glass as he moved it slowly back and forth.

He shifted in the seat. Bringing her here had been a mistake. If

Angie was calling the divorce off, there was no reason to keep her here at all. He'd take her to dinner. The resort had a great restaurant right out on the beach. Then he'd take her back tomorrow. No harm. No foul.

His glass hit the bar too hard. He glanced at the bartender. "Scotch this time, neat."

He should take her home. To New Orleans.

He wasn't going to.

CHAPTER EIGHT

A few hours, a facial, a sea salt scrub, a mani/pedi and a massage later, Lizzie didn't think it was possible to be any more relaxed. The girl at the salon had wanted to flat iron her hair but Lizzie wouldn't let her. Nic wouldn't like it. Then she realized she was making decisions about her appearance based on what she believed Nic would like and that really freaked her out. She was supposed to be getting Nic out of her system, not more entrenched.

She told herself she picked out the blue-green dress because it matched her eyes. She glanced down at the five inch surprisingly comfortable heels. A thin strip of leather encrusted with crystals crossed over her freshly painted toes and swirled up to wide cuffs covered with more crystals as they closed around her ankles. She should never have tried them on but it was too late now.

A girl never forgot her first pair of Jimmy Choos.

She reassured herself that the dress was not too short. At five three, dresses were always too long for her. This boutique specialized in ultra mini dresses designed for clubbing. She'd never worn anything so short before but when she paired the dress with the shoes, it gave her the illusion of long legs. She couldn't seem to take the outfit off. She didn't recognize herself. The plain, pale math major was long gone and the pretty but ditzy party girl who stared back at her was up to no good.

Perfect. She could be this girl for a week.

It would be like a mental vacation. She could worry about shoes, toenail polish and perfecting her tan. No functions, and calculations, or trying to prove that prime numbers could reveal the secrets of the universe…even if the answer to the universe wasn't a prime number. No creepy professor making her feel like a complete failure. She shivered, stuffing Hatton back past the barrier of this week. This week was fun and sun and kissing. Lots and lots of kissing. Whatever was left of her when the week was over, could worry about the universe.

There was a sharp tap on the dressing room door and Nic walked in before she could respond. She spun around as he shut the door behind him, turned and stopped. Stunned, he didn't move but his eyes swept over her with an intensity that lit small fires under her skin. He locked the door without taking his eyes off her. "Lizzie, you look...amazing."

Warm color brushed her cheeks. "You don't think it's too short?"

His eyes slid slowly up and down as he approached. "No, it's perfect. Keep it on. We're having dinner."

When he reached her, he surprised her by turning her toward her reflection. His eyes met hers in the mirror, then he leaned down to kiss the curve of her neck. Her eyes drifted shut and she leaned back into him, tilting her head to give him better access.

Warm fingers slipped into the draped opening at the back of the dress. She shivered as they traced over her rib cage to tease at the slight curve of her bare breasts. He stepped closer, his chest supporting her head so she could see them both in the mirror. She watched, fascinated, as his hand teased her under the soft layers of chiffon. Her nipples beaded into hard points that showed under the multiple layers of thin fabric. Color burned across her cheeks. He was watching her watch his hand.

"Soft." He breathed the words against the back of her neck, making the soft hairs dance. "So..."

"Small?" she inserted, completing his sentence, trying to break whatever spell he was casting. She'd seen the women he dated. She was nothing like them.

"You know better." His hand cupped the modest weight, his thumb teasing the tip. "You're perfect."

She melted into him. She was a sucker for flattery. Who knew?

Flattery from Nic was deadly, the sincerity behind it burned her alive.

Her eyes fluttered shut and her skin ached as he continued to tease her. He pulled her back tighter against his chest, and his fingers skimmed along her thigh easing the hem of the too- short dress higher. She stopped breathing as those fingertips teased the sensitive skin of her inner thigh. She caught his wrist when he reached the edge of the lace boy shorts, but she wasn't able to stop the lazy glide of his fingers across her skin. Or the release of liquid heat deep inside her.

"No, someone might come in." She gasped the words out, appalled at herself for being more concerned about getting caught than stopping him.

"The door's locked."

His fingers slipped inside the lace and her lungs stopped working. Electricity charged the liquid heat building in her and shock burned down her arms. He wouldn't. Not here. He couldn't.

He did.

Her mind and body went white hot.

He groaned against her neck as he stroked her. "Lizzie, you're drenched."

Blood scorched her cheeks and she tried to wrench away from him. The hand on her breast moved down to flatten against her abdomen. He wasn't going to let her go. The burn inside of her turned molten. Any minute now she would vaporize.

"I missed this," he whispered, as long fingers stroked deeper. His other hand smoothed down her belly, then around her until his arm was a tight a band across her, keeping her from sliding to the ground. "Open your eyes."

She struggled to process what was happening. Her knees threatened to buckle. Bones melted away. The crisp hair on his arm teased the sensitive skin on the underside of her breast. Was it possible to panic and die of pleasure at the same time? She was about to find out.

"Open your eyes," he repeated, the edge back in his voice, making her do things she couldn't admit she wanted to do. "Open them."

Her eyes opened and shock lanced through her. His arm was through her dress and his dark hand was lost in the scrap of lace. Lizzie's skin froze, melted, then froze again. Feeling his hands on her was one thing. Seeing it, seeing him again and the hunger in his eyes, well… it was too much.

"I can't." She turned her face away, shutting out the overwhelmingly erotic image.

"Look or I'll stop." His teeth grazed across her shoulder, his fingers ruthlessly demonstrating what she had to lose.

"Nic, please." She was begging now. She didn't know what she was begging him for. Not to make her watch? Not to keep turning her into this person she didn't know? Not to stop?

If he stopped, she would die.

He increased the pressure and rolled his fingers against her until she couldn't breathe. She gasped without making a sound, still unable to comprehend that anything could feel so good. His fingers continued until she coiled tight enough to break.

Then he stopped, dangling her over the edge. She writhed against his hand but it wasn't the same and she died as the gruff laughter warmed the skin of her neck. Was he punishing her?

"Look in the mirror, *bella*. See what I see. Just for a second. Look." The last word was a definite command. It overrode all the embarrassment keeping her eyes clamped shut.

She opened her eyes again but didn't recognize the girl locked possessively in his arms. That couldn't possibly be her.

"See? Beautiful."

Her breath caught and her lips parted as he resumed taking total control of her body, hell, her entire existence with each dangerous roll of his fingers. She didn't recognize herself in the wanton creature leaning back against the tall dark man who was doing wicked things to her. She couldn't tear her eyes away as he built the small nuclear explosion inside her. Her muscles seized then broke loose in a shattering wave of white hot pleasure as she watched herself fly apart like lightning in his hands.

Nic caught her before she collapsed. He sat down in one of the armchairs and pulled her into his lap, refusing to admit to himself how good it felt when she curled into him. He held her, while reaction shivered through her.

She hadn't made a sound. How could she be so quiet and come that hard? Amazing. "Okay?" A strange protective urge swept over him.

"I don't think I'll ever be okay."

The instinct to lose himself inside her right then was staggering, but Nic had never been controlled by his emotions or his sex drive.

"Don't make me do that again." She melted against his chest, pressing her head under his chin. Technically it might have been a cuddle, except Nic didn't cuddle but he liked how she felt curled against him, and he pulled her tighter against his chest, and rubbed his cheek against the top of her head.

"I'm going to make you do that a lot, beautiful girl, but I'll make sure we're at home next time." Nic shut his eyes hoping she didn't realize he'd said home…he'd meant alone.

She nodded. "Kay." The word whispered across his overheated skin.

"I couldn't help myself." He hurried to cover his slip. "It's these shoes. When I do lock you up, you'll be wearing these. They are spectacular." He'd meant it as a joke, but there wasn't a shred of humor in his words.

No, he meant them. He wanted to carry her off and lock her away and keep her all to himself. He didn't want anyone else near her.

She laughed. The sound played around in his chest, teasing at his heart, making it feel strangely light. "You haven't gotten the bill yet."

She slid away from him, unsteady on the five inch heels. She turned around, dazed and vulnerable. "What is this, Nic? What are we doing?"

Another protective instinct swelled inside him. Maybe he was getting in way over his head but instead of backing off, he did something he'd never done before. He tried to reassure her.

"Let's see, I'm taking you out to dinner." He kept it light and gentle. "We'll have some interesting wine. Talk about all sorts of unimportant things. Then I'll take you home and kiss you good night. I think you call that a date."

He wanted to see her smile all the time, except when she was screaming out his name the way he planned for her to as soon as he got her home…no, he meant alone.

"A date?" She wished the amusement in Nic's eyes wasn't turning her insides back into mush.

"Yes, what did you think?"

"That we're having fun."

"If you consider going insane fun, then I guess I'm having a lot of fun. Take your time. They'll hold our table as long as it takes."

She watched him leave in the mirror, the door closing behind him. Her legs were weak and her arms were too heavy. Curling up in the armchair he'd been sitting in and going to sleep was way too tempting.

A date. Really? A date meant possibilities, not a stolen week she'd already labeled a fling.

A week, she reminded herself. She could handle a week. A fun week to get him out of her system. She had to remember this was temporary. She couldn't let herself get so caught up in him that she forgot who she was. Or what she had to do.

When she stepped outside the dressing room a few minutes later, his eyes skimmed over her. The approval in his smile didn't quite match the admonition in his words. "You didn't follow my instructions."

She stopped short, her forehead creasing in concern as she frowned. She couldn't tell if he was teasing or not. Who did he think he was anyway? She wanted to tell him that he had no right to give her instructions then she remembered that arm candy probably always did as instructed. Still she wasn't playing dumb when she asked. "What instructions?" She honestly didn't know what he was talking about.

"Two dresses and a pair of shoes doesn't equal a lot."

"Oh." The word escaped. Was she supposed to apologize for not going crazy in the boutique? They were only here for a week and he knew she didn't want him buying her a bunch of clothes. "Wait." She stepped forward when he brushed past her toward the racks of hideously overpriced designer wear.

She watched, equally excited and horrified as he added more dresses, a teal silk robe with a huge poppy on the side, and a few outfits she had been drooling over earlier. Then he found the lingerie and Lizzie discovered she could turn multiple shades of pink and purple at the same time. Grateful there was no one else in the dress shop, she could hardly breathe until he told Anna he was satisfied.

"Nic." She leaned closer, lowering her voice. "Don't get all this. It's too much." She glanced down at her feet and tried to feel guilty. But the shoes were fantastic and there was no way she could feel anything but sexy in them. Oh, she'd have hell to pay later if her father or brother found out, but she would make sure that didn't happen.

"Humor me," he said, as they left the shop.

She leaned against him, balancing on the heels. "You're spoiling me."

"That's the idea," he said, pressing a kiss to her forehead.

"I could pay for this if I had my purse. I couldn't find it back at the house and my cell phone is in it too." She stopped talking when she saw his expression turn slightly guilty. Shock rippled through her "You didn't take it, did you? Because that would be a little scary."

He leaned down to kiss her forehead. "Paradise. Remember? No cell phones allowed and you don't need your wallet while you're with me."

"You have your phone."

"I'm not on vacation. Relax, Lizzie. It's safe."

Well, that was something. At least her cell phone was safe, because she certainly wasn't. She was trying to decide what she thought when Anna handed her the small bag that matched the Jimmy Choos. "I added a few things you might need," the lady confided.

Lizzie popped it open and found a lipstick, mints, tissue, powder, hand sanitizer and basically everything arm candy should be concerned with. She took a deep breath but it caught in her throat. She'd spent five hours in a resort full of telephones and it hadn't once occurred to her to ask to use one.

"You ready?" Nic asked, his smile telling her he'd thought the same thing. He held his hand out for her. "Choose fun, Lizzie."

She placed her hand in his and did exactly that.

The restaurant had a veranda right out on the beach. Wind chimes mixed with the sound of the surf as they were seated at the table closest to the water. Candles gave off a soothing warm glow and there were flowers everywhere. Lizzie didn't think she'd ever seen a more beautiful setting. She couldn't believe they had it all to themselves, but none of the other tables were occupied. The interior dining room was packed and people had been waiting for tables when the hostess walked them straight through.

There was already a bottle of wine open on the table and Nic waved off the server and poured their glasses himself. She sipped it cautiously. It was lighter than she expected and fruity. She set the glass back down. "Berries?"

"Not too dry, then?"

She took another careful sip. She was reeling from earlier and the setting was intoxicating enough. She didn't need to add more trouble to the mix with alcohol. "No."

The server returned with a menu for Lizzie. Her heart threatened to escape her throat as she hesitated before opening it. She blinked a few times, plastered on her best smile and tried to act normal. She hated being such a freak about food.

"Is there a problem with the menu? If you don't see anything you like…"

She shook her head. "No, I'm not hungry."

No surprises there. None of his first dates were ever hungry. "The fish is good."

She flinched. "There are mushrooms."

Okay, she didn't like mushrooms. He wanted to know what she did like, besides plain scrambled eggs. Nic reached across the table and took the oversized menu from her. The server hadn't given him one because all the chefs in his resorts knew his food requirements. He scanned the selection of specials. "The chicken is…" he stopped, when she shivered in revulsion. "You don't eat chicken?"

She took a quick sip of her wine. "No. Too many antibiotics and growth hormones."

"Free range or organic? No? But you do eat eggs?"

"Yes, and dairy. I couldn't live without ice cream."

"Then dessert's a no brainer?"

She smiled, and Nic felt the lightness return to his chest. He glanced back at the menu. "I'm going to take a guess and say no red meat or baby animals."

"No."

"Definitely not the suckling pig?" he teased her, looking back to see her struggling to smile as she turned a light shade of green.

"Definitely."

"That leaves fish."

The opening he'd given her was too delicious to pass up. She sighed tragically. "This fish is a problem because I don't have my cell phone."

His head snapped back. "You need your cell phone to order fish?"

"I have an app."

"An app? Are you counting calories?"

Lizzie swallowed hard. She couldn't answer that. She was pretty sure arm candy did not track their calories in their head a week at a time. "No, there's a Seafood Watch app. It helps find ocean friendly fish."

"Ocean friendly fish?"

She nodded. "The ones that aren't overfished. It can also let you know if mercury levels are too high and..." She trailed off when she registered the surprise on his face. "You don't want to hear all this."

Nic pulled his cell phone out of his pocket. "Not true. I think you'd better download it for me although I would hope the restaurants in our resorts already serve ocean friendly fish."

Lizzie reached for the phone and he caught her hand, his thumb brushing across her fingers before releasing the phone to her.

"Something you'd better know about me." He eased back in his chair. "I'm a pescetarian. I only eat seafood, eggs and dairy."

Warmth cascaded through her. "Me too. I haven't eaten meat since Stefan told me the truth about chicken nuggets."

Nic smothered a laugh. "I haven't eaten meat since I moved to Texas."

Her eyes widened but before she could ask what he meant, the server appeared at their table.

"Order for us. You don't need the menu. Tell her what you want."

What was it like going through life knowing everyone made sure you got everything you wanted the way you wanted it? Different worlds. She took a light breath and ordered. "I haven't had mahi-mahi this month."

"We have a special tonight," the server offered. "Mahi-mahi Grilled with a lemon glaze served with roasted balsamic Brussels sprouts."

"Do you like Brussels sprouts?" Nic asked her.

"Oddly, yes," she admitted. "The special sounds good."

Nic ordered the same. The server left as the sommelier arrived with more wine. Lizzie glanced around the empty dining room while Nic tasted the wine. The restaurant was lovely. Ceiling fans turned down low kept the air moving and the candles flickered against all the white tablecloths covering empty tables. Which was odd, the lobby had been packed when they walked through.

Surely, Nic wouldn't clear out an entire dining room so he and Lizzie could have dinner alone? No one had come into the boutique while she was there either, and she'd walked right in at the spa, past ladies flipping through magazines and drinking Mimosas while they waited.

She turned back to him. It was hard to believe he owned this entire resort. He could clear out the entire building if he wanted to.

The sommelier left and Nic turned his attention back to her.

"Nic, is it a good idea to keep all these tables empty?"

He shrugged. "I like my space."

She couldn't help comparing the menu prices versus the number of empty tables. Based on normal table turn over time, families could live on what it was costing Nic to keep the dining room empty but that wasn't what concerned Lizzie.

"Yes, but I'm sure your wait staff depend on tips." Her cheeks burned at the shocked expression on his face. She really needed to Google *how to be arm candy*. She had no idea what she was doing.

She cringed as he nodded at the dangerous looking man standing on the edge of the dining room. She'd noticed him in the lobby earlier and as he approached their table she realized he wore a sidearm under the understated gray suit.

"Tag, ask the manager to seat these tables."

Tag glanced at Lizzie, surprise lifting his eyebrows although the rest of his expression didn't flicker. "I'll take care of it."

"Who was that?" Lizzie asked, as Tag moved away.

"Tag is head of my security."

"You have security?"

Nic nodded. "I'm afraid so."

Alarm prickled through her as the server arrived with their salads. She lost the chance to ask more questions. *Don't forget who he is, Lizzie*, she told herself as she set the pot of salad dressing aside, careful not to let it touch the spring mix. Salad dressing was a menace.

"No dressing?"

She shook her head, not wanting to meet his eyes. He was really going to think she was a freak. "Do you have any idea what can fall into dressing?"

"I see your point."

Stunned, she watched him transfer the strawberries from his salad to hers. Lizzie caught her breath. This really was a date. She was on a date with Nic, and it didn't feel at all like a first date He'd even remembered she loved strawberries.

"You have the strangest expression on your face."

She didn't doubt it. She felt strange. The whole world seemed to be tilted two degrees differently than she was. Enough to throw her off, but not enough for anyone else to notice. Except for Nic. Nothing got by him.

"I'm not dreaming." The truth escaped her before she could think of something clever to say. More hot color swept over her face. Someone needed to invent a laser therapy to stop the blushing response. Lizzie would happily be their first test subject.

"You're wide awake." He leaned back in his chair, a teasing, and slightly smug smile playing at the corners of his mouth. She could still feel that mouth moving along her shoulders, and his hands scalding her skin. "Do you dream about me a lot?"

The arrogance of the question broke through the peculiar feeling of everything being familiar and strange at the same time.

"I bet you always wake up before the good part?" His deep voice took on a hoarseness that shimmered all over her skin, then went deeper, stoking her inner glow into a raging bonfire.

Nic watched the emotions play over her face. The wine, the candlelight warming her creamy skin was starting to get to him and he didn't like not knowing what he was going to do next. Except he felt a strange sense of anticipation. He hadn't felt it in so long it had taken a while for him to recognize it.

He hadn't realized how bored he'd been. Had been for a long time. He was only thirty-one but lately he'd felt ancient. Not anymore. The ennui was gone.

"What did you mean you stopped eating meat when you moved to Texas? Isn't that steak country?"

Nic shrugged. "Obviously, I didn't want to be there. I refused to eat anything but fish because I assumed all they ate was beef. It was childish but Claudia was so eager to play happy family, she had the cook prepare special meals for me."

"Sounds like she was trying."

"She was." He remembered how hard Claudia had worked to make him feel welcome. "But I was an angry kid."

"Claudia's your stepmother?"

He nodded.

"Angie's your half-sister?"

The fish arrived and Nic used it as an excuse not to answer. He watched her carefully lift her fork. When she tasted a bite and smiled, he relaxed back into his chair.

"The fish is perfect." She smiled then returned to the subject he'd hoped dinner would distract her from. "What about your mother?"

Maybe it was the careful tone of her voice, or the gentleness in her expression but Nic found himself answering her questions. "She died when I was six."

"How old were you when you moved to Texas?"

He watched, fascinated as she blinked back tears. Tears for him? How odd. He shook the strange feeling teasing at him and continued the story he never told anyone. A story that was somehow easier to tell Lizzie.

"Ten." Nic paused, swallowed back the rest of the story. He didn't want to lie to Lizzie but he wasn't ready for her to know the truth. He reached for the wine bottle and topped off their glasses and the words started spilling out of him before he could stop himself. "I was at boarding school. I broke my arm and Claudia used it as an excuse to bring me to Texas."

His heart stopped. He'd never talked about his childhood. Had never wanted to, but telling Lizzie took the sting out of the trauma he kept buried. She was easy to talk to. She smiled, her gentle expression understanding without being invasive. Then she surprised him by leading the subject in a different direction. "I guess public school in Texas was a big shock?"

Lizzie sipped her wine and pretended she didn't notice the relief sweeping over Nic. He'd already told her more than he'd meant to. She knew because he kept trying to slide behind his calm façade.

"It was," he agreed. "For one thing it was co-ed."

"Not a bad thing?"

He shook his head. "No, not a bad thing. They didn't have a rugby team so I played football."

He had to be teasing her. "You? Played football? Seriously?"

"I was the kicker."

It was easier to picture him in rugby shorts and socks than football pads but she could believe him as a kicker. "I'll bet you dated all the cheerleaders."

Her heart raced at his slowly, sexy smile. "A few. Were you a cheerleader?"

A cheerleader? Her? No, they hadn't let math geeks on the squad at her school. "No, Jen and I went to high school in Toulouse. The cheerleaders there are picked at birth."

"Toulouse?"

"Small town between Slidell and Baton Rouge. We lived there after Katrina for a few years."

"You lost your home in the storm?" The gentleness in his tone soothed along her skin, beating back the chill that always accompanied the memories of Katrina. Lizzie never talked about the days following the hurricane. She didn't want to think about it and talking about them dragged it all up again.

"We were lucky. We got out of the city and stayed at a friend's farm. We always stayed there in the past when there were storms. They have horses and we'd ride, have a big BBQ and go home."

"Katrina was different?"

Lizzie pushed the fish around her plate and let the candlelight flickering off the china distract her. "It kept coming. It was a category three when it destroyed the farm but we were lucky. Mr. Masters has a helicopter and he flew us to Atlanta. We stayed there until Dad and Stefan found a place in Toulouse. We lived there until Mom and Dad compromised on moving to Slidell. Dad wanted to build our house back in the city but Mom refused to live on that side of the Pontchartrain again."

She focused on Nic, not wanting to think about Katrina. She had no right to be upset anyway. They'd been lucky. The X on their house hadn't had a body count.

"No cheerleading?" he teased, distracting her from the memories tightening her throat.

"No cheerleading," she agreed, the nightmare of Katrina sliding away.

Jet black eyebrows narrowed at her. "What have I told you about looking at me like that?"

"Like what?"

"Like you're starving." His voice was hoarse again.

She glanced away, the dark magic swirling around them becoming too much for her. "Nic, please tell me I'm not the only one feeling this. I think I'm losing my mind."

She was reaching for her wine glass when his fingers caught hers. "No," he rasped. "You're not."

She watched, fascinated as he stroked his thumb across her knuckles. He turned her hand over and teased the tender skin on the inside of her wrist. Chills ran up her arm. "I don't know if I can do this."

He spoke slowly, a teasing tone offsetting the seriousness of what he said next. "I'm not sure we have a choice."

The darkness in his voice surrounded her and the ambient noise from the restaurant fell away. The craziness in her mind quieted down. She couldn't take her eyes away from the contrast of his tanned fingers, circling around her wrist. She could feel her blood thickening with each lazy round of his thumb.

Time simply had no meaning any longer. When he spoke, she was startled by the sound.

"We should get going. Finish your wine. Then I'll show you the beach."

A few minutes later, she was walking down the soft sand, her new shoes dangling from one hand and her other hand lost in his. The moon was high and bright in the sky bathing the beach in silvery light. It was a gorgeous night and better than anything she'd ever dreamed.

He stopped her and pulled her around to face him. She kept her arm extended for a minute, then let him pull her to him. His mouth brushed against her forehead. "I didn't take your phone, *bella*. It's on the charger in my office. Your purse is sitting next to it on my desk. If you'd bothered to snoop through my things, you would have found them right away. But you didn't, did you?" he whispered, his arms tightening around her. "You were by yourself most of the morning and I bet you didn't open a drawer."

She shrugged. Did arm candy snoop? She really didn't care. She flattened her hands against his hard chest, then threw her head back. "Stop wasting moonlight, Nic. Kiss me."

He nodded, accepting her change of topic without hesitation. "How can I say no to that?" His hand curved around the back of her head and he kissed her. It was a gentle, searching, scorching kiss she'd never ever forget. The way Italian princes must have kissed centuries ago. Fairytales and moonbeams wove around her and she sighed when he raised his head.

It was a few minutes before she could open her eyes. It was all so perfect that it was hard to remember that it wasn't real. It felt real, it tasted real, but it was only temporary. They only had a week. Then the crystal shoes were going back.

"Dinner was delicious." She sighed, as they continued back to the resort.

"Successful first date?"

She nodded, glancing up at him. She smiled when she saw his relaxed expression. He seemed younger, more approachable. Nothing like the harsh businessman she'd arrived with earlier. She slid her arm through his and leaned into him. "Perfect."

Later, when the Aston Martin came to a stop in the garage, Lizzie's heart tried to escape her chest. She leaned back against the seat, her face turned toward Nic watching him put the car into park, turn the engine off, push his not-so-steady fingers through his hair. He'd been beautiful in the moonlight on the beach and he was just as gorgeous under the stark fluorescent light in the enormous garage. She loved watching him. It didn't matter what he was doing. Fishing, cooking, dancing, breathing. Every move he made was a singular work of art and she could drown in the view for a lifetime and never notice.

He turned to her then, his eyelids low and his lips not touching. He watched her too. The intensity of his gaze burned through layers of skin and muscle, right to her bones. She ached for him like she never had before.

His hands curved around her face, then his mouth moved hard over hers. His tongue pressed deep, filling her with his taste. Spicy with traces of the wine they'd had at dinner and the mint he'd popped into his mouth when he thought she wasn't looking.

Her fingers slid into his hair and she held his head while he took the kiss deeper, taking them too close to the edge. His mouth lifted so they could breathe but his forehead touched hers. They stared at each other, breathing too hard and unwilling to be the first to let go.

"Lizzie," he whispered, his breathing ragged. "Back in New Orleans, I rushed you. I don't want to tonight. I'm going to kiss you again, then I'll take a guest room."

"But—"

Fingers covered her mouth.

"Get a good night's sleep because we're taking the boat out early."

He eased away from her, sucked in a ragged breath and got out of the convertible in one graceful move. Stunned, she stared at the space he'd occupied. The passenger door opening startled her out of the daze and she glanced at him. His expression was unreadable but his eyes were warm and his mouth did not have that hard edge to it. She was pretty sure if she put her ear to his chest she'd find his heart banging as erratically as hers.

As soon as they were inside the house she turned to speak but he was kissing her again. Her arms went around him and she held on while he turned them both inside out. He lifted his head.

"Goodnight, *bella*."

"Goodnight, Nic." She started to turn away from him, then turned back. "You know I'm going to dream about you now."

"Try not to wake up before the good part."

He kissed her again. "I'll see you in the morning."

She found her cell phone the second she stepped into his office. It was right on his desk where he'd said it was. Her red beaded bag next to it. She took it off the charger and slipped back into the master bedroom. As soon as she turned it on a barrage of text messages and e-mails set off notifications.

Most of them were from Jen wanting to know why she wasn't answering her phone.

Lizzie swallowed hard and turned the location setting off on her phone in case anyone got clever about finding her. She was an adult. She didn't have to explain where she was. Except Jen had resorted to a voice mail and that meant she was worried.

This was not going to be a short phone call so she took the phone into the master bathroom and decided to give the whirlpool tub a spin. She sat down on the edge of the tub and called Jen back.

"Where are you?" Jen demanded a second later when she answered.

Lizzie twirled her finger through the hot water steaming up the bathroom and switched to speaker phone. "Key Largo."

"Key Largo?" Jen echoed, her voice anything but calm. "What are you doing in Key Largo? We don't even know anyone in Key Largo, Lizzie."

"Nic Maretti," Lizzie said simply, as if it explained everything. And actually, since it was Jen, it kind of did.

"Noooooo way." Jen breathed out the word with shock and awe.

"Way," Lizzie chirped, not wanting the conversation to get too serious. Jen knew she'd had a crush on Nic forever, but she hadn't told Jen what happened the night of the wedding. She wasn't ready to share that yet and it felt weird not telling Jen everything.

"You're serious?" Jen balked. "You're in Key Largo with Nic Maretti?"

Lizzie stripped off the blue-green dress and carefully draped it over the vanity stool. "Yeah, why is that so hard to believe?"

The water was heavenly as she stepped into it.

"Because you are supposed to be at school."

"I sort of finished early." She groaned as water surrounded her. She stretched out in the tub and decided she was apartment shopping until she found one with a real bathtub.

"What are you doing?"

"Bubble bath." Lizzie laughed. "Alone."

Jen laughed and Lizzie relaxed even more.

"So are you going to tell me why you're in Key Largo with Nic Maretti?"

Lizzie laughed softly. "He brought me down here to distract me from Rogan."

"And have you been?" Jen teased. "Distracted?"

"Oh, you have no freaking idea."

"So you and he…uh…did you?"

"You're married now. You can say sex."

"I could say sex before." Jen got quiet on the other end of the line suddenly and some of Lizzie's delight faded. "You always kidded around saying you were saving yourself for him, I didn't realize you actually meant it."

"Well, I didn't know I would get to mean it."

"You don't think he's a little old for you?"

"Uh, hello, Stefan is too old for you except that he's immature for his age so it doesn't matter. And trust me, Nic is so not immature for his age. Besides, we're just having fun. I don't think wedding bells are chiming in the distance. He's not a forever kind of guy, Jen," Lizzie explained. Saying it out loud, and hearing it out loud, made her stomach twist painfully.

"Then why are you involved with him?" Jen asked, adding quickly, "And Stefan is not immature for his age."

"He so is. What did he say when he found out about the zipper? Or lack of one?"

Jen sighed. "I'm not speaking to him. Do you have any idea what that dress cost?"

Lizzie sputtered with laughter, making water slosh against the side of the tub.

"Lizzie," Jen said, her voice taking on that wary but gentle tone. "This is me. Remember? The one person on the planet who actually knows you. You wouldn't have gone with him to Key Largo if you weren't serious."

"The thing is…" Lizzie sat up in the water. "This is my chance to finally get him out of my system. I've had a crush on him for so long, I'm not sure who I am without it."

"Maybe it's not a crush."

"Okay, what? Obsession? I don't have time for it. I can't daydream in class about him anymore. These professors aren't fooled. They can actually tell if I'm paying attention or not."

"Oh, you mean school just got real for you?" Jen laughed. "Now you know how the rest of us feel."

"Shut up."

"Be careful, Lizzie."

"We're just having fun. I went to the spa today, then we had an amazing dinner, and walked on the beach. Tomorrow we're taking his boat out and I'm going to work on my tan."

"I kind of hate you right now," Jen grumbled.

"I'll be back in New Orleans by the end of the week."

"Okay, you've convinced me," Jen assured her. "Now, as soon as we hang up you can start trying to convince yourself."

"I kind of hate you back."

"I'll have pancakes waiting for you when you get back."

"I'll be fine."

"If he hurts you, Mac and Stefan won't get a chance to kill him. They won't be able to find his body, Lizzie. I mean it."

"Jen, I swear, I know what I'm doing. I will still need those pancakes, but this will all be fine. Trust me."

Jen groaned. "Now I'm really worried."

CHAPTER NINE

It was the perfect day to spend on the water. Big fluffy clouds floated across the bright blue sky and reflected in the calm clear water. The sun was warm but the air was cool. On the deck of Nic's fishing trawler, Lizzie relaxed in a lounge chair and tried not to think about anything.

"You okay?" He handed her a travel mug of coffee.

She nodded, forcing a smile.

"Lizzie—" he sat on the edge of the lounger, "—don't make the mistake of thinking you're the only one who can't feel the ground under your feet."

He kissed her forehead, then levered up to go do whatever it was he needed to do to get the boat ready to go. She watched him, no longer faking a smile but determined she was not going to read more into this than there was but Nic didn't make it easy.

By midmorning, she was torturing him. She'd stripped down to her bikini and was rubbing sunscreen on all the skin the bikini left bare. Which was most of her. Nic had been free to get his gear together, bait his hooks, and drop his lines. He'd been fishing for several uninterrupted hours when the scrape of a lounge chair startled him. He glanced over his shoulder to find her adjusting the chair to maximize the sun. Her back was to him as she scooted the chair around. She bent over and Nic's body turned to steel while his brain shut off.

There was a hard tug on his line and he ignored it. Her bikini stretched across those perfect curves and had Nic choking on his own breath trying to get oxygen into his lungs.

She straightened, and turned to grin at him. She knew he was watching her. "Want to do my back?"

She waved the bottle of sunscreen at him. She was teasing him and the way she smiled, her face lit up like Christmas, made him smile back at her. He shrugged helplessly. He wanted to spread sunscreen on more than her back. Instead he held up his hands. "I've had my hands in all this bait."

Her smile went away as she shuddered. "I'm good. I don't need any help."

He grinned and went back to his lines. When it got too quiet, he was about to go look for her when she stepped out of the cabin holding two bottles of water. She closed the distance between them, the shells and charm on the sarong clinking together.

Nic looked down at her feet and his throat went dry. His eyes fixed on the silver rings on several of her toes and the cherry red toenail polish. He had the strangest urge to pull those rings off one by one with his teeth.

She dangled a bottled water in front of him. He took it, grateful for something cold.

He swallowed most of the water in one gulp and when he could speak without sounding like he had sandpaper in his throat, he asked, "Getting ready for lunch?"

She took a sip of her water and replaced the cap. "No, I'm good. Unless you're hungry."

"The kitchen's fully stocked. I'm sure you can find something you can eat."

"Oh." She sounded nervous. "I'm in charge of lunch?"

"Should I be worried?"

"Probably. Jen doesn't allow me in the kitchen anymore. She tried to teach me to cook but I think I take too long getting things ready. She gave me cookie dough once and it took me ten minutes to get all the slices right."

"You sliced cookie dough?"

"The premade kind. In the tube."

"Oh." Nic stifled a laugh. He could see her concentrating on getting all the slices the same.

"If one slice is larger than the other, one will get done faster so not all the cookies will reach peak yumminess."

"That would be bad," he agreed, charmed again when color dusted her cheeks.

"I shouldn't have told you."

This time he shrugged. "I prefer cannoli to cookies."

Her bright smile almost blocked out the sun. "Oh really? I have a great recipe for cannoli."

"I can't wait to hear it."

She nodded. "Yeah, you drive down to Carrollton Avenue and stop in at Brocato's. They come out perfect every time."

Nic shook his head in disbelief as he watched her walk away. How could she be so cute and sexy at the same time?

Nervous, Lizzie stared at the kitchenette like she would an army of advancing battle robots. She didn't have a chance but she had to try. The boat's galley was more compact than the kitchen at his house, so it should have been less intimidating. She hadn't been kidding about being hopeless earlier. Jen had given up trying to teach her anything a long time ago.

"What would Jen do?" Lizzie asked out loud as she opened the refrigerator. "Oh…" She almost passed out in relief when she found it full of elaborate platters of gourmet cheeses and fruits. Lunch was going to be a snap.

Lizzie couldn't cook but she could set a mean table. Later, she had a table for two set up under the canvas canopy. She'd found fresh basil and lemons and made a centerpiece. She wanted to photograph it so she could pin it or send it to Jen. She groaned and realized she'd left her phone on Nic's charger and forgotten all about it.

"This looks good and those lemons are perfectly sliced."

She laughed, pushed him away playfully. He pulled her chair out for her. "Such a gentleman."

They drank a light red wine and ate crackers with cheese and fruit. The canvas canopy blocked out the sun but nothing could stop the cool, clean ocean air. The water was calm and there was no one for miles.

"This is wonderful." Lizzie sighed. "How can you stand to leave this place?"

"I hate to leave this place. It's the one place I have to myself."

"Except for now," she reminded him.

"Yes, but see how useful you are." He waved at the empty plates between them. "This gourmet feast you prepared was delicious."

"Did it earn me a place in your crew?" She grinned.

He plucked a strawberry out of a bowl of mixed berries and held it up for her. She leaned across the small table and opened her mouth. The berry was cold and crisp and juice ran down her chin as she bit down.

When she licked the juice away with her tongue, she almost laughed at the pained expression on his face. "Delicious," she admitted.

"I think I can definitely find a place for you on my crew."

"Oh, then I'll need a uniform."

"Come here." He pushed back from the table.

She took her time standing and moving toward him. She loved the way his eyes skimmed all over her. She stopped in front of him, standing between his legs staring down at him. His hands went to her waist before sliding up her bare rib cage. She loved the feel of his hands there and the way his thumbs swept over her abdomen.

"You won't need a uniform."

She smiled and caught her breath as his thumbs moved to tease her nipples. They beaded into hard points and the pressure of his thumbs made them ache. She grabbed a strawberry to distract him and held it for him. She watched him bite down on the strawberry with strong white teeth, then ducked down and traced the trickle of juice at the corner of his mouth with her tongue.

He tugged her forward. She lost her balance and fell into his lap as he swallowed the strawberry. He kissed her. Wine, strawberries and Nic was more than Lizzie could take.

"You are delicious."

She stretched. Light-headed, she settled down against his shoulder and gave into the weight pulling at her eyelids. "I think I had too much wine."

His index finger pressed against her lower lip. "Thank you for lunch."

Another first for her. She smiled, kissing the tip of his finger. She was having all kinds of first times with Nic. The wine, the rocking of the boat, and the heat from Nic's body were all too much and she lost the battle with her eyelids and fell asleep before she knew it.

A splash roused Lizzie from the catnap she was dosing in and out of. Another splash had her up and looking around. She spotted a neat pile of clothes by the stern. She leaned over the side of the boat and found him in the ocean treading water.

"Are you crazy?"

He wiped the water off his face. "I needed to cool off. Come in."

Lizzie shivered, the sun was already starting to set and the water was darker. "There are creatures. Jellyfish, seaweed. I don't do oceans, Nic. I like the beach."

"Some mermaid you are," he teased, swimming back toward the boat.

"Mermaid? What makes you think I'm a mermaid?"

"Your hair," he told her. "Definitely mermaid hair."

Lizzie grinned then a second later dove into the warm water.

"What about the creatures?" he asked as she surfaced next to him. She shrugged. "Mermaid. Remember?"

She splashed him in the face then pushed away from him, enjoying the warm sea water on her skin. They played in the water for a while, laughing and splashing and kissing until Nic dragged them both back to the boat before they drowned because they couldn't stop touching each other.

He levered onto the swimming platform, then pulled her next to him.

"You want to stay out here tonight or go back in?"

"Stay on the boat?"

He nodded. "Cabin's comfortable."

"You think that's a good idea? You may not be safe. Mermaids can be dangerous." He might not be safe anyway. Her hands wanted to smooth away the water droplets clinging to the fine hairs on his chest. She'd never realized how sexy chest hair could be. She wanted to rub her whole body all over him.

"I'll take my chances. You don't scare me, mermaid or not."

A second later, Lizzie got her wish as crisp hairs met soft skin and a bonfire blew up between them. She pulled her mouth away this time, and ran a sizzling line of open-mouthed kisses along his jaw, down his throat until she was tracing the lines of his pectoral with her tongue. He was delicious. He tasted like the ocean and Lizzie wanted to taste all of him.

He stopped her when her mouth trailed down. She was about to trace his navel with her tongue when he flipped her to her back on the swimming platform and blocked out the afternoon sun.

"My turn."

"It's always your turn."

His slow sexy smile held her in thrall as he moved over her, droplets of ocean sliding from his hair to her skin.

"Tell me where you want me to kiss you next." His voice was at least two octaves lower this time. It redefined sexy. "Lizzie," he warned, drawing her name out and smiling at the same time he tried to sound dire.

She pretended to think, rolling her eyes around as if it were a hard decision. When one dark eyebrow lifted, she tapped her cheek, turning it to him. "Here."

"Good choice." He pressed a gentle kiss against her cheek. "My turn to pick."

She choked back a shriek when he pushed one black triangle of her bikini top aside then closed his mouth over one aching breast. His tongue teased her ruthlessly, but not for long enough. Then he made a move for her other one and she tried to wrench away from him. "My turn."

His tongue flicked out in one quick circle. "No, matching set counts as one."

She giggled then yelped as he teased her other nipple until she wasn't sure if she was laughing or crying or trying to breathe. His teeth nipped at her and a slight edge of pain sliced through her. Her eyes flew open and she found him studying her reaction.

"You like that, don't you?" His voice was hoarse. He rolled her tight bud between his finger and thumb as he watched her closely, not letting her break eye contact. Her lips parted as another arrow darted through her. "Don't you?" He increased the pressure.

"Yes." The husky tone of her voice called something dangerous out of him. He straightened and pulled her to her feet. "Nic, what's wrong?" Concern shook her.

He crushed her against his chest. "I'm not inside you, that's what's wrong."

Heat seared through her. "You can fix that, right?" she teased.

He was silent a full heartbeat then the most amazing thing happened. He laughed and it turned him into a complete stranger. She'd never heard him really laugh before. Chuckle maybe, but not the rich, full laughter that made her knees go weak.

"I may have a plan," he agreed, urging her toward the deck lounger. Confused, she stumbled. "Knees," he rasped against her ear and she dropped to her knees on the end of the heavy deck lounge chair.

He pulled the bikini top ties loose and it fell away. His hands closed over her breasts, massaging and teasing until she was delirious. She turned her face into his neck as he rolled her nipples harder. There was the slightest edge of pain but it sharpened the pleasure. The muscles in her back flexed involuntarily and she shivered in reaction.

Overwhelmed, she couldn't think. He spoke against her ear, warm raspy words asking her to do dirty things. Fire licked through her and she got her body to do anything but burn. His tongue traced the spiral of her ear as he continued the slow pressure on her nipples, torturing them until Lizzie admitted to herself she liked it when he got a little rough with her.

"You got to see what I see, now I want you to feel what I feel."

"I do feel it." She whimpered, her whole body shaking.

"Show me," he whispered against her ear. "Touch yourself for me."

The hunger in those raspy words sliced through any inhibitions she had. She wanted to comply but her body wouldn't cooperate with her brain. "I can't." The words rattled past her teeth and she couldn't stop shaking.

"I'll help you," he whispered, taking her right hand and lacing his fingers through hers.

"Nic." She tried to jerk away from him but he flattened her hand against her stomach and held her tight against his chest. She didn't think she could do this. The idea of touching herself in front of him paralyzed her with a drugging combination of embarrassment and excitement.

He tugged the strings at her hips loose and the two triangles of the bikini bottoms fell away. "There is no one else here," he assured her. "It's just us."

She was losing all sense of herself. The edges of her reality were blurred and all she could feel was the heat from Nic's body pressed tight against her back and the sound of his voice calling out the wicked part of her that wanted to do anything he asked.

"I've got you." He moved her hand lower, curving her fingers until she felt her own slick heat and then reality joined her bikini on the deck as it fell away.

He rolled her fingers and every part of her burned. Making her share something so intimate with him unlocked layers and layers of pleasure inside her. She got drunk on discovering each one before she floated straight out of reality.

"*Bella*, let go." The quiet words were like silk on her skin and Lizzie surrendered to the knowledge she would never be the same again.

His name escaped from her lips in a harsh gasp as the orgasm consumed her. He let go of her hand, and used his own to push her further into oblivion and she died, not understanding why he could do these things to her. Why she let him. He turned her around and pushed her back down on the lounge chair, spread her legs until her feet touched the ground on either side of her. She pushed to her toes when he slid his hand under her hips and lifted her to his mouth.

His tongue moved over her much more slowly than his hand. Too slowly. Her fingers clawed into his hair and she felt him chuckle, his breath sending chills racing across her skin.

"Nic," she pleaded, her body coiling tighter and tighter as she fought to suck in oxygen. "Please...I need..."

"I know what you need," he rumbled, licking her deep until she cried from the pain of so much pleasure.

He dangled her over the edge, building something sharp and bright inside her. She didn't think she could come again. It was too far away. She couldn't quite reach it. Whimpering as he pushed hard fingers deep inside her, she lost her mind when he crooked them and the bloom began. He stroked that spot inside her, coaxing the orgasm into a frenzy until it ripped her apart piece by piece. The release wouldn't stop. She burst into tears when she realized another wave was hitting before the last one receded.

His hands moved and she cried out in protest, "Don't stop."

"Hold on."

Relief speared through her when he ripped the condom wrapper. She forced heavy lids open and watched him roll on the thin barrier. He moved over her, blocking out the world.

"Tell me what you want." He nudged at her, ruthlessly teasing her as she lifted her hips, trying to take him in.

"I need you," Lizzie hissed, biting into his bottom lip, surprising him into pushing deep.

"Nothing should feel this good," he rasped into her ear. "Nothing has ever felt like this."

She wasn't sure if he was aware he was speaking out loud. The words were so low, they were practically growls but they spun liquid pleasure through her, taking her higher as his body rocked them toward oblivion.

There was nothing but the heat of him deep inside her. He lifted her hips, pushing deeper. She tried to wrap her legs around his waist as his hands flattened on either side of her hips. Then he was on his knees on the lounger, wrapping his hands around her waist and pulling her up as he continued to strip her down to nothing but pure sensation.

He was so strong. Every move he made was controlled and powerful and the thing he was coaxing awake inside her now was going to destroy them. Pleas tightened his expression into fierce concentration. She pulled him closer and pressed her palm to his cheek. He sucked her fingers into his mouth. Her orgasm came out of nowhere, catching both of them off guard as she detonated around him and he let himself go, pounding into her then rearing back. His neck almost snapped as his face crashed into exquisite pain. The sound coming from his chest was primal and violent and so ecstatic it sent Lizzie straight into another rogue wave.

Brown eyes clashed with blue. She tried to smile at him but her facial muscles weren't listening. None of her muscles listened. She was boneless and floating and she wanted to stay where she was the rest of her life.

He lowered his weight toward her. She expected him to lie down beside her and pull her into his chest. Instead, she caught her breath, tears sparking at the back of her eyes as emotion clogged her throat. He moved down her body, his cheek resting on her belly as he tried to catch his breath. Lizzie's fingers sank into his hair, sifting through the silky waves. He sighed and stayed there, resting his head on her, making her wish the world would go ahead and end because nothing could ever top this moment.

Emotions cascaded over her. He wiped the moisture off her cheeks. She closed her eyes, sucked in a ragged breath and tried to smile. Nic moved then, doing what she had expected before, curving around her, surrounding her with his warmth, making her forget the world was not a safe place.

She didn't know how long they slept while the boat swayed on the gentle sea. She dozed, feeling safe and complete, something she hadn't felt in a long time.

Later, the air turned cool. She woke with Nic curved around her but he wasn't asleep.

"Why are you smiling?" he asked.

She wanted now to last forever. "Three orgasms? Something would be wrong if I weren't smiling."

"You're keeping score?" His smug smile was back. "And I think it was four."

She traced his smile with her index finger, stopping in the center of his bottom lip. "You made me lose count." She couldn't believe it. She'd never lost count in her life.

"Good." He kissed the tip of her finger. "I need to go check my lines. You aren't going to disappear on me, are you?"

"You mean swim back out to sea?"

He moved away from her and gathered her bikini and sarong. He dropped them in her lap then kissed her hard. "Don't disappear."

She tied the sarong around her waist then sat back down on the lounger. She pulled her knees to her chin and rested her cheek on them. Had it really happened?

When he wasn't touching her it felt like a dream. Her legs ached, and electricity popped and snapped along her body. She wished she hadn't fallen asleep. Maybe they could have talked. She'd felt so close to him for a few minutes, but with him gone she wasn't sure what to do next.

Nic's fishing lines were fine but he took his time reeling them in and reeling himself in, which proved to be more difficult than it had ever been. Something had happened. They'd connected on a level that had nothing to do with his body joining with hers. When their physical connection was broken, the other remained. Nic wasn't sure it would ever go away.

This trip had been a huge mistake, but making love to her had not been. Shock whispered to him, growing exponentially until it threatened to explode out of his chest. The difference was they hadn't had sex. They'd made love.

At least he had been making love. He wasn't sure about Lizzie, although she seemed to be giving him everything.

Now he had lost his mind. Nic held his breath, bracing himself for the suffocating pressure. The chill in his stomach. The claustrophobic reaction. The instinct to run.

Instead, there was a strange sense of peace. Like he wasn't alone anymore. The idea was too alien to consider. Nic had never been lonely. He'd been perfectly happy in the organized world he created for himself, surrounded by people he cared about but never letting them get too close. Lizzie had barged right in, breaching his defenses. He hadn't even tried to put up a fight.

He waited, staring out to sea, his tackle forgotten as his very understanding of himself split open and spilled out on the deck.

A week, he reminded himself. Then he was flying to Hong Kong. The trip would clear his head, set him back on track. He could do a week.

Relief speared him when he found her asleep on a lounge chair. Part of him had been listening out for a splash in case she decided to run again.

She sighed and mumbled. She was beautiful sleeping, the delicate lines of her face relaxed as she spoke in low tones. Numbers? It sounded like a bunch of nonsense until he realized with a faint shock it sounded like she was calculating something. Nic frowned but continued to listen, intrigued by the numbers she whispered. She was full of surprises. He carried her downstairs to the cabin, smiling as she curled onto her side.

He left her reluctantly, called his security team to let them know they were not coming in. He took his time securing the boat for the night. Afterwards, leaning against the railing, he watched stars flicker in the dark sky. The water was calm and the moon was high. Normally a night like this would have him up for hours, sitting on the fly deck, glad to be away from the world and enjoying the universe' light show.

Not tonight. He wasn't where he wanted to be. He closed his eyes and sighed in defeat. His body came to life just thinking about her. Why couldn't they stay here forever? He glanced over his shoulder, imagining her in his bed asleep, her hair a glorious mess on his pillow and his dark gray sheets draping around creamy limbs. As much as he loved being on the open water at night, he wanted to be with her more.

She was asleep when Nic stepped back into the cabin. She'd flipped onto her back, her arm across the space where he should be. The bed linens had slipped down to her waist and they tangled in her legs. She was laid out for him like some exotic feast. A feast with cherry red toenails. And Nic was starving.

Smiling when his knee hit the bed, she held out her arms for him without opening her eyes. His name escaped on her next breath. Then he was lost in her, with no desire to find his way back.

CHAPTER TEN

Lizzie watched striped fish dart in and out of coral. She couldn't believe she was diving. They'd gone on a snorkeling cruise earlier in the week and Lizzie had loved it so much, she agreed to try diving. Nic had been right. It was amazing.

"Try it once," he'd said. "If you don't like it, we won't go."

He knew one of the local dive instructors. After spending a day giving her a crash course, Reston took them on a short dive and Lizzie fell in love. Swimming along the protected coral reefs was unlike anything she'd ever experienced. There were so many colors. So much life. All of it a living art. Awed by the beauty and peace surrounding her, her mind was quiet and she experienced real freedom for the first time.

The instructor swam up and tapped his watch and Lizzie nodded. It was time to go. Reluctantly, she swam toward the sunlight and broke the surface of the water at the same time Nic did. They climbed back into the boat and started removing their gear.

"See, mermaid," Nic teased.

"That was amazing." Happiness radiated from her like a small sun. "Thank you for taking me, Nic. I would have never done this without you."

He nodded and stripped back down to his swimming shorts. The ride back to shore was quiet. They sat on the edge of the boat, his arm around her shoulders as they watched land grow larger and larger. "I have something special planned for dinner," he told her, leaning to press a kiss to her temple.

She hadn't expected him to be so affectionate, but if they were near each other he was touching her. A casual arm around her shoulders, his fingers laced with hers, or even their feet touching under a table if they were eating. He always maintained contact. The barrier between Nic and the rest of the world didn't include her.

Her plan to get over him had failed miserably.

There would be no getting over Nic.

"Special?"

"Very exclusive," he promised.

"We'd better go change." She glanced down at her worn khaki shorts and the tacky bright lime green tourist T-shirt she'd knotted at her waist.

"No, they'll let us in." He grinned at her, his sunglasses hiding what he was thinking.

She knew he was having fun. He was wearing a matching T-shirt in the same electric lime green but the silly T-shirt worked on him. He raised it from tacky tourist to island cool.

Lizzie laughed when they pulled up at a shabby building desperately in need of a paint job. Bikes, motorcycles, cars and trucks were crammed into a tiny parking lot and a line of people waiting to get in. The sign over the building said Mickey's in fading red letters.

"Popular spot." Lizzie grinned.

"Mickey was a professional kite boarder. He opened this place to have something to do when the wind wasn't good."

"Seriously?"

"I'm serious, but the word got out about his fish tacos and he had to expand and hire staff so he could stay open."

"Mr. Maretti." A guy in striped board shorts and no shirt waved at them from the front of the line.

"That's us." Nic grinned his "I told you so" at her.

"You aren't going to clear out the rest of the restaurant too, are you?"

"Are you kidding? There would be a riot."

Nic leaned back in his chair, his arm resting on the railing next to their table on the back porch. He watched Lizzie chew the last bite of her fourth fish taco. She was licking her fingers and Nic was having a hard time not grabbing her hands and pulling her across the table so he could lick them for her.

She knew it too, because she was taking her time, watching him with a mischievous smile that amused and tortured him at the same time.

He'd thought she was lovely at the wedding. She'd been drop-dead sexy in Miami. She'd been a sensual dream come true in the turquoise dress she'd worn on their first official date. Now, sitting across the red-checked vinyl tablecloth, her skin glowing with a warm honey tan, and her hair streaked lighter by the sun and blown into loose waves by the ocean air, she was perfection. Right down to the light freckles the sun had scattered across her nose.

Nic had no idea how he was going to let her go. He wanted to wrap her in a net, put her on his boat and sail out to sea.

"Did you save room for dessert?" The chirpy server interrupted Lizzie's playful seduction.

"No," they said in unison.

The server shrugged and left the check on the table.

"Last day tomorrow," Nic said. "What did you want to do?"

"Take the boat out," she suggested.

"Take the boat out," he repeated, leaning across the table and catching her hands in his. "And keep going. How does that sound?"

She grinned, not taking him seriously for a second. "Sounds perfect. Except for the meeting in Hong Kong you can't reschedule again."

He sighed, sorry once again he'd answered the call from Pam a few days ago. "I'll be gone a week. When I get back…"

A huge slice of coconut cream pie hit the middle of the vinyl-covered table. "What's this bullshit I hear about no dessert?"

Lizzie watched a tall scruffy guy grab their ticket despite Nic's protest. "Maretti, your cash is no good here." He stuck out his hand to Lizzie and grinned. "I'm Mickey."

"I'm Lizzie," she said, shaking his hand momentarily dazzled by his million-watt smile.

He was wearing a faded T-shirt with the Mickey's logo, board shorts, no shoes, a scraggly blond beard and a haircut so short it must be growing out from a recent shave.

"You're adorable," Mickey corrected, then grabbed a chair and sat down with them. Lizzie met Nic's warning glance across the table and almost laughed out loud. Was he jealous? "Your taste is improving,

Maretti."

"I hear you've been late on your payments," Nic shot back. He sounded serious but she knew better. Mickey did too. He tipped his head back and laughed.

"I paid you off years ago." He turned to Lizzie. "I had a shack and was doing fine. This guy comes along and tells me I should expand. So I think maybe a food truck and a couple of picnic tables but no, he mentions me to some food critic and the next thing I know some food network big shots are down here challenging me to cook-offs, eating my food and telling the world. Now I have to work seven days a week and had to buy this building and I have people lining up every day. I was retired until Nic Maretti ruined it."

Lizzie laughed, something softening inside her at Nic's discomfort with Mickey's obvious gratitude.

"He paid me back with T-shirts sales alone," Nic explained.

Mickey grinned at Lizzie. "He's a good guy but he doesn't like for anyone to know it."

"You could have gotten a small business loan," Nic reminded him.

"Yes, but the paperwork." Mickey shivered in disgust. "You know how many times they make you sign your name? Reston said you've been diving a couple of times."

"Yeah, he came out and gave Lizzie a class."

"Yeah." Mickey winked at her. "He mentioned that too. It's all over the island you brought a girl with you this time. Lots of excitement in the air. Don't forget I cater too."

Lizzie almost spit her water across the table. "I'm sorry." She grabbed a napkin and tried not to cough.

"I like her," Mickey announced. "Try the pie, Lizzie. I make it myself."

"He doesn't make it himself," Nic assured her. "Reston doing okay? He avoided all my questions. Said everything was all good."

"Yeah, a group of Asian businessmen who decided they needed diving lessons and stayed an extra week to explore more reefs kept him pretty busy a few months back. I think they're back on track. Amanda's in her third trimester." He turned to Lizzie. "Amanda's my sister."

"I met her," Lizzie said, remembering the girl in the office who was ready to give birth any day. "She said they're having a boy."

Mickey nodded. "They've been trying for a while to have kids. Spent their life savings on IVF, almost lost their house to it. If a certain convention hadn't come through town, I'm not sure what they would've done. Make him eat some pie, Lizzie. He loves coconut."

Mickey stood and shook Nic's hand again. "Let me know next time you're headed this way. Found a new fishing spot we need to check out."

"Will do," Nic assured him.

Lizzie watched Mickey walk away, shaking hands and visiting other tables. "You loaned him the money for this place?" She tried a bite of the pie and nearly died of pleasure.

"More like forced him to take it," Nic admitted. "He started a food truck business when he blew out his knee in New Zealand a few years ago."

"This place is popular." Lizzie glanced around again. All the tables were full. "You loaned Jen money to start the bakery too, didn't you?"

"We made the loan through the investment company I have with your brother. The business plan was solid."

"Food service is high risk. You like to gamble, don't you?" Lizzie teased him. "Sometimes you win, sometimes you don't?"

Nic laughed. "I always win, Lizzie. You should know that by now."

She sighed, giving in and eating more pie. "I'm not sure I could figure you out if I spent the rest of my life trying."

His smile was unreadable but the heat in his eyes was pretty clear.

"You should try some of this," she insisted, pushing the plate toward him. "So you own resorts all over the world and you're a venture capitalist?" she asked carefully, aware he was uncomfortable with her questions. She'd learned this week that Nic didn't like to talk about himself.

"I like to invest in small businesses," he admitted. "Sometimes I loan the money."

"Or sometimes you recommend their businesses to visiting Asian businessmen? Those businessmen wouldn't happen to be from Hong Kong?"

Nic's smile was almost embarrassed. "Hong Kong is a big place."

"I'll bet it is." Lizzie let him off the hook, a new kind of warmth glowing inside her. She finally cut a piece of pie and held up her fork for him. "You're one of the good guys, aren't you?"

"I make money on all this, Lizzie. I'm not a charity organization." He met her halfway across the table and let her feed him the pie. By the time she pulled the fork out of his mouth, she could barely breathe. He smiled as he slowly licked his lips. "And I'm not that good."

She opened her mouth and found she didn't have enough air in her lungs to respond. He took full advantage and kissed her. Her eyes fluttered shut and her last thought was the pie really was the best she'd ever tasted.

The last day on the boat and Nic was too restless to fish, until she decided she wanted to fish too. She surprised him by already knowing what she was doing.

"I'm Mac Sellers' daughter. You think he never took me fishing? I hunt too."

"You hunt?" He couldn't believe it. "As in you go into the woods and come out with a dead animal."

She blushed. "Actually, Dad, Stefan and Rogan quit letting me go when they realized they never got a deer when I was with them. Apparently, I'm too noisy."

"You did it on purpose?"

"Damn straight." She laughed. "No deer ever died on my watch. Oh, I think I got something." She jerked the rod back with surprising strength then reeled the fish in slowly.

When it broke water, Nic helped her bring it in. The second he had the hook out of the shiny red fish's mouth, she said, "Okay, throw him back."

"Are you serious?" He paused before throwing the fish in the cooler with the others he'd caught earlier. "This is dinner."

Lizzie shook her head, hand on her hips. "It's not dinner if I see his face, Nic. Throw him back."

He opened his mouth to protest.

"Now. Throw him back."

The fish hit the water with a small splash and swam off. "No more fishing for you, we'll starve," he teased her.

She threw her arms around his neck and kissed him but as soon as he moved to touch her, she yelped and jumped back. "Fish hands. Don't touch me."

"You do know this is a fishing boat." He laughed as she darted away from him.

"I'll make it up to you. I promise."

"Yes, you will. Now go find us some lunch."

He watched her disappear, too bewitched to mourn the loss of a good size red snapper. He imagined her dressed in camo, tromping loudly through the forest scaring the wildlife away. He laughed to himself, and didn't stop smiling when he cast out another line.

He couldn't remember the last time he'd smiled so much. He was always smiling around her, unless he was kissing her. It wasn't always serious. She was fun, he realized. Everything was more fun with Lizzie.

He loved having her around. She fit into all the jagged edges of his life, filling them with sunshine and laughter and companionable silences. Things Nic had never realized were missing. He finally understood what Pam had been trying to tell him about spending too much time alone.

He wasn't looking forward to tomorrow when he dropped her off in New Orleans. In fact, he was dreading it. He set his rod and reel aside and decided to go find her. They didn't have much time left and he didn't want to waste any of it.

She wasn't in the galley. He found her stretched out on the bow, leaning back on her arms, her head back with her face toward the sun. Sunscreen glistened on her skin and she smelled like coconut and paradise. For a moment he wasn't sure if his lungs would ever work again because she literally took his breath away.

She'd reminded him of a mermaid the first time he met her. She'd stood out in the crowded ballroom, her hair spilling all around her shoulders. Now sunning herself on his boat, he could almost believe she was a mythical sea creature he'd caught in his net. All she needed was an iridescent fin and a shell comb.

When she caught him watching, the smile curving her lush mouth wiped every thought from his mind. "Everything all right?"

She gave a fake and somewhat dramatic sigh, then wiggled her toes. Nic's throat went dry as the silver toe ring taunted him. "My toenail polish is all wrong." She made it sound like a national disaster as she flexed her toes so he could see the red polish.

His teeth ground together. It was ridiculous to get so wound up over her toes but he couldn't help it. They looked delicious. "Tragic," he agreed in the same world-weary tone. "We could go back to the resort. I'm sure the spa can book you for an emergency pedicure."

She tilted her head and pouted at him. She was teasing but there was nothing funny about her mouth when she pretended to pout. It gave Nic all kinds of wicked ideas. "Why? Can't you helicopter someone out here to fix them for me?"

She wasn't serious, but if she had been, he wouldn't have hesitated to fly someone out to change her toenail polish. It would take one phone call and he wouldn't give a damn what anyone said. Then she laughed and the sound brought a lightness back to his chest. For a moment, he couldn't move.

Lizzie laughed. For an instant he'd believed her. "You know I'm kidding, right?"

He nodded.

"You could, couldn't you? Make a phone call and someone would be out here ASAP."

He pushed his fingers through his dark hair. It had grown longer this week and the sun had found some streaks in it. She hoped he didn't notice because it softened his hard edges, made him seem younger. He wasn't that old, but sometimes his eyes were positively ancient.

"Yes." Something shut down in him and he turned away from her, focusing on the horizon. "Or I'd get Pam to arrange it."

"She must be some assistant."

"Pam is more than an assistant. She runs all my companies, with the exception of my Asian offices, and my uncle runs De Santis for the foreseeable future but I'll have to take it over eventually and it's not something I can delegate."

"De Santis?" she echoed, humor draining out of her quickly. "You're going to run De Santis Farms?"

He nodded, his expression deceptively calm. "It's not a secret. My uncle has no children."

No, it wasn't a secret. Lizzie knew his mother had been a De Santis but it had never occurred to her Nic would inherit all of De Santis Farms.

De Santis Farms' wine, cheese and luxury foods were a household name. The De Santis family was one of the oldest families in Italy. She'd seen a documentary once on the De Santis vineyards in Tuscany. Their vineyard was over five hundred years old and their wine labels hinted that they could trace their family back to the Romans.

They were definitely from different worlds. Lizzie knew nothing about her father's family. Her mother's family could trace several generations straight back into the Bayous of South Louisiana. Unlike

Rogan's family, who could trace back to *Le Grand Derangement*, when the British deported the Acadians in the 1700s from Nova Scotia, Nadine Sellers' family had not kept up with a family history.

The gap between them widened. Nic was so far out of her league she wondered what she was doing on his boat.

"Lizzie, don't—"

She shook her head, cutting off his raspy words with her own. "If you're heir to the De Santis fortune, why didn't you grow up in Italy?"

"I told you, my mother died."

Something in the way he said it didn't ring true. "Your father remarried and moved to Texas."

"Stepfather," Nic corrected.

Her jaw dropped as he flinched. Pain flickered briefly in his eyes a second before he closed down like a fortress.

"Forget what I said." He turned away from her again, grabbing the boat's railing, his knuckles turning white as he stared out to sea.

This time, she couldn't leave it alone like she had the other night at dinner. Nic in pain was hard to get her head around. She'd never imagined anything could touch him, much less hurt him.

"Nic." She moved to stand next to him, not touching him but close enough to feel the electrical current running between them.

"It's a long story, Lizzie."

"I like stories." She covered one of his clenched fists with hers and his grip on the metal relaxed.

"Legally, he's my father." He sighed heavily, not turning to her but not as shut off as before. "His name is on my birth certificate."

"But he's not your biological father?"

Nic shook his head. "No."

"Do you know who your real father is?"

He flinched before she finished the question and his hand tightened on the railing again. "When my grandfather discovered my mother was pregnant, De Santis paid Andreas Maretti a lot of money to marry her. They didn't want the De Santis heir to be a bastard."

She watched him, the wind ruffling his hair and the line of strain around his mouth. He spoke the words like they were about someone else. There was no emotion. No anything.

"Why didn't she marry your real father? This isn't the middle ages."

"He wouldn't marry her. My uncle explained he didn't want my mother exposed to his world."

"What does that even mean?"

"Believe me, Lizzie, as bad as Andreas is, my real father is infinitely worse." Bitterness and resignation seeped into his voice. Emotions she would never have attributed to him.

"That is so messed up."

"You're right. It's messed up."

"Why were you with Maretti if he's not your real father? If your uncle has no children, why didn't they…" She trailed off at the stricken look on his face. "Nic." Her words were barely a whisper.

"Are you sure you want to hear this?" he asked, reaching for her and pulling her into his arms so she was standing between him and the railing.

"Yes." Instinct told her he needed to talk, even if he didn't want to.

Her hands curved around the cool metal, as his arms went around her, his hands resting on the railing next to hers. Caging her in. She didn't mind, sighing as he leaned into her.

"The agreement was Andreas would receive his money in two lump sums. One when they married and the rest when they divorced. They agreed the marriage would last two years and he would receive a generous monthly allowance. Then Andreas decided he liked receiving the monthly allowance and the final payment was not enough. He delayed the divorce."

"He got greedy?" she asked.

"No. He was born greedy. He got arrogant, thinking he could milk my grandfather out of more money. It worked for a while then my mother became terminally ill and died before he could divorce her. My grandfather cut Andreas off. No divorce, no settlement, no big pay out for Andreas."

"He took you instead?"

His arms tightened around her. "And dropped me off at boarding school."

Lizzie's eyes closed as she put the pieces together. "He left you there until your stepmother found out about you?"

"Yes."

"Your uncle or your grandfather didn't do anything?"

"Why would they? It was a prestigious boarding school, maybe not the one they would have chosen for me but Andreas was suing them for his settlement and maintenance for me. They decided to wait it out rather than pay him another dime. "

"You're not serious?"

Nic shrugged, his voice back to emotionless again. "He would've kept coming back for more, Lizzie. It's who he is."

"So they just left you there? What about holidays? You didn't spend those in Texas until you were ten so…"

He was gritting his teeth and Lizzie felt her stomach drop.

"Nic?" She blinked back tears as she turned and wrapped her arms around him.

"I want to take you to Italy." His voice was gruff as he changed the subject without warning. "I inherited my mother's part of the estate when my grandfather died. Her villa is surrounded by vineyards as far as the eye can see."

Lizzie let it go, stamping on the heartbreak images of a small boy all alone at a boarding school at Christmas. Nic wouldn't appreciate the drama. She pressed her face against his chest and felt the tension in him ease as she asked, "Do you have one of those vats? We can stomp on grapes."

He rested his cheek against the top of her head. "I'll buy you one and you can stomp on grapes for me. It will be my own private vintage."

"Selfish," she whispered, her eyes closing as she let the images build in her mind. She could picture an old terracotta villa surrounded by vineyards and tall cypress trees.

"I'll do the cooking but you have to do the laundry."

"I don't do laundry," she whispered. "I'm not domestic."

His mouth pressed against her temple. "Maybe I'll take you to Milan for a few days, buy you more shoes."

She nodded, losing herself in the fantasy. She could learn how to do laundry. How hard could it be? "We could take your Ferrari?" She was kidding until his expression said there was a Ferrari at his mother's home.

"We'd take the helicopter, it's faster."

"Helicopter?" She swallowed, her throat tightening as the fantasy got way too real. "You have a helicopter?"

"Or two," he admitted.

Her hands lingered on his chest, her fingers tingling from the contact. She didn't want to think about how different their lives were. He might come from a rarefied social strata but Lizzie had spent every Christmas of her life with her parents.

"Don't you dare feel sorry for me," he whispered.

She tightened her hold on him. "I don't. I'm angry at them. Families aren't supposed to be that way."

"I'm starting to get that."

She stepped back as much as the rail would allow. "Andreas is your stepfather? So Angie is...She doesn't know, does she?" Lizzie whispered. "Don't tell her, Nic. She doesn't need to know. It doesn't change anything, does it?"

"No, it doesn't change anything." He stepped back from her and for a moment she didn't want to let him go. "You want a drink?" he asked.

"Sure." She nodded. "Got any of those little umbrellas?"

"I'll check."

When he walked away, she wanted to chase him and tackle hug him until it was all better but she doubted it would help. She wondered if anything could make it better. She couldn't imagine what Nic's childhood had been like. Her parents had always been around. Always been there for her and she'd had Stefan, Jen and Rogan. She'd been surrounded all her life by a close loving family. Had Nic ever been surrounded by people who cared about him?

It explained so much about him. Why he was so detached. Why the world never seemed to touch him. Now the things she'd thought were so sexy suddenly took on a bleakness. She wanted to scream at the injustice of it.

Her breath caught again and her heart broke for real this time as all her childhood fantasies about Nic Maretti shattered around her. She clutched the rail before her knees could give way. He was not the fallen angel of her fantasies. He was human. A flesh and blood man with real feelings, no matter how deep they were buried.

He was also a good man. He helped people without taking credit. He cared enough about his employees to learn their names and remember them. He defended and protected his family. He adored his nephew. He had a sly sense of humor and a way of getting her to do things she would never do on her own.

The detached elegant European playboy billionaire façade began to crumble away along with the crush she'd had on him. The man left standing was a million times more complicated and fascinating. Lizzie would walk through fire for him if he asked her.

Her crush faded with the sunlight, and Lizzie fell hard, and fast, and forever.

CHAPTER ELEVEN

Had he completely lost his mind?

Why had he told Lizzie Angie wasn't his real sister? Along with all the other dirty secrets he'd never told another soul.

If a brick wall had been handy, Nic would have introduced it to his forehead. He pulled the wet bar cabinet doors open and poured himself way too much scotch. He knocked it back and willed his brain to erase the memory of her pity.

Nic didn't need anyone to feel sorry for him. He'd spent a few holidays alone. Big deal. He'd also spent some with friends. It hadn't been that bad. Character building, one of his professors had told him. Learning to rely on himself and trust his own instincts had served him well over the years. Yes, he would inherit a substantial fortune from his mother's family, but he'd made more than he would ever need on his own.

Nic had always considered himself self-made. No one had ever done a damned thing for him. He'd taken the miniscule amount of money his uncle had been forced to give him at eighteen and turned it into his own Empire. Nic Maretti did not need anyone's help. He didn't need anyone.

He sank down on the nearest seat and brooded. He sipped his drink, then brooded some more.

He might not need Lizzie feeling sorry for him, but if he was brutally honest with himself it didn't feel as awful as he expected. He downed the rest of his drink, pushed to his feet, and tried to shake off the crazy.

Except, the crazy felt kind of good. He might be losing his mind but there was a lightness to his chest and skin. The air around him felt sweeter. He groaned. He wasn't losing his mind. He'd already lost it.

He couldn't believe he'd told her that Andreas wasn't his real father. Hell, Pam didn't even know that. The words had slipped out of him and it didn't matter that some of the weight he'd carried for years had lifted off his shoulders too. He should have kept his mouth shut.

As far as Nic was concerned, tomorrow couldn't come fast enough. The sooner he got Lizzie back to New Orleans, the better.

Pain squeezed his chest hard.

He didn't want to take her back to New Orleans. He didn't want the week to end. He wasn't ready to give her up. He wanted more time with her. He did want to take her to Italy and show her where he'd been born.

He had no idea who he was anymore. Lizzie had him in a complicated tangle of emotions. She made him feel all sorts of things he had no desire to feel and as a result of the web she'd spun him into, now he was feeling pain and rejection he'd refused to feel since he'd stood at the warped glass window of an ancient dorm room and watched Andreas Maretti get in a taxi without once glancing back.

He remembered feeling cold that day but not really caring as the taxi pulled away leaving him in a strange place for an indefinite period of time. His beautiful mother was dead. She was not coming back so there was no point in being homesick for the house she no longer filled with laughter and music. He remembered the last time she was able to speak to him. She told him to be strong and not cry. So he was and he didn't. When the winter break came, most of the students returned to their families while Nic was left to spend his first Christmas after his mother died alone.

When a large box had arrived postmarked from Italy, Nic had refused to open it. He'd given it to the staff that had stayed behind at school for the few students who had not gone to be with their families

With far more maturity than a six-year-old should have, he decided he didn't need Maretti, or the De Santis family. They had ceased to exist for him until he broke his arm playing Rugby and Claudia had arrived, her heart in the right place but unaware of what she set in motion when she took Nic to Texas.

He'd stuffed all those memories away years ago and had avoided feeling anything about his childhood for over two decades. He wasn't about to start now. He didn't like the way Lizzie was laying waste to the well-ordered calm he'd created when a grieving six-year-old boy had decided he didn't need or want anyone.

But he liked Lizzie. He liked spending time with her. Her sense of humor. He liked never having to tell her something twice. Most of all, he liked the way she wanted him. She trembled with need every time he got near her. She came alive when he touched her and never held back anything. She gave him everything she had to give and didn't ask for anything back. She didn't want anything from him. Hadn't complained about a thing.

Lizzie didn't seem to care about his money, his name or his family connections. No, she wanted him. Just Nic. Not Nicolas De Santis Maretti. He wasn't sure if he'd ever met anyone who was interested in him and not what he was worth. He'd been more relaxed and more himself this past week than he'd ever been.

He dreaded tomorrow. He didn't want to be alone. Feeling exposed for the first time in years, he decided the trip to Hong Kong needed to happen. He could get some distance and clear his head.

He found her where he'd left her. She was leaning against the railing staring out to sea. She was lovely in the fading light as she scanned the horizon. An ache started inside him again and he forgot everything he decided minutes ago.

"Ready to go back in?" he asked, when he joined her at the railing.

"No." She shook her head. "Everything is so peaceful here. How can you stand to leave this place?"

Warmth spread through him at the sigh she released. He couldn't stand to leave this place. He loved it here. He loved it more with her. "Sometimes I can't stand to leave."

She nodded, but kept her face turned away.

"Lizzie." He was about to break every single rule he had about women. "Tomorrow—"

"This week's been great, Nic." She spoke quickly so he couldn't. "Let's not ruin it with messy goodbyes."

He should have been struck dumb by his good fortune. A woman who didn't believe in messy goodbyes? A few weeks ago that described his perfect woman. Now, watching Lizzie walk away from him, it pissed him off.

So he went after her, throwing all his rules overboard. They were his rules. He decided when and if they mattered. He caught her arm and pulled her back around. "What if I'm not satisfied with a week? What then?"

"What?"

"What if it's not enough?" The rules didn't apply to Lizzie.

Not enough?

The words bounced around inside her.

"Lizzie, tomorrow is not goodbye."

She backed away. "Yes, but I don't think…" She forgot what she was going to say in the middle of the sentence.

Concentration was impossible while he focused on her with such intensity.

"You don't think…what?"

She was so tempted to give in but the longer she stayed with him the more it would hurt when it was over. "My life is kind of—"

"Complicated? You've said that already. Mine is too. Try again."

"We hardly know each other."

"All the more reason I want more time with you."

"For what, exactly? Sex?"

"Sex? You think this is about sex?"

She backed up when he moved. "Isn't it?"

A darkness seemed to roll over him like a thunder cloud. He lowered his face until they were eye to eye. "We have never just had sex, Lizzie."

He kissed her then, teasing the corner of her mouth, tasting the slight swell of her bottom lip before sliding his tongue inside to tangle with hers. "You feel that? Like you're drowning and it's not happening fast enough?"

She nodded, tears burning at the corners of her eyes.

"Is it always like this? Do you feel like you're falling off the earth when the blue-haired boy kisses you?"

"No," she whispered, her lungs stopping when he smiled with smug satisfaction.

He kissed her again. Her arms went around his neck and she ran head first into the blaze.

"The others?" he asked, not lifting his mouth from hers as he teased her.

"What others?" She kissed him back and it took a second to realize he'd pulled back from her. Not physically. He stepped right back behind his stoic façade. She wanted to fall through the deck straight into the ocean and never come back.

She opened her eyes and froze at the darkness in his expression.

"What are you saying?"

The chill in his voice told her she didn't need to say anything. "What were we talking about?"

"I knew you were inexperienced but…"

Lizzie shivered as the chill leaked out of his voice and straight into her. She pushed away from him, but he didn't let her go. "Why are you making this a thing?"

"You're twenty-one years old. How is this even possible?"

Stunned he was angry, she felt her own temper start to sizzle. "Not that I owe you an explanation, but well, I…I told you we switched high schools after Katrina. There wasn't anyone…"She wrenched away from him and he finally let her go.

"Not even blue-haired boy?"

Lizzie sucked down the outrage and resisted the urge to slap him right across his beautiful smug face. "He's a friend, okay? I didn't meet him until after…"

"After?" He prompted.

Lizzie shook her head. Not for all the tea in China was she going to tell him that he was the reason she'd never been with anyone else. She injected as much artic freeze as she could in her tone. "None of this is any of your business, Nic."

"Nonc of my business?" He shook his head in disbelief. "Are you serious? You had plenty of opportunities and time to tell me. You rode up that elevator with me knowing I had no idea it was your first time. You should have told me, Lizzie. I could've hurt you."

His last words were like a bomb going off between them. Lizzie looked away. "I was afraid you'd stop," she admitted, shattering the eerie silence between them. "I didn't want you to stop."

He pushed his fingers through his hair and backed up to the railing. "I can't believe this. That's your excuse? You didn't want me to stop?"

She nodded. It had made sense at the time.

"So you used me?"

"What?" Her attention snapped back up to him. "That's ridiculous."

"You were ready to get rid of your V card and I was convenient?"

Her jaw dropped. "Seriously?"

He shrugged. "Explain it to me then. Why did you lie to me?"

"I didn't lie!" she exploded back at him. "Not telling you something so personal is not lying."

"Lies by omission. Same thing." He shoved his fists into his pockets and turned away from her. "How do you know I would've stopped?" he demanded, but most of his anger had drifted away. Now it was worse. He was disappointed.

"You would have stopped," she said softly.

"I'd like to think I would've stopped, but the truth is I probably wouldn't have. You're not that easy to resist, *bella*."

"Oh." She didn't know what else to say.

"But I would've handled it differently."

"It was perfect."

"You ran the first chance you got." He pulled his hands out of his pockets and gripped the railing.

"I told you what happened..."

"Yeah. You panicked." He swung back around to face her. "Has it occurred to you if I'd known it was your first time, and I'd taken things slower, you wouldn't have panicked? You would've stayed the night and things would be very different right now."

"No, I still would've left. I had class on Monday."

Genuine surprise, then doubt flickered across his face. "I could've flown you back to school and we could've spent Sunday together. Possibly the next weekend too."

"Flown me? What do you mean you would have flown me?"

His expression closed down and Lizzie knew.

"You have a plane too? Of course you do." She threw her arms up before he could respond. "Why not? You have a Ferrari, two helicopters, of course you have a plane."

He crossed his arms again. "A jet."

"What?"

"It's a jet, not a plane. I need an aircraft capable of international flights."

She nodded, hysterical laughter bubbling up her throat. "Oh sorry, my bad. A jet."

"That's right. The same jet that is flying you back to New Orleans tomorrow."

She shook her head in disbelief. He couldn't be real. None of this seemed real anymore. "You really do make Tony Stark look destitute, don't you?"

If she'd thought he was shut down before, she'd been wrong. Now he was a fortress. A complete stranger stood in front of her and said, "I honestly don't know what I'm worth but if it's important to you, you can ask Pam."

"Believe me," she assured him, "I don't want to know."

"Can I believe you? I'm trying to decide."

Her breath caught as the knife went deep into her chest. "Why wait until tomorrow? Let's go back today. I can be ready in an hour."

He was right behind her before she could move. Arms went around her and she fought him off, but he was bigger and stronger and he had her trapped tight against his chest. "I'm sorry," he rasped.

She was stunned because from what she'd learned about Nic, he never apologized. "I don't care. Let me go."

"You think I can let you go now?" He loosened his hold when she stopped struggling. "There's been no one else?"

"No." She lowered her eyes in defeat, once again unable to lie to him.

"And you didn't sleep with Adam because?"

Her fingers curled into fists. "Sometimes I really hate you."

"Answer the question, Lizzie."

She closed her eyes tight and took a deep breath. "Because I'd already met you. Okay? Are you satisfied?"

He turned her around, pressed her back against the wall. Dark eyes swirling with anger searched her face. "Say that again."

"I didn't want anyone else after I met you."

His palm pressed against her cheek. The incredulous expression on his face breaking her apart and putting her back together at the same time. She was in so far over her head that she knew she would never make it back. This thing she had for him was insidious. An addiction. A weakness she couldn't afford. A brass ring she knew better than to grab for.

But she was going for it anyway. She had no choice. The instinct was in her genetic code.

"We're not done." The words grated across her skin as his head dipped toward hers, hovering over her trapped lips. "We may never be done."

"It won't work," she whispered, clinging to him so she wouldn't fall off the earth.

"It's working perfectly." Nic smiled against her throat. Then he was kissing her again, stealing the last of her sanity before lifting his head. "Mine," he whispered, brushing his lips across her cheek. "Mine."

She wasn't going to survive him. She should walk away now. She should go back to school and focus on convincing Hatton she deserved a spot in the doctoral program. Going back to the real world was the best choice. The choice that would make her family proud. The choice that wouldn't leave her shattered and humiliated. The only choice.

Besides, the girl Nic liked was not her. She wasn't the light-hearted party girl. She was a focused, academic with her future mapped out. She didn't take risks. She didn't like chaos unless it was on a quantum level. School and research had always been her focus. It was all planned out. She had to follow the path but the man licking fire across her skin was making it harder and harder to check off those boxes. Because she didn't have a going-insane-over-a-dangerously- sexy Italian gazillionaire on her list of things to do. She didn't fling herself knowingly against impossible dreams she knew would destroy her.

"I'm not yours," she told him. "You don't know me, Nic. Not really. The girl you think you know isn't me."

He frowned, his head snapping back. "What?"

"You've seen me at parties, or weddings, but that's not me. You wouldn't give me a second glance if you passed me on the street."

"I wouldn't pass you by."

She swallowed hard again, clenching her fingers into fists so her hands would stop shaking as she stumbled back. "We wouldn't be on the same street. I don't live in your world."

He tilted his head, watching her closely, seeing through her. Or was he seeing her.

"Do you think I care where you're from?"

He sounded so sincere. He probably meant it. For now.

Who knew how long now would last. Because Nic wouldn't stay. He never stayed.

"It's not where I'm from. It's where I'm going. I have plans, things I want to do and I can't do them with you."

"What things?" he demanded again.

"Graduate school things," she shot back at him. "Research. You're...distracting. I won't be able to concentrate if you're around."

"Like now?" An arrogant smile transformed his features. He liked that he distracted her.

"Exactly like now."

"Now you aren't in school. I'll distract you all I want."

When he reached for her, her fingers slid into his hair and she kissed him first. His eyelids fluttered shut and his entire body turned to steel as he let her explore his mouth. His arm tightened around her back, pulling her up until Lizzie gave in and let him take her weight. She curled her legs around lean hips and kissed him like there was no tomorrow. Because she no longer wanted to deal with tomorrow.

Then he took over, devouring her, invading her system and moving through her like a narcotic. There was something desperate in the way he touched her and the way she wanted more.

"You're cheating."

"I always get what I want."

She tightened her body around him as he walked her down to the cabin below deck.

He bent over the bed and lowered her down to the mattress. She let go of him, pushing the shirt off his shoulders so he had no choice but to pull it off, then her hands flattened on his chest then moved around to his back, stroking up and down, then down farther to a flat stomach that led to lean hips she wanted to sink her teeth into.

"*Bella,*" he whispered against her mouth, catching her roving hands. "Am I distracting you?" he rasped against her ear his hands running down her overheated skin, fingers sliding between her legs and sinking deep.

She couldn't find the breath to answer. She endured the exquisite torture of his fingers. The intensity of it grew with each purposeful circle of his thumb, scorching away her sanity.

"You like being distracted, don't you?"

Lizzie arched, moaning as he teased her. "Yes." She hissed the word out.

"Do you want me to stop?" He nipped at her ear.

A harsh laugh escaped her. "Do you want me to kill you?"

"What makes you think you aren't?"

Then hard fingers plundered even deeper, pushing her head first into the blaze.

She was burning alive and cried in relief when he ripped open the condom wrapper. He reached for her, wasting no time moving over her, positioning himself then teasing her with his fingers again until she whimpered. He pushed hard and deep and flattened one hand against her back when she bowed off the bed, keeping her body arched as he moved deeper into her.

With each push and pull of his body, he stole more of her. She could feel herself slipping away. Her mind struggled against the chaos of too much beauty and sensation. Too much emotion. Too much everything. For once the numbers she relied on to explain her reality no longer made any sense. Numbers, functions and formulas danced, rushing around in a fiery swirl, no longer making sense. They wanted to burst into light and blaze until they burned out.

Lizzie went up in flames so hot she couldn't let go. The universe seemed to shrink down to the connection between their bodies. Nic went deeper, moved harder with each thrust until Lizzie could no longer feel where she started and Nic ended. Her eyes flew open again as her mind tried to make sense of what was happening. Her brain faltered. For the first time in her life her mind went blank. A cascade failure of heat, light, and chaos blew through her like a solar wind.

Then what used to be Lizzie understood it all.

It was all clear. She finally understood that she would never understand. They were too complicated. There was no solution. She and Nic were an uncountable set.

"Stay with me." Gentle words pulled her back from the abyss spreading out in front of her. "Stay with me."

How could she stay? There was no way to stay. Dark matter formed right in front of her. It wrapped around her, slid under her skin and into her veins like liquid lightning. She tried to hold on but the burn was reaching deep into her muscles. He whispered against her ear, holding her back with him as her whole body threatened to dissolve into light. His voice kept her solid while he drove in and out creating something new and dangerous inside her. She clung to him helpless as the dark matter went supernova hurling her in a million different directions and breathing life back into every fantasy she'd ever had about him.

Still he whispered to her, "Mine. Mine. Mine."

"Mine. *Ragazza pericolosa.*" He groaned against her throat and the distant part of her brain still functioning knew he was lost. A second later, Nic blew apart, dragging them into an event horizon where everything stopped and the light turned inside out.

Oblivion, Lizzie decided, was perfect.

Later, draped across his chest, fighting sleep because she didn't want the sun to rise, she said, "I should have told you. I'm sorry."

His arm tightened around her and he pressed a kiss to the top of her head. She turned her face to his, smiling at the sated and tousled man smiling back at her. Her heart ached. How was she going to leave him tomorrow?

He kissed her again. "Don't lie to me again, Lizzie. I can forgive a lot of things but not that."

The drive to Miami was quiet but this time Lizzie was awake for all of it. She spent a lot of time watching the water pass by. It made her strangely homesick for New Orleans. She and Jen always tried to hold their breath when they crossed the Pontchartrain but the bridge out of the Keys was too long.

When they hit the turnpike, Nic's phone rang. The sound was so alien it took Lizzie a minute to realize what it was. She froze. She'd forgotten about her phone. She hadn't checked it once since talking to Jen. She hadn't gone this long without a cell phone since Katrina.

"Rogan and Angie are flying back with us." He darted another glance at her as he ended the call. He dropped the phone on the console caught her hand, pulling it to rest on his thigh.

"Is she going to be upset if I'm on the plane?"

He squeezed her hand. "My jet. My rules."

"Jet," Lizzie corrected herself. The water was so clear.

He lifted her fingers to his mouth for a gentle kiss.

He believed everything was settled. He thought because he wanted something the universe would change direction to make sure it happened. Lizzie knew better. If the universe suspected you needed or wanted something too much, it would take it away. Because anything that good, the universe wanted for itself.

When they pulled up at the airstrip, Lizzie wasn't sure why she was so shocked. Had she expected a single engine plane? Really? She should know better by now. No, the private jet was huge, but then it would need to be if he was flying around the world checking his five-star resorts and casinos.

She stepped out of the luxury SUV. It probably cost a year's tuition. She took a deep breath and reminded herself to stop forgetting who and what Nic was. It was so hard to remember he had more money than some small countries. She just saw a beautiful man, who smiled more often and looked years younger than he had a week ago.

She followed him up the steps and into the interior of the jet. It redefined luxury for her in a way she hadn't dreamed of. The plane was a masterpiece of understated elegance. It screamed money that didn't care it was money. It didn't have the traditional rows of seats. It had captain-style chairs gathered around a huge flat screen TV. Nothing felt like the inside of an airplane.

Nic steered her into one of the butter-soft captain chairs. "I'll be right back."

A quick kiss on the forehead and he left her to meet with his pilot. She was surfing through movie options when he returned a few minutes later.

"You finding everything you need?"

She set the remote control down and leaned back in the comfortable chair. "I guess. You live in a different stratosphere."

"You'll get used to it."

"I don't see how. I've never seen anything like this plane."

"You aren't exactly impoverished, Lizzie."

"Me? I own a car, a smart phone and some really great shoes. This—" she waved her arm around, "—different planet."

He sat down on the low table in front of her. "Your father owns the tallest building in New Orleans and just signed an eight-figure deal with Alexander Volikov to supply parts for Volikovneft's deep water drilling platforms."

Lizzie shrugged. "He doesn't have a private jet."

"He does have a mansion on Lake Pontchartrain."

"He built it after Katrina because my mother didn't want to live in the city anymore. We're new money. There's no way I'm at home here in your luxury jet after spending the week on your yacht."

"Fishing trawler," he corrected. "My yacht's at Lake Como."

"See? That's exactly what I mean." She bit her lip and tried not to laugh at him. She wasn't trying to be funny. "I bet you have a house there too."

He shrugged, then gave her his slow sexy smile. Spellbound, she couldn't look away.

"A little place in Bellagio. We'll visit when we go to Italy."

"I have one question."

"I'm afraid." He caught her hands, pulling her forward until she had no choice but to stand with him. Then he switched places and she was in his lap.

She laughed, trying to get comfortable and moving around more than necessary. He hissed in reaction then settled her across his legs. She pouted a little and rested her head on his shoulder.

"Ask your question."

Her fingers played with the top button of the linen shirt he wore. "Do you have flight attendants who double as strippers?"

His eyebrows rose. "No, but if you're offering to dance for me, I'll have a pole installed straight away."

"I have two left feet."

"Liar, I have danced with you on more than one occasion."

"All of which led to serious trouble."

He lifted his head. "I love trouble, Lizzie. Haven't you figured that out yet? Now open your mouth, *bella*, and let me kiss you properly before we're interrupted."

She smiled at his unearthly beautiful face and wished on every shooting star she'd ever seen. Then he kissed her properly.

Lizzie hadn't expected Angie to be nice to her, but she also hadn't expected her to act like she didn't exist. Granted, she had Zachary with her and spent most of her time entertaining the little boy while Rogan installed his travel seat.

Lizzie took her cue from her and pretended everything was fine. It was easy to do since the strain lining Rogan's face was gone. He was happy, so Lizzie was happy for him.

He gave her a questioning look when he set Zachary down. Zachary threw himself at Nic. Lizzie smiled when Nic swung him up high and spoke to him in Italian. Zachary laughed and tried to answer in English. Nic raised an eyebrow and the little boy giggled out a few words back in stilted Italian as he patted Nic's face with his hands.

"You okay, *cher*?" Rogan dragged her attention away from the exchange when he leaned down to kiss her on the cheek.

"I'm tired."

"I'm not going to ask any more questions, because it would be wrong to beat the shit out of him before the plane takes off."

"Don't you dare."

Rogan tapped her nose with his index finger. Something he'd done since she was a kid. It always made her smile. "You say the word and he's toast."

"I like him, Rogan." She held her breath for Rogan's reaction. It was wonderfully anti-climactic.

"I can see that." He straightened. "I need to pick out a movie before Zachary does."

"Things are good?" Lizzie asked, giving him what she hoped was an encouraging smile.

"We're getting there."

Zachary beat him to it and spent the beginning of the flight dancing with lemurs, and running back and forth between his father and uncle until he stopped and passed out, snoring loudly while Angie tucked him into his travel seat. While they were occupied with their son, Nic pulled Lizzie out of her seat.

"Hungry?" He pulled her into the surprisingly large galley. He shut the door, backed her up against it. "I'm starving."

His mouth sealed over hers and she sighed. Her arms went around him while he melted every bone in her body. He was starving for her. She was for him too and she kissed him back with an intensity she hadn't known she was capable of but it might be their last kiss, and she wanted to remember the way it felt to be in his arms.

He lifted his head. "This isn't a goodbye kiss."

His next kiss was brutal, and when he raised his head his expression was worse. Her lips throbbed as she raked her front teeth over her bottom lip to keep it from trembling. "Nic, I—"

Fingers pressed against her mouth. "We've done everything backwards. When I get back, we'll have dinner and see where it goes."

She nodded and let a tiny spark of hope scrape off her heart. "Okay," she agreed, letting herself believe him despite the warning sirens and red flags going off in her mind. "Dinner."

He kissed her again, pulling her deep into his body and turning that tiny spark into a bonfire. It was a dangerous kiss and gave her too much hope and worse, made it seem safe to dream. She poured herself back into the kiss, wanting to leave her mark on him the way he was leaving his on her. She wanted it to resonate through him until he returned to her. Because she wanted him to return. More than she wanted her next breath.

The sun was high and hot in New Orleans and the humidity was like a heavy wet blanket but it was nothing compared to the suffocating weight settling on her chest. Hitching her bag over her shoulders, she took the first step. Then the next step, then the next until she felt Louisiana under her feet and for the first time, it didn't help to be back home.

Nothing was going to help.

Then an arm slid around her waist and kept her from tipping out of the world. She turned into him, sighing when his arms closed around her. His palm rested against the back of her head and she leaned into his chest. The world stopped and for a perfect moment all the pain was gone.

Time had no meaning for her when he held her. Reality no longer mattered. The strength of his body and his clean spicy scent were all she needed. She'd been a fool to think she could walk away from him in one piece. She drank in the perfect moment, trying to memorize every detail and hoping they would stay like this forever.

He lifted his head, the tenderness in his expression warming her in ways nothing else could. Then he started walking her toward a familiar Escalade. Her heart stopped. This was it. Everything squeezed tight inside her and she turned into Nic, pressing her forehead into his shoulder. His hand stroked the back of her head. He kissed her temple.

"Don't disappear."

"I won't."

"Promise me, Lizzie. I'll be back as soon as I can."

"I promise." The words escaped from her heart before her brain had a chance to weigh in.

He smiled, an odd smile she wasn't sure how to take. Then he opened the car door for her and stepped back so she could get in. Every instinct she had told her to grab hold of him and make him take her with him. Getting in the car was a big mistake. Letting him leave was a bigger one.

Nic urged her inside. "Dream about me," he whispered in her ear, then spoke to his sister when she jerked the front door open and slid inside. Angie answered without turning around, waving a dismissive hand at him.

"Be safe." Lizzie forced herself not to jump right back out of the SUV as he shut her door.

"I'll see you in a week."

Then the door was closed between them. She was amazed at how much it hurt. She'd known it wouldn't be fun but she hadn't been prepared for the hollowness and dread. A week. She could do a week. A week away from him would be good. Maybe she could get some perspective back.

"Touching."

She ignored the sneering comment and watched Nic and Rogan talking. Zachary was on Rogan's shoulder but he kept reaching for Nic. He threw himself at his uncle who caught him easily then hugged him close to his chest.

Lizzie wasn't sure how much more her heart could take.

Angie turned in her seat, when Lizzie didn't acknowledge her. "Don't think for one minute he's serious about you."

"Don't start."

"My brother's affairs last about six weeks. They end with a beautiful diamond bracelet chosen by his girl Friday, Pam, and delivered with lots of roses and good wishes." Angie's eyes flicked over her. "You barely lasted a week."

Lizzie sucked in a breath, trying to stay calm. "He had meetings he couldn't reschedule."

Angie laughed. "Meetings? In Hong Kong? Oh, Lizzie." Angie sighed, false compassion making her smile cruel. "Hong Kong is code for Xia Chang."

The name pricked at her. Xia Chang sounded familiar. "Who?" she asked before she could stop herself.

"Who?" Angie pushed her hair behind her ear. "Xia Chang is the only long-term relationship Nic's ever had. They've been together for years, Lizzie. Surely, you've seen pictures of her. They hit the gossip blogs and tabloid anytime Nic is in Hong Kong."

Lizzie swallowed hard and resisted the urge to dig her cell phone out of her purse. She refused to fall apart in front of Angie. "I'm not listening to you, Angie. Give it up."

"You fell for him, didn't you? He said you would. Why do you think he took you to the Keys? He wanted to get you away from my husband but now Rogan and I are back together and he's done with you. He's flying back to her like he always does."

Lizzie sucked in a ragged breath as each word hit her like a dart, breaking her skin and shattering her insides. "That's not true."

"Why would I lie? If you don't believe me, Google her. It's Xia with an X." Angie smirked. "I'm sure there'll be photographs all over the Internet in a few days."

Lizzie started to tell Angie to go to hell, but all the hatred and animosity staring back at her stopped her.

"Now you know how it feels when the man you want wants someone else." Her voice broke and she turned around. "Or maybe you get a thrill being the other woman."

Ice burned through Lizzie but before she could react Rogan opened the back door and strapped his exhausted son into his car seat.

"Zio Nic," Zachary pleaded, grabbing handfuls of Rogan's hair. "Want Zio Nic."

It was the same thing Lizzie wanted to yell. Zachary's cries gutted what was left of her.

"I know, buddy. He'll be back soon." Rogan kissed his son's forehead, then extricated his hair from tiny fists. Even drowning in pain, Lizzie could see what a good father Rogan was and how much more settled he seemed with his family back.

Lizzie knew it would take one word, one repetition of the vitriol Angie had flung at her and Rogan's reconciliation with his wife would be over. She couldn't do it. She wanted him to be happy. When he glanced at her with concerned green eyes, she forced herself to swallow it all down and smile.

"Lizzie? He'll be back in a few days."

She nodded and dashed back a stray tear with the edge of her hand. "I know. I'm tired and ready to get home."

"You want us to drop you at your parents' house or Jen and Stefan's?"

"Jen's." She turned toward the window in time to see Nic going up the stairs to the jet. Maybe he would look back.

He should have looked back.

She waited.

The door of the jet shut behind him at the same time Rogan shut Zachary's door.

She bit the inside of her lip until she tasted blood and the burning tears backed off.

He hadn't looked back. Not once.

Her hand covered her mouth and she swallowed it all back down. She was not going to fall apart. She leaned her forehead against the window, the glass cool on her hot skin. She needed numbers. She wanted to lose herself in her research and not think about anything but gaps fluctuations.

CHAPTER TWELVE

Nic stared at his cell phone for another half second before it went skidding across the glossy wood conference table. It crashed into an abandoned glass of water, which upended and splashed water across the table. He ignored the water dripping onto the carpet and ripped the Windsor knot at his neck loose.

It didn't help. He still couldn't breathe.

He'd cleared the conference room a few minutes ago when he couldn't listen to any more reports, projections or labor issues. It hadn't occurred to him to step out of the room. He'd abruptly ended the meeting and kicked everyone out. No one had protested. They had calmly gathered their things and left him alone to brood.

He should have never let her off the plane.

He retrieved his cell phone, then opened his photos. She smiled at him, blue eyes dancing straight through him. He'd snapped the photograph of her when she'd been sunbathing, careful to only get her face. He pushed the heel of his hand hard against his forehead and tried to shake off the falling sensation.

He should never have let her leave the house. He should've kept her in the Keys.

Why wasn't she answering her phone?

There was a soft tap on the door before it opened halfway, and Xia appeared. "Nic. We have a reception in an hour."

Nic dropped the phone on the conference table and went to stare out at the crowded skyline. The stunning view was lost on him. Everything was gray. "You'll have to apologize for me. I'm not up to another party. The fundraiser the other night was enough."

Her smile was mild as she straightened an imaginary wrinkle from the white jacket she wore. "What should I say?"

"Tell them I have jet lag."

"Nic." She surprised him when she joined him at the window instead of slipping out discreetly. She held out the phone he'd left on the conference table. Lizzie's picture was open on the screen. "Is she the reason you've been in such a black mood? Oh, don't answer, I can see it all over you."

"She's not answering her phone," he admitted gruffly. He shoved his hands in his pockets and glanced back over his shoulder at her.

She was fighting a smile and it surprised him so much he turned around. "You think this is funny?"

She shook her head slowly, letting the smile take over her expression. "Have you looked in the mirror? When was the last time you shaved?"

One hand left his pocket and he was surprised his normal scruff was a lot fuller than he normally allowed. "You're taking this rather well."

Her smile widened, revealing her rare sense of humor. "You wanted me to tear my hair out and cry?"

"Maybe," he admitted, turning to gaze out at the city that had always been his refuge. Now it was overwhelming. Too busy. He should never have left the Keys.

"Oh." She brushed his concern aside. "I did two years ago. But I could have refused the job offer and everything would have stayed the same."

Nic chuckled. "I made you the offer because I knew you were tired of me."

"You were getting too old." Her smile was indulgent and clearly amused. "If this girl is different, you may want to make some adjustments in how you approach relationships. In fact, whatever your first instinct is, you should do the opposite."

"I'm that bad?"

Her smile never flickered. "At some point, you are going to have to let your walls down. Not everyone is waiting outside for a chance to steal part of you."

"She's not waiting for me."

"I find that hard to believe." She waved a hand at him. "Go home. If she's not waiting, find her."

"Chase after her?"

"What is your first instinct?"

Nic's jaw tightened as he realized his first instinct was to say the hell with her. If she didn't want to talk to him, fine. Anger burned in his gut and the excruciating hole in his chest expanded.

She shook her head, before he could answer. "Do the opposite."

"You want me to crawl on my knees and beg?"

"Will it make you feel worse than you do now?"

Nothing could feel worse than this black despair clawing at him. "I hate when you make sense."

"Go home. Everything is under control here. You can fly out tonight."

When the door shut behind her, he checked his phone. No texts. No missed calls. Nothing. He started to hit redial and stopped himself. Calling was doing no good. Instead, he called Pam to see if she could get the next available flight time for his jet. With any luck he'd be in the air before morning.

"Every slice of cheese doesn't have to be straight, Lizzie."

Jen stepped up to the kitchen island where Lizzie had a line of bread slices spaced across the island. She blinked back tears. She couldn't put cheese on sandwiches right.

"Lizzie," Jen whispered, moving to hug her again. "You can't keep up like this."

Lizzie backed up quickly, her arms going up in the air, palms out. "You knew better than to ask me to help. I'm hopeless in the kitchen."

Jen's shoulder's sagged. "That isn't what I meant."

Jen was getting fed up with her because she wasn't telling her about Florida. Lizzie couldn't talk about it yet. Not without her skin peeling off.

Jared leaned over her shoulder and started moving cheese slices so they were uneven again. "They're like Stepford sandwiches."

"Who are you again, you bald-headed freak?" Lizzie meant to sound snappy and sarcastic but snappy eluded her. She sounded tired.

Jared rubbed his super short hair and grinned. "You don't like it?"

Lizzie sighed. She was so tired. She couldn't get enough sleep. "I didn't say that. I don't know why you cut it."

"He lost a bet." Jen snickered. "He won't say which one."

Jared grinned and went back to disrupting her carefully placed cheese. It should have all felt familiar, despite Jared's freakishly short hair, but Jen and Stefan's home didn't feel like her home anymore. Jen and Stefan were married. The knowledge kept ringing through her with a sharp edge she hadn't expected.

Everything was different. They were different. Closer. Lizzie wasn't used to feeling like a third wheel with her best friend and brother but they weren't a trio anymore. Jen and Stefan were best friends and she was the little sister. She'd wanted Jen to be her real sister all her life, another one of her childish dreams had come true and bitten her on the ass.

She was never going to learn. She dashed back a stray tear and realized the room had gone quiet. Jared and Jen were watching her too closely. Concern softened their expressions and it undid Lizzie. They felt sorry for her? Could she be any more humiliated?

"The cheese will melt anyway," Jen reassured her and finished piling turkey and roast beef on the bread. "Here, you can have extra smoked gouda." Jen added another slice to Lizzie's cheese sandwich.

"Why don't I get extra smoked gouda?" Jared snatched a slice when Jen wasn't looking.

"You can have extra." Jen added extra cheese on Jared's sandwich.

"If he's getting extra cheese, then I'd better get some." Stefan stepped into the doorway, caught the upper jam with both hands, and stretched.

Jen shook her head and added more cheese to Stefan's. Lizzie couldn't work up a smile when Stefan grabbed one of the sandwiches off the pan and bit into it before Jen could get it back.

"Those aren't finished!" Jen yelled at him, surprising Lizzie.

It was strange seeing Jen so unguarded with Stefan. He'd gotten a lot more than he bargained for with Jen. He was enjoying it too if his expression was any indication.

Lizzie smiled as Stefan held his sandwich over his head. "Tasted good to me," Stefan insisted, waving the sandwich before taking another bite.

Disgusted, Jen dropped her arms and went back to finish the others. "I was going to toast them."

"I'm starving and you're making me two, right? The hippie's sourdough is better untoasted."

"See." Jared smirked at Jen. "What did I tell you?"

Jen eyed them with disgusted amusement. "I liked it better when you two hated each other."

"I still hate him," Stefan assured her around another mouthful of sandwich.

Jared batted his eyelashes at Stefan. "Not as much as I hate you."

Stefan rolled his eyes and ate his sandwich. What planet was she on? Stefan hated bread. He never ate carbs. Now he swallowed down a sandwich and grabbed a handful of homemade potato chips.

"What did I tell you, Lizzie?" Jen smirked. "Total bromance."

Jared made gagging noises while Stefan almost spit the food out of his mouth. Normally Lizzie would have enjoyed their banter. She normally would say something like *have you two picked out your china pattern yet?*

Now, she was too tired and all of it seemed to be happening at a great distance. She was so disconnected. Panic slicked up her throat as she realized it wasn't everyone else. It was her. She'd changed. She was the one who was different.

It took her a minute to realize they were all staring at her again. They were concerned and sympathetic. Lizzie couldn't stand much more of it.

Stefan broke the strained silence. "So you got nothing?"

"What?"

"This is the part where you back up Jen with some smart-ass comment we all pretend to understand."

"Oh." She tried to think of something to throw him off but wasn't quick enough.

"What's going on with you?" Stefan demanded, shaking off the calming hand Jen put on his bicep.

Lizzie forced a cough, not wanting to lie but not wanting to have the conversation she knew would follow an honest answer. She wasn't sure where to start or if she could explain it anyway. "I don't feel good. Allergies?"

"That's what you're going with?" Stefan opened the refrigerator and grabbed bottled waters. He tossed one to Jared, who caught it without looking. "Allergies?"

"She does look kind of sick." Jared grinned.

"Don't help me," she snapped back, then took the first painless breath she'd had all morning.

"It wouldn't have anything to do with the voice mails and text messages from Nic Maretti asking if you're okay and why you won't answer your phone, would it?"

Lizzie coughed for real, then choked on air. "Messages?"

"Yeah, messages." He tipped his water back but his eyes never left her as he drained half the bottle.

Lizzie shrugged. "I don't know. You'll have to ask Nic."

"Nic's in Hong Kong."

Lizzie flinched. She knew where Nic was and she knew who Nic was with. Angie hadn't been lying. A photograph of Nic and Xia Chang had appeared on an Italian gossip blog. She couldn't read the article but she didn't have to. There were enough photographs to tell the story.

Xia Chang was everything she was not. Tall, sleek, elegant with a thick curtain of glossy black hair and a face so beautiful, Lizzie couldn't blame Nic.

They were at a formal black and white charity ball. Nic was dangerous in the jet black tuxedo and long black tie. Xia leaned on his arm in a white gown glossier than her hair. Lizzie couldn't fault the dress. It skimmed her perfect figure but was neither tight nor revealing. The sheer long sleeves and high neck suited her regal bearing.

And her shoes. Lizzie had tortured herself by enlarging the photograph so she could see the understated pointy toe white pumps with razor thin black heels. They were perfect too, offering nothing for Lizzie to sneer at.

Lizzie had examined the photographs in detail, drowning in a sharp and jagged jealousy that had hacked so deep it felt like a poison she would never be able to rid herself of. With her now, it made her want to run away and never stop.

"Lizzie." The concern in Jen's voice dragged her back to the present.

She opened her mouth to reassure them, but nothing came out. Her throat was too tight. Breathing was starting to be an issue. She wiped her hand across her face. Great. She was crying again. Damn it.

"I'm going to kill him." Stefan hissed.

She shook her head, managing a weak, "I'm fine."

"You are the exact opposite of fine."

She flinched at the harshness of Stefan's tone. He was angry at the situation, not her, but she was so raw it still hurt. She forced her mouth into a painful smile. Her facial muscles were ready to shatter. "I don't have time to be anything other than okay, besides, he already has a girlfriend and—"

"Wait. What?" Jen's concern dissolve into anger. "You went to Florida with him when you knew he had a girlfriend?"

"You went to Florida with him?" Stefan exploded, then turned on

Jen. "You knew she was in Florida?"

Jen's apologetic grin didn't help.

"What if I did?" Lizzie snapped, pulling his attention back to her. "I'm not a kid anymore and I didn't know he had a girlfriend until Angie told me. That's why I won't call him back. Satisfied?"

"Angie?" Jen's surprise caught her off guard. "She may not be the most reliable source of information, you know. You should talk to Nic."

Should she talk to Nic? Would she be able to without humiliating herself? Not likely. "No, it's better this way. I can't get involved with anyone right now. I have to teach this fall and I'm trying to get into Dr. Pak's research group. I have way too much I need to focus on." She sucked back another ragged breath. She backed up, holding up her hands in defense when Jen tried to move toward her. "Please, don't. I promise you. I'm going to be okay."

She knew they didn't believe her but before they could say anything the back door slammed open and Rogan exploded into the kitchen breathing fire and brimstone. "You! Hippie!"

"Chill." Jared caught the envelope Rogan slammed against his chest. "What is your damage?"

"I want a divorce. Right fucking now. Do whatever it is you lawyers do."

Lizzie relaxed, grateful all the attention had swung away from her. Then happy, fun Jared left the building. Scary Jared appeared as he flipped through the papers. "Is this for real?"

"Yeah. Delivered by special courier less than an hour ago." Rogan caught the long neck beer Stefan tossed him.

"Divorce papers?" Lizzie swallowed. "I thought everything was okay."

Rogan's chin dropped. "Yeah, after I dropped you off World War III broke out. I'm done. She's gone too far this time."

"Adultery is hard to prove." Jared shoved the papers back into the envelope as the room went silent.

"Adultery?" Stefan threw his empty bottle in the trash. "With who? Lizzie? Did they name her?"

"Yes." Rogan turned toward Lizzie at the same time, regret and shame darkening his green eyes. "I'm so sorry, kiddo."

"What?" Lizzie whispered, as she quietly stepped out of her body. "Because she saw us dancing together?"

"I've seen you dance, Lizzie, and it's hot," Jared teased.

She turned on him. "You are not helping!"

"You told me not to help you."

Lizzie groaned as Jared grinned at her.

Jen grabbed the papers from Jared. "It really names Lizzie? Do people still do that? Has Angie lost her mind?"

"It's not true." Her stomach twisted. "No one will believe it."

"It doesn't matter." Jared was serious again. "With everything going on with Judge Robicheaux and your family, if the news media gets a whiff of this, it'll be all over the news. The media will lap it up because it will keep the Robicheaux case interesting in the news."

"So now you're a media expert too?" Lizzie groaned, sitting down hard on a barstool. This couldn't be happening.

"I won't fight her for custody if she agrees to stay in New Orleans and we can work out visitation," Rogan said.

"You can't do that," Lizzie said. "I don't care what they say about me. I don't want you to lose your son because of me."

Rogan shook his head. "It's not because of you."

"No," Stefan snapped. "This is all Andreas Maretti bullshit. I'll bet you money he's behind it. He's angry we got the Volikovneft deal. Now, he's bailed Judge Robicheaux out of jail."

"You're not serious?" Lizzie was on her feet again.

"Completely serious." Jen sighed. "It happened while you were in Florida, but so far he's been keeping a low profile."

"He's not going to try anything else," Stefan said. "The whole world is watching him."

"No, he's just regrouping." Jared added. "My brother is building a hell of a case against him but it's not going to be easy. Everybody owes that old man favors." Jared straightened all the paperwork up, put it back in the envelope, then checked his watch. "And speaking of my brother, Grant is probably on the golf course. I'll take this to him. He loves me when I interrupt his golf game."

"I don't want Rogan to lose custody." Lizzie whispered.

"He won't," Stefan snapped. "You were right not to take Nic's calls. Stay away from him, Lizzie. That whole family is nothing but trouble."

CHAPTER THIRTEEN

"Who the hell is that?" Stefan groaned as Jen rolled away from him after the doorbell went off for the third time. "This had better be good."

"I'll go." She grabbed her robe from the floor where Stefan had thrown it earlier. "It's probably Jared."

The doorbell chimed again.

"Fuck." He swung off the bed and grabbed his jeans, wincing as he eased up the zipper. Whoever was pressing their doorbell was seriously risking their life. "No, stay here. It's not the hippie. He walks in when he wants to." He grabbed his T-shirt then headed for the stairs, taking them two at a time while he pulled the shirt over his head.

He jerked the door open and his head snapped back. He hadn't expected Nic Maretti on his front porch looking all impatient and aggravated. Stefan leaned against the doorframe blocking the entrance. He was not about to let Maretti in. "You got some kind of death wish, Maretti?"

Nic's expression didn't flicker. "Where is she?"

Stefan shook his head, fingers squeezing into a fist and resisting the urge to plant it in Nic's face. It wouldn't take much to wipe his bored expression off his face. Instead, he said, "Not here."

"Stefan." Jen slid her arm around his waist, reminding him to be civilized. "Come in, Nic, I'll make coffee."

Stefan huffed, his anger fading now that she was touching him. Still pride demanded he put up a protest. "This is not a social call. You don't have to make him coffee."

She backed away from him and folded her arms across her chest, giving him a fierce look. He should deck Maretti, take her back upstairs and finish what she'd started. Then she raised her eyebrow at him, ready to take him on and he forgot everything except how much he loved her.

He stepped back away from the door and waved Nic in. "Yeah, fine. Whatever. Come on in, it's all about the Southern Hospitality at the Sellers house."

Nic had not slept. He wasn't hungry yet, somehow he found himself in the most amazing kitchen he'd ever seen while Jen scrambled eggs and Sellers prowled around, grumbling that he didn't do coffee.

"How do you like your eggs, Nic?" she asked, ignoring her husband.

"Just salt."

"No cheese?" Jen asked, a strange smile on her face. "Bacon?"

"No cheese and definitely not bacon. I don't eat meat."

"You don't eat meat?" Stefan stopped dumping coffee in the coffee pot and glanced over his shoulder.

"No."

Jen and Stefan exchanged a strange look and tried not to laugh.

Nic did not have time for this.

"I want bacon." The scruffy musician Nic had caught Lizzie dancing with at Trick's walked into the kitchen. He was half-awake as he headed straight for the coffee. He pulled a coffee mug down from a cabinet. Did he live here too?

"What the hell are you doing here?" Stefan demanded.

Unconcerned, the guy shrugged as he poured himself of cup of coffee, sipped it then spit it out in the sink despite Jen's horrified protests. "You call this coffee? Jen, you know better than to let him play with the coffee pot."

"Screw you." Stefan jerked the refrigerator open and grabbed a bottle of water. "You aren't supposed to be here."

"I was hiding in the Carriage house until you two finished your thing. About time too, I'm starving. Oh, hey, Nic."

"Have we met?" Nic asked, not impressed by the musician's sudden grin.

"Jared Marshall. You loaned me a bunch of money. Thanks, by the way. You should come by the bakery if you're going to be in town awhile. Check out the best investment you ever made."

Nic had trouble reconciling this unkempt boy with the brilliant business plan he'd read. Marshall had been all over Lizzie at Trick's but today he looked different. His hair was all gone. "You're Jared Marshall?"

"Soon to be the late Jared Marshall," Stefan grumbled.

"Chill, Sellers. It's not like I was in the house. Unless you want some pointers."

Jen's hand flattened on Stefan's chest before he could reach the younger guy. "Cool it, Jared."

"What?" Jared laughed. "I want extra cheese. Give me that, you're doing it wrong." He grabbed the skillet away from Jen and began folding the eggs exactly the same way she had. "Go stand by your man before he rips my head off. I don't want to die on an empty stomach."

"My eggs had better be perfect," Stefan warned him, dropping down on a barstool. "Extra cheese."

"Extra cheese," Jared mimicked him in a little kid's voice. Then scraped the eggs onto a plate. "Hey, these are plain. Is Lizzie here?"

"Those are for Nic." Jen pushed the plate across the island to Nic. "You want coffee, Nic?" She poured him a mug before he could refuse it.

"She's not here? Where is she?" Nic had no intentions of eating the fluffy mass of yellow on his plate. Then his stomach grumbled so he had a few bites. The eggs were perfect and the coffee was delicious. Then he realized he couldn't remember the last time he'd eaten anything.

They all ignored his question again. Stefan stared suspiciously at the plate of eggs Jared handed him. "You better not have spit in them."

"Dude, you've been watching me the whole time."

"Ignore them," Jen said. "I live for the day they grow up."

Nic set his coffee cup down. "This is all very charming but I need to know where Lizzie is."

Jared grinned, nodding at a brown envelope lying in the middle of the island. "There's your first clue."

All eyes were on him again, but this time no one was laughing. He reached for the envelope, knowing instinctively the contents were a game changer. When he pulled the papers out and flipped through them, every cell in his body turned inside out.

"You didn't know?" Jen asked.

"No."

"This is Andreas, isn't it?" Stefan nodded at the paperwork Nic was crushing in his hands.

"No one else would be this stupid. Does Lizzie know about this?"

"Yes," Jen answered him.

"She and Rogan ran away together." Stefan smirked.

"Yeah," Jared said. "They're tired of hiding their love."

"Who are we to stand in their way?" Stefan added, then he and hippie bumped fists.

Nic decided neither would live long enough to grow up. "You do realize Andreas will have a private investigator following them? Angie would never have signed off on this without some sort of proof."

"Proof?" Stefan's barstool slid several feet away from him as he came to his feet in one threatening motion. "Fuck him and his private investigator. There is no proof. Your father is done fucking with my family. It's bad enough he's bankrolling that snake of a judge but if he and Angie try to drag my sister through the mud, we will rain hell down on all of you. If Lizzie wanted Rogan, they'd be married with kids by now. They'd be a whole lot happier with each other than tangled up with your family."

Nic considered everything Sellers said, his mind sharp and calm. When Sellers finished, he waited. The silence stretched until it was at a breaking point. Nic had learned a long time ago that sometimes the best negotiation tool was to say nothing and Sellers was not a negotiator. It was one of the things Nic had always liked about him and his loyalty to his family. Sellers was a good guy and he was not wrong.

"Fuck you," Sellers snapped, backing down.

Nic blinked, his voice calm and cool. "You were expecting me to argue with you?"

"No." Stefan's voice was icy with disdain. "I expect you to leave my sister the hell alone."

"That is not going to happen. I'm going to get Lizzie then I'll deal with Andreas. Now where are they?"

"Orange Beach," Jen said. "Lizzie likes to go to the beach when she's upset."

Nic inclined his head. "Thank you. Do not call them and warn them I'm on the way. You owe me, Sellers," he reminded Stefan and the younger man backed down.

"This was a good idea." Lizzie sighed as the sea breeze and the sound of waves hitting the shore washed over the balcony.

"Yeah." Rogan joined her on the balcony. He pulled one of the chairs up to the railing, sat down and kicked back, resting his heels on the metal ledge. "You going to be okay?"

Lizzie nodded, pushing the hair the breeze flattened across her face behind her ears.

"I'll make sure she leaves you out of the divorce, kiddo. I promise."

"I don't want to talk about it." She sat down next to him. Tired and wiped out from the drive, she was too restless to go to bed but too exhausted to do anything constructive. "It's okay."

Rogan sighed. "You know, the Marettis aren't like us. They look down on the rest of us like we're their subjects."

"Nic's not like that."

"Nic's worse. Eventually he'll be the De Santis heir, so don't think he doesn't watch the world from his ivory tower."

"I used to think he was disconnected," she said. "But Nic's more complicated."

If he did watch the world from an ivory tower, it's because the people who should have loved him and grounded him had failed him. Not because he believed he was better than everyone else. Guilt stabbed at her stomach. She wanted to be the person to break through the walls surrounding him but she knew she would destroy herself in the process.

The doorbell rang and Lizzie jumped up, eager to brush off the sudden remorse. Maybe she should have answered those calls. "I'll get it."

"Bring me back a beer." He caught her hand as she brushed past him.

"Okay, but you're only having one more."

"Whatever."

"We're not getting drunk," she called over her shoulder as she opened the front door.

She turned back to the open door and her heart stopped. They were so getting drunk. As fast as possible.

"Do you want me to set them down for you?" the delivery man asked, smiling at her from around a monstrous bouquet of red roses as long as her arm.

"Sure." She stood aside so he could set them on the kitchen's raised breakfast bar. They were blood red and the condo was already filling with their sickening scent.

"Thank you."

She couldn't take her eyes off the roses. They could've been a dozen snakes on sticks and she would have been less afraid to reach for the white card stuck in the middle.

"Oh, and don't forget this."

He handed her a small box and told her the gratuity had been taken care of too. Good thing, because tipping him was the last thing on Lizzie's mind. She stood a long time, the small blue wrapped package in her bloodless fingers.

The sliding glass doors opened behind her.

"What the fuck?"

She spun around so quickly reaching for the roses before he could see them and ended up knocking them off the raised bar. Her entire body cringed as rose petals, water and glass shattered all around her bare feet. The vase missed her toes by a hair's breath. The glass spray burned as it ripped against her lower calves and ankles like briars in the woods.

"Don't move." Rogan sounded like he was at the other end of a tunnel. She ignored him and knelt down to pick up the white card before it was soaked.

"Lizzie, wait." He grabbed the shoes he'd left by the sliding glass door. "Hang on and I'll get you."

It was too late. She waved him off and sat down hard in the middle of the mess, glass and thorns scratching her feet. The biting pain was nothing compared to the ice burning through her system. She hadn't known anything could hurt so much.

This was what you wanted, she reminded herself. What had she expected when she ignored his phone calls and text messages? Did she think he'd quietly disappear?

How could he be so cruel? He wasn't a vicious person.

She ripped open the envelope and anger surged up so fast for a moment she thought she was going to be sick.

Our week was great, cara, but we're too different.

Even knowing what to expect, pain seared through her like wild fire and she forgot how to breathe. This was why she hadn't wanted to get involved with him. This was why she had wanted to keep her distance. It hurt so much she couldn't think straight. She wanted to curl up in a ball and die. It was a million times worse than she'd predicted.

It was more than Lizzie could bear. She gave in and let it consume her. She let go. What difference did it make?

Wait, how had he known where she was?

Lizzie paused, an eerie calm settled over her as the logical part of her brain flickered back on and kicked her freaked out heart to the curb. Everything froze and her mind separated from the emotions trying to smother her.

Nic had never called her *cara*.

Pam would never make a mistake like that on the card. Pam wouldn't have sent her red roses. She would've sent her pale pink roses. Lizzie knew this because she'd made a Pinterest board called *Future Reference for Pam* one night while she and Nic were goofing around. Nic had dared her to do it so she'd had no choice. She'd filled it with black roses, pink roses, Italian travel tips, and the world's most expensive diamond bracelets.

Nic hadn't sent the roses.

Lizzie closed her eyes against the truth. Nic would never send her roses.

But Angie would.

That bitch! That unbelievable harpy.

This was all Angie. She must have someone following Rogan.

Lizzie swallowed hard. Coming down here with Rogan had been a huge mistake. They were using her to try and take away his son and now she'd given them live ammunition.

Hands reached under her arms to pull her up but she fought him off. Rogan sat down in the middle of the floor with her and pulled small shards of glass out of her feet and ankles, then he cleaned up the cuts.

"They will never find his body, Lizzie, I promise."

She nodded, unable to speak as she opened the package and found a shiny gold bangle. She dragged in a ragged breath as her suspicions were confirmed. Pam would never have sent something so cheap and tacky. Pulling her arm back when Rogan tried to take it away from her, she slipped it over her hand. The cool metal burned her skin. She shivered. Angie really hated her.

"He had no right...damn it." Rogan hissed as a stray piece of glass nicked his finger.

"Rogan." She didn't want to say the words out loud. They were going to cut him deeper than the glass had. "Nic didn't send these."

Rogan stopped. "Who else would?"

"Angie told me he always ended his relationships with roses and a bracelet."

Color left Rogan's face as he moved to sit next to her, resting his arm on one bent knee while her head tipped down on his shoulder.

"She believes you and I are a thing," Lizzie said sadly. "She knows we're down here together, proving her right. I'm so sorry. If you lose Zachary because of me…"

"Hey, hey, don't go there. I'm not losing Zachary and none of this is your fault. It was my idea for you to go to Miami, remember?"

"It was a mistake."

"I know my wife, Lizzie. She should know me better than to think I'd cheat on her but I've been doing some thinking and I agree with Stefan. Her father is behind this. There's no telling what the psycho has said to her. Stop worrying."

"Rogan." She nudged him with her shoulder. "You have told her you and I aren't… I would never…I mean…gross."

"Okay, thanks, because you know my ego is at its peak right now," he grumbled, but there was humor under his faint Cajun lilt. "She tried to put a knife through your back, why are you making excuses for her?"

Lizzie couldn't believe it herself. "Because sending me these flowers was vicious. I can't believe you would be in love with someone who can be this cruel. Either you completely misjudged her or she's in so much pain she doesn't know what she's doing. Can't you see that?"

"I can now." He sighed.

"You need to talk to her. She won't believe me and coming down here, we've made it worse. She must have someone following you or how would she know. You need to call her."

"I need a drink." Rogan pushed to his feet, then pulled her up to hers. "If it makes you feel any better, if she did send those flowers I promise you she's curled up in bed sick to her stomach waiting for the axe to fall."

"You should call her now."

"I'm afraid of what I'd say to her. I'll call her in the morning."

She stared at him for a minute then nodded. "Okay. Do we have orange juice?"

"In the freezer. I'll be right back," Rogan said.

She was on her way to get the whipped cream vodka she'd spotted earlier in the refrigerator when she spotted the Silver Patrón on the top shelf. She couldn't remember the last time she'd had tequila. She remembered having a great time.

"You said we weren't getting drunk," Rogan said as she levered up on the counter so she could reach the bottle.

Lizzie slid down to the floor. "That was before I realized how screwed both of us are."

A few hours later she sat in the middle of the floor, a long stem rose minus the rosebud and thorns between her teeth, as Rogan tried to flip a coin into the tequila shot she'd dropped into the bottom of a pitcher. Lizzie laughed because he kept dropping the quarter.

"Shut up." He flipped the quarter and miss the pitcher again.

"Ha!" she announced, grabbed the shot and handed it to him.

"I hate tequila," he said.

"Fine." She downed it and set the shot glass upside down.

"You've had enough."

He wasn't wrong. "I should have stuck to the vodka."

"I should have stuck to beer."

"See, we're so screwed up, it's sad. We should go dancing."

"Dancing?" Rogan shook his head. "I'm not sure I can stand. We should go to bed."

"Now that would be something." Lizzie giggled.

He groaned and leaned back on the floor, staring at the ceiling. "Not what I meant."

"You're not my type anyway," she said. "You're not bossy enough."

"Okay, now that's way too much information."

"Nic is very bossy," she rambled on.

"Enough," he warned, leaning up and grabbing the rose stem away from her. "You should go take a shower and throw up before you go to bed."

She grinned, the tequila was making everything so much better. Her whole body moved up and down when she sighed. Her skin felt so good. She raised her arms over her head and stretched. She and Silver Patrón were going to be best friends forever. "Maybe you should try being bossy," she suggested as she returned to the project she was working on. "Angie might like it, I know I do."

"Okay, we're done," Rogan announced, struggling to his feet. He grabbed all the alcohol and turned for the kitchen.

"I'm just saying..." She shrugged, continuing to snap thorns off the roses she'd rescued from the garbage can sometime after her third or fourth shot.

"We're not having this conversation. Who the hell is that?"

"Who is what?" She scattered more rose petals across the intersecting lines.

"You can't hear someone banging on the door?" he asked, as he went to answer it.

"I thought it was in my head." she called after him as he disappeared down the hall.

Then she heard voices, and her BFF tequila turned on her savagely and the world started to spin.

"Where is she?" Nic exploded into the room, looking around then down. Then he took a step back in shock.

Nic stared down at the floor so stunned he couldn't speak at first. Lizzie was sitting cross-legged in the middle of the great room floor. Rose stems minus the buds were arranged in front of her and she was setting rose petals in random places. She seemed to take her time with each one, then changed her mind and moved them around.

"What the hell is this?"

"It's a Lizzie thing," Rogan dismissed, waving his hand toward her. "We never understand when she does stuff like this."

He looked back to Lizzie. Her eyes started at his shoes and slowly moved up. By the time she reached his face and gave him a slowly dreamy smile, Nic was burnt to a crisp. She was definitely intoxicated. Her legs were bare and she'd changed her toenail polish color to a bright green that matched the baseball T-shirt she was wearing. The shirt had bright green varsity leathers spelling...*mathlete*?

All the anger that had fueled him across the Atlantic deserted him. There were dark smudges under her eyes and cheekbones were too pronounced. Xia had been right. He was glad he'd come. Dropping to his knees and begging wasn't going to be necessary. Something else was going on here. She hadn't been blowing him off. She'd been miserable too. The world seemed to right itself but he needed to get her out of here. They could go back to Florida and do what he'd wanted to do in the first place. Take the boat out and not come back.

"What is this?" he asked, stepping closer.

Her eyes widened in surprise. "A complex plane."

CHAPTER FOURTEEN

She liked his shoes, she decided as she stared at the leather loafers. She loved the black jeans. Her eyes kept going up and up and sighing. The leather jacket and black T-shirt gave him a slightly dangerous edge. He was the guy she'd danced with at Trick's. The man she'd gone up to the suite with. A thrill teased at her belly. She shouldn't be so glad to see him but she totally was.

"A what?" he asked again.

"A complex plane. I'm looking for zeroes," she explained, trying not to roll her eyes. How could he not know what a complex plane was? Maybe because it wasn't a complex jet. She giggled and moved the petals around again.

"Zeroes?"

"Nontrivial zeroes." Some of the petals weren't correct, so she rearranged them. "If I could find one that isn't on this line…but I don't believe there are any."

"What line?"

"The half line." Lizzie's smile faded. Nic didn't know what nontrivial zeroes were? Oh, wait, she wasn't supposed to tell Nic about her math problem but the stupid tequila had made her forget. She winced as pain sliced into her right hand. She examined it curiously, surprised to see blood seeping out from between her fingers. "Oh, I forgot the thorns."

She started to open her fist but Nic pulled her to her feet before she could. He had her in the kitchen with her hand under running water before she fully comprehended what he was doing. Then the stinging started and she tried to jerk it back but he made her keep it there until it ran clear.

"Let me go, it hurts."

"Be still." His finger traced over the bangle and started to slip it off her wrist. "Where did you get this?" His jaw was clenched. She'd never seem him so angry. Nic didn't like her anymore. Then she remembered. He'd come for the cute and ditsy girl. He'd gotten drunk and despondent math genius. No wonder he wasn't happy.

"It's mine." She wanted to keep the bangle. She'd already given too much away.

. Rogan set an open first aid kit on the counter. Nic took out an alcohol wipe. The square package reminded her of a condom, and she giggled.

He stopped and met her eyes. "You think this is funny?"

The giggle died a quick death and she tried to be serious. "No."

She hissed as the alcohol stung the cuts, but the worst part was when he bunched some gauze together and pressed it hard into her palm with his thumb.

"That hurts, Nic. Stop."

"Be still."

She kept trying to pull her hand away but his grip was like a vise. She gave up and slumped in the barstool he'd put her on. He was hurting her but he smelled so good.

"Where did the roses and bracelet come from?" The question was directed at Rogan, who glanced at Lizzie but didn't answer.

"Your sister really hates me," she said in a conspiratorial whisper, pulling his attention away from Rogan. "I mean, like really hates me. I've never had someone hate me so much. Not even Dr. Hatton and he thinks I don't pay attention in class but at least the bracelet she sent me was pretty and the roses may help me win a million dollars so—"

"You think Angie sent them?"

Lizzie shrugged. "It's not like you sent them. We weren't together long enough for me to get roses."

His eyes narrowed on her and she choked back a nervous giggle. Her answer must have been wrong because his expression went black. Funny, she didn't usually miss test questions.

"We're still together."

They were? She was pretty sure they were not together. No, if they were together she wouldn't hurt so much. "I don't think so."

"You're wrong."

Maybe he would kiss her and make it all go away.

He didn't, he watched her. "I'll deal with Angie."

"I'll deal with Angie," Rogan said. "She in Houston?"

"I think so." Nic pulled his cell phone out of his pocket and handed it to Rogan. "Call Pam, she'll find her. Leave my phone on your way out. Tag's downstairs. He can take you to the airport."

Rogan's head went back but he didn't say anything. Lizzie bit back a smile. Rogan wasn't used to taking orders. He normally gave them. She was surprised at the curt nod as he backed off and did what Nic told him to do.

She'd never seen Rogan back down from anyone. The only reason he and Stefan didn't butt heads was because they'd beaten the crap out of each other in fifth grade. They'd been best friends ever since.

She wondered if Nic had ever had a best friend. Probably not. It was all she could do not to run her fingers through his hair. He needed a haircut.

"Be still while I wrap this up."

She straightened and tried to behave but he was being all bossy. The harsh look on his face and dangerously quiet words were getting her worked up. She struggled not to squirm on the barstool but she was starting to ache as the heat simmered deep inside her, turning parts of her liquid. "You're mad at me."

"I'm getting you out of here." He taped off the gauze and set it aside.

"No." She blinked back tears. "No, no, no. I'm not going anywhere with you."

She squeaked when his arm snaked around her waist. "You aren't going anywhere else without me again," he informed her. "Except maybe a shower."

"I've had far too much tequila for a shower to do any good." She rubbed against him to make sure she wasn't imagining things. Bossy she liked. Angry not so much. "Don't be mad. I can't take another person hating me."

His hand flattened at the small of her back. "Does it feel like I hate you?"

She shook her head, unable to speak.

He caught himself from lowering his head and kissing her which made her mood plummet. "We're going to talk first but not until you're coherent."

"I'm coherent," she told his throat. He had the sexiest throat she'd ever seen. "I'm trying to solve the Riemann hypothesis."

"With rose petals and stems?"

"Uh huh." She wondered if his throat tasted as good as it looked.

"And blood and alcohol." She lowered her voice in another conspiratorial whisper. "But I don't think it can be solved. It's unsolvable. Like us."

He stepped back and she tried to slide down from the barstool but the ground wouldn't stop tilting. Nic leaned down and slid his arms under her legs and shoulders then lifted her up. She sighed, resting her head on his shoulder.

"I'm going to miss this part," she admitted, then forgot about everything else but tasting the bronze skin of his throat. He tasted so good and she loved the rumbly sound he made in his chest. She licked him next, and yes, her hypothesis was correct, he made the rumbly sound again but louder. She kissed him some more, loving the taste of the warm skin inside his collar and the way his fingers tightened on her.

Maybe she could solve her Nic problem. She might not get a million dollars but her prize would be so much better.

"What's the Riemann hypothesis?"

She smiled. Nobody she cared about was ever interested in her work. Maybe Nic would be different. Maybe he might understand some of it. "It's the holy grail of mathematics."

"It's that important?"

She sighed. Maybe everything might be okay after all. "Yeah, it's a millennium problem. There's a million dollar prize if someone proves it, but if it's proven it will bring down the Internet, destroy e-commerce. No one's password would be safe."

"And you still want to prove it?"

"It's the most important unanswered question. Some people are trying to disprove it by finding a nontrivial zero that's not on the half line, but no one has and I don't think you win the million dollars if you disprove it."

"You want a million dollars that bad?"

"No." She sighed. "I wouldn't take the money. The guy who proved Poincaré conjecture didn't take the prize money."

"You want to solve a million dollar math problem but not for the million dollars."

"I'm not making any sense, am I?"

He shook his head but the corner of his mouth was ticking up and Lizzie decided it was good to be back with the center of her universe. The world was a cold place without him. "Not much," he agreed, reaching past her.

She opened her mouth to explain that prime numbers were random but still had structure when icy water crashed down on her. She shrieked and danced up and down as he held her under the water while her lovely buzz went right down the drain and she sobered up involuntarily.

"I hate you."

"No you don't."

"I think I would know if I hated you or not."

He reached past her and turned the warm water up. It didn't help. Her clothes were plastered to her and she was freezing. He worked the wet T-shirt over her head and threw it to the floor of the shower. The loud *thwap* of soaked cotton hitting tile distracted her from the fingers working the button loose on her shorts. "You don't hate me."

She turned her head and his mouth landed on her cheek. He trailed a line of scorching kisses down her jaw, then her throat. Her bra joined her T-shirt then his fingers moved to the edge of the white cotton panties. They were sheer against her wet skin.

He slanted his mouth over hers before she could protest. His fingers dipped into her underwear, finding hot slick heat and making her moan. Her shoulders fell back against the tile wall and she tried to catch her breath. He pushed the soaked cotton down her legs, holding her steady as she lifted one foot then the other. He kissed her again, pushing his knee between her trembling legs, the hairs on his chest and legs teasing her skin until her skin rippled in reaction.

She didn't remember him taking off his clothes. She had no problem with it.

He licked the outer shell of her ear. Lizzie shivered, as wet on the inside as she was on the outside, but she wasn't freezing anymore. He kissed his way down to capture one aching breast. He sucked the stinging peak hard into his mouth, torturing it until she was delirious. Her fingers tangled in his hair and she cried out with each hard pull of his mouth.

He kissed his way to the other one, his hands at her waist thumbs below her belly, holding her still, rubbing the sensitive skin and making it next to impossible to stand. Her hands bit into his shoulders but she didn't try to stop him. She needed his mouth and hands on her.

Then his mouth moved lower as he dropped to his knees.

"No," she whispered, her fingers digging into his shoulders. "It's my turn."

He smiled against her abdomen. "You get a turn when you sober up."

"I'm sober," she insisted, then groaned as his tongue dipped into her belly button. "I'm completely...oh, wait..." Then she couldn't speak anymore. Not words anyway. Just his name.

His hands moved lower, his thumbs sliding down the sensitive skin below her belly to the tops of her thighs. She made a valiant effort to keep her legs together, but his mouth moved lower, licking her until she forgot all about her turn.

Her stomach contracted and she melted, knowing what was coming, what he would reduce her to, but her body blatantly ignored all the alarms going off in her brain. His thumb pressed against the inside of one of her thighs, opening her up for him. She jerked, trying to escape and get closer at the same time. He pushed her harder against the wall and took the rest of her weight with his shoulders while she tried not to scream.

Then he was there, his tongue licking across her before parting her trembling flesh with his fingers. He explored her with his tongue, lashing deep inside, finding sensitive spots and teasing them into a frenzy. She was dying.

His tongue trailed up to trace excruciatingly slow circles around the tight bud of her clit before sucking it into his mouth. The lazy rhythm had her breathing his name out or maybe screaming it but her hips urged him to speed up the torture. He chuckled and continued the slow, sanity stealing spirals.

Whimpering gave way to sharp hisses and tiny cries. He spun her up into a pleasure so sharp and so sweet she was sure it would destroy her but she would die if he stopped. The coil wound tighter inside her, sparking and burning what was left of her. Fingers invaded her swollen flesh while his tongue continued to torment her. The slight edge of pain cut the coils loose. Her eyes flew wide open and she opened her mouth to scream, then froze as his fingers crooked inside her and one endless heartbeat later, Lizzie broke free. Orgasm after orgasm assaulted her, turning her into someone mindless, weak and utterly incapable of stopping him from doing it again and again until she was no longer in her body. She was out there somewhere, radiant and free and flying into the sun.

Sometime in the next century, he straightened coming to his full height in front of her. His breathing was as erratic as hers. His hand cupped her face, his thumb pressing down on her trembling lower lip.

"My turn," she whispered, or begged. She wasn't sure.

His smile was slow and her eyes met his as his thumb pressed deeper into her mouth.

"I'm not drunk." She swirled her tongue around his thumb and slid her hands from his shoulders, down his chest until they wrapped around the burning length of his cock. "At least not on alcohol and besides, you promised."

"I did?" He gasped, his head falling back as she stroked him. His thumb left her mouth as his fingers curled into a fist and hit the tile next to her head.

"Should I get on my knees and beg?" she asked nicely, in the sweetest voice she could muster.

His body turned to steel right in front of her and for a moment he couldn't speak. When he did, it was more of a growl. "You ever done this, Lizzie?"

Her smile was slow as she shook her head. A wild and primitive instinct took hold of him. She licked her lips. "You'll have to show me how."

"Get on your knees." His words were little more than a growl, but Lizzie caught the unsteadiness underneath them and heat roared through her. Then he was pressing her down to her knees and she caught hold of his hair roughened thighs so she wouldn't tip over. "Open your mouth."

Her fingers pressed into hard muscles of his legs as he rubbed the tip of the granite hard erection across her lips. The swollen head was softer than she expected and her first taste of him went straight to her head.

"Open your mouth and breathe through your nose." He teased her with another swipe, as his other hand stroked the top of her head. "I'll do the rest."

He nudged at her mouth, stroked her face and watched her with an intensity that speared right through her. Her smile turned sly as she kissed the tip, loving the way he shuddered. She kissed him again then traced the entire hard length of him with her tongue. His hand left her cheek and tightened in her hair. She wrapped her uninjured hand around the hard base of his cock and paid him back for her slow torture by taking her time. She groaned as he stretched her, gliding over her tongue, filling her mouth. Her eyes rolled back as she swirled her tongue around him.

Warmth flooded her at his sharp intake of breath. He breathed out her name, then curt instructions she tried to follow, then unintelligible sounds that may have been Italian or jungle cat. Lizzie wasn't sure and she really didn't care. Her curious nature got the best of her and she decided to find out on her own what he liked.

Because he totally lied. He didn't do any of the work. Unless work was defined as intermittent growls and beating one fist against the tile wall over her head while Lizzie learned how to make him lose his mind. She understood every sound, every harsh cry, growl and hiss escaped him even though there wasn't a single word in English.

He let go of her head and braced his other hand against wall. She took him deep, his salty taste filling her senses as she tried to find a rhythm with her mouth and tongue. She felt it roll through him the second she got it right and the power burned through her was intoxicating. He was all hers. She'd reduced him to his most primitive savage self, stripped him of everything except his need for her.

His hand caught the back of her head and he tried to stop her before it was too late. For a moment Lizzie couldn't breathe as he touched her throat, cutting off her air until her eyes watered. After that he couldn't escape her and his fist pounding against the tile was all the warning she got before she drowned in him because she couldn't swallow fast enough.

And she loved it. Every primitive second of it and she wanted to do it again.

She let him go and he came crashing down next to her, his face dazed with shock. She licked her lips provocatively and almost laughed at the way his eyes fixated on her mouth. His chest heaved, but his eyes never left her. He couldn't speak, she realized, and knowing she'd done that to him did something wild to her. Her whole body rippled with it.

She grabbed the mesh sponge and bath gel and worked the pear scented lather into his chest and arms and shoulders. He caught her wrist when she moved lower.

"Wait." He groaned. "I need another minute."

He let her wash his hair instead and it was impossible to say who enjoyed it more. He practically purred as she massaged the shampoo into his scalp with her good hand. Then she was in his arms, slick skin against slick skin. Arms and legs tangled together until they formed a knot she never wanted to undo. She rested her cheek on his shoulder and stared straight ahead. Maybe they could stay here.

Maybe the rest of the world would go away.

She sighed and smiled when he hardened against her. He didn't make a move to go any farther. Instead, his fingers trailed lazily down her back until he whispered in her ear, "Beautiful girl, are you going to let me do everything I want to do to you?"

Heat sheared through her again and the throbbing ache between her legs roared back to life. She nodded unable to lift her head. She tried to protest when he stood, taking her with him but he kissed her until she slumped against the wall shaking and useless and ready for whatever he wanted to do.

"Good, because I have this fantasy."

Wildfire streaked through her as he turned her toward the wall. She imagined all kinds of dirty things they could do in a shower. Before she could turn to see what he was doing, his hands were working shampoo through the long strands.

He was washing her hair? A thick wave of pleasure unlocked inside her.

"You have a thing for my hair, don't you?"

"Yes, and if you ever cut it, I won't be responsible for my actions."

He kissed her while the soap rinsed away. It was tender and searching and a whole host of other things she wasn't prepared to admit yet.

When he reached past her to turn off the water, she was clinging to him. Or they were clinging to each other. She couldn't let go of him. As long as they were touching, the world stayed away. Lizzie would have given anything to stay in that moment with him and escape the rest of the world.

CHAPTER FIFTEEN

Nic toweled her dry, then dried himself with the same towel. There was something so intimate about him using the same towel. She shivered a little, tears pricking her eyes. She turned away and dove for her toothbrush before he noticed the emotions overwhelming her again.

She ran the brush under water and watched him in the mirror as he stepped back into his jeans. Such a shame. She paused brushing her teeth when he shoved his arms through the sleeves of his T-shirt and pulled it down to tuck it into his jeans. It was a crime to cover his body in clothes.

His eyes met hers in the mirror and she turned bright poppy red. "You just brought me to my knees and you're blushing?"

She almost went to her knees again, as his words set her insides on fire. The sound of his voice was enough now. He stepped up behind her. "Don't look," she said, her words slurred around the toothpaste. She rinsed off the tooth brush and tapped it on the sink. He was watching her. "Don't look!"

"You don't want to spit toothpaste out in front of me?"

She shook her head.

His smile was incredulous. "Toothpaste? Seriously? When a minute ago you—"

"Okay! Shut up." She grabbed a handful of water and swished it around in her mouth. She spit it out as daintily as she could, but she shouldn't have worried. He swung her around and crushed her mouth with his so fast and so hard, she lost her balance. He caught her and set her on the vanity, never breaking contact with her mouth.

"Cinnamon," he teased against her lips as he plundered them, making noises deep in his throat as if she was the best thing he'd ever tasted. He lifted his head, his eyes warm, scorching her as they searched her face. "You knew I didn't send those roses, didn't you?"

She nodded, sliding off the vanity. "I don't know how she knew to send them here, unless she's having Rogan followed." She grabbed her Princeton T-shirt she'd slept in last night and started to pull it over her head.

"I'm sure they are." He caught hold of her shirt while he spoke and pulled it back off her.

"What are you doing?" she sputtered, whirling around.

"You don't wear another man's clothes."

Suddenly, Lizzie wasn't cold anymore. "Have you lost your mind? It's my shirt."

He'd already shrugged out of the cream cotton long-sleeved shirt he'd been wearing earlier over the V-neck T-shirt. He held it up for her so she could put her arms through it.

She huffed in indignation, then shoved her arms through the soft cotton sleeve. She choked back the sigh of pleasure as the fabric moved over her skin. It was warm and it smelled like him. She'd never admit it but she should've stolen it herself.

"Caveman," she called him, pouting so she wouldn't smile.

The Caveman refused to let her do up the buttons. She stood still while he closed up the front of the shirt, then rolled up the sleeves.

"Possessive much?"

"Very much," he warned her, his fingers sliding up the exposed skin of her neck, his thumb skimming up her throat until it pressed under her chin, tilting her head back. "You keep pouting, and I'll show you how possessive I can be. If you don't want to wear my shirt, fine." His smile was one shade away from evil. "Give it back."

Arrogant jerk. He knew she wouldn't part with it now. "It's mine now," she warned him. "You're never getting it back."

He leaned to kiss her and stopped midway. His eyes widened. "Why do you have a Princeton T-shirt?"

A chill flickered down Lizzie's spine making her nervous. Unsure what to say, she answered with a question. "Because I'm in graduate school?"

He straightened, his expression closed off as he backed away from her. "At Princeton?"

She nodded, stepping into the cut off shorts she'd been wearing earlier. "It's not a secret."

"Why Princeton?"

"Do you know who John Nash is? They made a movie about him

when I was a kid. Had the *Gladiator* guy in it."

"It sounds familiar."

"The movie made me curious so I read his biography. He went to Princeton."

"You wanted to go to Princeton because of some guy in a movie?"

She smiled sadly. "He's not just some guy. He's one of the most brilliant mathematicians in the world. He won a Noble Prize."

"You're studying math? At Princeton?" Shock rippled off him in a freezing cold wave.

She'd gotten over the way people reacted when they found out what she did but with Nic, it felt like the world was coming to an end. "Or I discovered life on Mars. Which is easier to believe?"

He ignored her sarcasm. "So zeroes, complex planes and some hypothesis destroying the Internet wasn't the tequila talking?"

"No."

"The mathlete T-shirt. Not ironic?"

Her hands went to her waist. "I told you I wasn't a cheerleader. You never asked any other questions."

His eyes were so hard, his gaze felt like cut glass scraping over her skin. "You knew I had no idea. Were you having a laugh at my expense or was it like your virginity and none of my business?"

Lizzie took a deep breath and folded her arms across her chest. A blue pill would come in handy right about now because she wanted to be anywhere else.

"Has anything been the truth from you, Lizzie?"

Screw the blue pill. She wasn't running anymore. "I tried to tell you I wasn't that girl."

"You deliberately misled me. What else have you lied about?"

She swallowed a painful lump in her throat. "I've never lied to you."

He pushed his hands through his hair then shook his head again. Then he found his shoes and started putting them on. "I've told you before, lies by omission are still lies."

Her lungs weren't working. She needed fresh air. She needed to get away from him because she was either going to fall apart or murder him or both. She wasn't sure which. She knew he was leaving so she was determined to beat him to it. She headed straight for the door then stopped.

Lies by omission? Seriously? Who the hell did he think he was?

She spun around and faced him. "I may not have told you all my dirty secrets, but you didn't tell me yours either. At least my secret wasn't that I was already in a long-term relationship."

It would have been an impressive exit if his hand hadn't shot out and slammed the door as she opened it. His hand stayed flat against the door over her head.

"Run that by me again?"

All the hairs at the back of her neck rose. She turned around and he was closer. This time, she didn't care. "Did you think Angie wouldn't tell me? Because the second you shut me up in the car with her, she threw Xia Chang at me."

"What?" The word escaped on a choked breath as he moved away from her like she'd burned him. "What did she say?"

"What do you think? She was manic telling me about the woman you really love and how she's the only long-term relationship you've ever had. You play around with other women when you aren't in Hong Kong. Xia overlooks it because you always go back to her." Lizzie squeezed her eyes shut. The words hurt so much she needed a minute. "You were going back to Hong Kong because you were done with me."

"And you believed her?" He wasn't looking at her now. His fists were thrust in his jeans and his back was to her.

"I didn't want to but there are photographs all over the Internet. I can see why you would be in love with her. She's perfect for you."

"Yes," he agreed, cutting her to the bone. "She is. She trusts me and she doesn't hide who she is from me but—"

He stopped at her strangled gasp. She turned away before he could see her, and leaned against the door, willing herself to stay on her feet. He hadn't denied any of it. Pain burned down her skin. The last spark of hope flicked out. She'd hoped maybe Angie had been lying to hurt her. The little spark had been the only thing anchoring her to the ground. Now it was gone.

It was shockingly anticlimactic. The world didn't have the decency to end. How could the earth keep spinning while she bled out?

She could feel the doorknob under her fingers and wrenching it open was easier than she expected.

Nic watched Lizzie stumble out of the room. Despite all his instincts telling him to stop her, he stayed rooted to the spot. Betrayal had blindsided him and he just couldn't move. He should be used to it by now. Everyone eventually destroyed his trust in them. Maybe he expected too much from people.

Coming from his sister, it was more than he could bear. He'd practically given Andreas Maretti two billion dollars because he didn't want Angie's family to lose everything. He'd invested money in Angie's husband's company. He'd let Angie work for his company although it meant employing additional people to make sure she didn't make things worse.

She was the one person in the world he considered family and what had she done? Minutes after he'd confided in her that Lizzie meant something to him so could she please make an effort to get along with her? She'd told Lizzie a pack of lies and destroyed something Nic was only beginning to appreciate. He imagined he could feel the knife Angie had plunged into his back when she told Lizzie all the lies.

But the real gut wrenching betrayal was Lizzie believing them.

She should've known better. She should have trusted him.

She should have answered his phone calls. Instead she'd run away. Again. Like she was trying to do right now.

"Stop!" He'd followed her into the hall without realizing that he'd moved.

She froze in front of the door.

He cleared his voice and softened his tone. "The pictures. Were they of the Black and White ball?"

She nodded but kept her back to him.

"It was business, Lizzie. A charity fundraiser. I'm on the board. I couldn't get out of it."

"Oh." Sarcasm drowned her usual sunny tone. She turned and leaned back against the door. She was pale and the pain in her eyes took his breath away. His first instinct was to kiss her and make all this go away but he was pretty sure if he touched her right now she would scratch his eyes out. "That makes it so much better."

He took a step toward her, trying not to let the smug satisfaction coursing through him show on his face. She was so jealous she was trembling. The hope it gave him was like a shot of adrenalin straight to his heart. "If you had answered my calls, I could've explained but you didn't, did you? You grabbed hold of everything she said and used it as another excuse to run."

"That's not true. I didn't run."

"You always run, Lizzie. Look what you're doing right now."

"I'm leaving because you've turned me into the person your sister accused me of being. How could you? How?"

Her knees gave way and she started to slide down the door. It broke something in him watching her. "It's not what you think, *bella*."

"No!" She waved her arms at him as if trying to ward him off. "I don't want to hear it. I want you to go."

Nic wasn't going anywhere. He took a few careful steps toward her. "You are so beautiful, Lizzie, it's hard to look at you straight on."

"Don't." Her reply was muffled but he heard the sob.

"The first time I saw you, you took my breath away. You were dancing with your father and I couldn't believe innocence like that still existed. I asked you to dance to prove to myself it was an illusion, but you made me forget my own name. You have no idea what you did to me. What you still do to me. I lay awake at night and I can feel you all around me. Taste you, smell you. Then I open my eyes and none of it's real. Because not once have you ever trusted me enough to be honest."

Lizzie gasped as his words hit home. "No."

"Angie lied to you." The words were jagged as they ripped out of him. "You believed every word of it without giving me a chance to defend myself."

Had she hurt him? It hardly seemed possible. Annoy him? Maybe. But hurt him?

Well, she had and the guilt hurt worse than anything.

"We were in a relationship but it ended two years ago when she took over my Asian Division. But when we were together, it wasn't exclusive. It was more business than anything else. She knows everyone who's anyone." His smile was bleak. "She's about twelve years older than me, and marriage has never been on Xia's agenda."

She believed him. Every word. Even though it made her feel worse. So much for being a grown up. She should have answered her phone. She should have given him a chance to explain. Her eyes closed and she dragged in a jagged breath. She didn't know what else to do. She pulled her cell phone out of her pocket, hit the call back button and held it up to her ear.

When his smart phone rang a second later, the shocked expression on his face made it difficult not to laugh. But she knew she'd just end up crying. "You might want to get that." Her throat was so sore she could hardly speak. "I'm calling you back. I'm an idiot."

"No." He closed the distance between them as he said, "It's my fault. We should never have left the Keys." Then his hands were on her face, his thumbs sweeping away escaping tears. "We should go back there now."

She leaned her face into his touch.

"Next time you run, *bella*." He cleared his throat, his voice sounding as raspy as hers. "You run to me, not away from me."

"Okay." She took another deep breath. "I'm so sorry. I didn't want to believe her. It's just that we don't add up."

"That's not true." His other hand moved into her hair, soothing around to her neck.

She tried to smile at him, but failed miserably. "Do you know anything about set theory?"

His thumb stroked her cheekbone. "Not a thing."

"Some sets are too complicated to count." She tried to explain, knowing he wasn't going to get it. No one ever got her. "We're like that. We're uncountable. Your sister hates me. Your father hates my family. My father hates your father. Your sister thinks Rogan and I are cheating and on and on. It's too much, too complicated."

"None of that has anything to do with us."

"You don't understand. If we were just irrational numbers I think we'd be okay but the uncountable thing is hard to overcome. We don't make sense together."

His smile caught her off guard. "Who cares if we don't make sense?"

"I care." She moved her face away from his hand. "I don't like when things don't make sense. I need for them to make sense."

"I get that, but this…us…" He waved his hand back and forth between them. "It may never make sense."

"You still don't understand. I was playing dress up."

"Dress up?"

"Decorative girl. Ditzy fun Lizzie. All about shoes, toenail polish and achieving the perfect tan. That's not me."

"You don't like to paint your toenails?" He stared down at the green polish on her toes.

She covered up the toes, one foot with her other foot. "No, yes—"

"You pretended to like diving?" He was watching her for any sign of weakness.

"No." Her voice shook as hope threatened to destroy her all over again. "I loved diving. It was one of the best experiences of my life."

"The orgasms?" His voice rolled over her like silk as one hand moved down her back. "Were you faking those too?"

"No." Her eyes fluttered shut and she swallowed. The wall was at her back and he blocked out the world from the front.

"You know what I think?"

Lethargy stole through her as one hand went to her waist and the other around her neck.

"No." The world would be so much easier if she could tell what he was thinking?

"I think you can be a genius and wear great shoes. You can be whatever girl you want to be as long as we're together and you said it, Lizzie, you can't take it back now. We're a set."

Her heart skipped a beat. Hope flickered inside her. Was it possible? "You don't mind?"

"Mind what?" He tilted his head in confusion.

"My math problem?"

He straightened, his mouth opening and closing on a silent Oh. Then a slow, sexy smile transformed his face into an unearthly beauty and Lizzie stopped breathing. The world stopped turning. Everything ceased to exist but them.

"Are you asking me if I mind—" he paused, his expression serious, "—that you make Tony Stark look stupid?"

Time stopped. Shock coursed through her as he turned her joke around on her. Her jaw parted and laughter started to escape. He got her. He really did. Joy sparked inside her as he leaned to kiss her but before he could she pushed to her tiptoes threw her arms around his neck and kissed him first.

Hard.

Pushing into his mouth, devouring him, clawing his shirt up and over his head. Her mouth was on his throat, kissing and licking him. Nic groaned, his head falling back. She breathed his name against his skin. When he tried to take back control, she fought back with her mouth and tongue. "My turn."

She levered up forcing him to catch her weight. She curled her legs around his hips. He'd given up control and it went straight to Lizzie's head. His taste streamed through her, slowed everything down and turned her to honey inside. She needed to punish him and make up for everything. She needed to stake her claim. She used her mouth to brand hot kisses at the base of his throat anywhere she could get to while he walked them into the great room and sat down on one of the large club chairs.

She straddled him, her knees going to either side of him, but didn't stop kissing him. His hands were free so he tried to slide them under her shirt. She batted them away. "Stop it," she warned him without removing her lips from his skin. "You're distracting me and it's my turn."

"I like distracting you." He gasped.

She nipped him then.

"Okay." He groaned in surrender and his head fell back on the chair. "You can have my next turn too."

Lizzie raised her head and smiled down at him. She kissed his forehead and the tip of his nose, then indulged herself by letting her fingers drift down to those classical cheekbones. He didn't try to stop her as she explored every chiseled hollow, touched every angle before rubbing the backs of her hand against the shadowy scruff.

"I need to shave," he muttered, his eyelids heavy as he relaxed into her touch.

"I like the scruff." She continued her exploration, smoothing his eyebrows with her thumbs. Her thumbs moved up to make a small arc on his forehead, then massaged from the bridge of his nose to his hairline, then down his temples, lingering when a small sigh of pleasure escaped him. Her fingers moved down the sides of his face, skimming over his cheekbones, his jaw and across the slight dent of his bottom lip. "Leave the scruff."

His hand covered her fingers and pressed them against his mouth as he spoke. "Yes, ma'am. No shaving."

She captured some of his beard between her fingers and tugged. "Maybe a trim."

He opened his eyes, his face more relaxed than she'd ever seen him. His eyes were warm and open and she could see Nic. The real Nic. The human being who needed affection as much as he needed oxygen. He hadn't had much, she realized. The elegant women he'd dated until now didn't want to mess up their makeup. She couldn't imagine Xia Chang ruffling her fingers through his hair.

She pressed a leisurely kiss to the middle of his forehead, emotion burning her throat as she blinked back tears.

"I missed you." His whisper was more of a rumble.

Lizzie squeezed her eyes shut because she knew he wouldn't appreciate knowing her heart was breaking for the isolated little boy who, through no help from the family who had failed him on every level, had grown into a good man.

She couldn't leave him now, not until he asked her to go. She knew it was the height of stupidity to think she was different from the women who had passed through his life. They had all wanted to be different too.

Except, she suspected Nic might actually need her. As astonishing as that might be, she knew on an instinctive level it was true and that he likely did not understand it yet. She, on the other hand, didn't need anything from Nic. She wanted him. She was choosing him and her family would understand and support her. Maybe her family could be the family Nic deserved.

"You're so serious all of a sudden," he teased her.

"I'm usually serious." She sat back so she could see his face. "I hope you're not too disappointed?"

"Disappointed? With what?"

"Me." Her chin dropped. "Boring math geek Lizzie."

"Boring?" His hands landed on her hips and he moved her until the hard ridge in his jeans had her hissing in response. "Do I feel bored to you?"

Her head fell back as she said, "No, you definitely don't feel bored."

"How do I feel?" The rasp in his voice made her smile wicked.

She rocked against him. "Impressive."

He sat up, and steadied her when she lost balance. "You didn't make anything up," he said against her mouth. "You feel the same. You taste the same. Same girl. My girl."

She blinked back more stupid tears. She was going to see about having her tear ducts removed. His fingertips brushed the moisture off her cheeks and she gave him a helpless smile.

"I can't help it. I cry when I see old people in coffee shops, cute puppy pictures…"

"You feel things so deeply." He smoothed the stray tears back. "Everything will be okay, Lizzie. Trust me."

She did trust him, she realized. She absolutely did.

His cell phone rang dragging them back to reality. He kept her in his lap while he talked to Pam. She had to bat away grabby hands more than once but the tone of his voice never changed. "We've got a flight time in two hours. How quickly can you be ready to go?"

"Go where?"

"Houston. I've got a few things to sort out then we can go wherever you want."

"Key Largo. I want to go diving again."

"Or Italy. I've always wanted to go diving in Portofino."

Her shoulders slumped. "I don't have a passport."

"I'll get Pam on it."

"What would we do without Pam?"

As soon as the plane was in the air, Lizzie found take out from her favorite Thai restaurant. Pam again. Lizzie couldn't wait to finally meet wonder woman in person.

While the food warmed in the microwave, she searched for paper plates but found fine china instead. She sighed. She was going to have to get used to things like this. She traced the dark blue and gold Maretti logo in the center of the gold-rimmed plate. Nic had probably never eaten off a paper plate. The microwave dinged. She arranged the food on the plates and took them back to the main cabin.

Nic had opened a bottle of wine and had two glasses waiting. "Ah, you made dinner. Looks good."

"I love Pam." Lizzie grinned.

She squeezed lime quarters on the noodles while he tried to steal the eggplant out of her curry. She pretended to get upset, even though she hated eggplant. She'd missed these silly moments. She dreaded losing the comfortable silences. The filled holes in her life numbers couldn't reach. Numbers weren't enough. She needed Nic too.

"This does not count as a date," she warned him as she headed to the galley. "Do you want coffee? I can manage coffee."

"Sounds great."

She joined him a few minutes later with two steaming cups.

"What a good flight attendant you are," he said when she handed him the cup.

She couldn't help the giggle bubbling out of her. "I need a uniform. Something short and made from the early sixties. Oh, and a pillbox hat."

"And go-go boots?"

"Definitely go-go boots."

"What color?" He set his coffee down and held his hand out for her.

"Hot pink."

"Come here," he growled.

She shook her head. "We're not supposed to fraternize, you know. I'm not allowed to flirt with anyone but the captain."

His arm snaked around her waist. He caught her coffee cup before it went flying and she fell back in his lap.

"What color panties would you wear under this super short mod dress?"

"Oh." She pouted, looking over her shoulder at him with a sly, wicked smile. "The boss won't allow us to wear panties. He hates panty lines."

"Smart girl." He was purring now instead of growling and Lizzie couldn't decide which one she liked better.

"He does these surprise inspections," she said, breathless as his fingers slipped the button at her waist band loose and his hand slid inside her shorts. "If he finds us wearing panties he…oh…wow…"

His fingers sank deeper inside her. "Is this what he does?"

She nodded unable to speak any longer.

"You wear panties to tease him, don't you?"

She nodded, hissing as he tortured her with long, sure strokes teased at the ache building inside her.

"I don't think I'm doing this right," Nic said against her ear, sucking the tender lobe into his mouth and setting her skin on fire.

"You're doing it right." She breathed out the words, her head resting back on her shoulder as her eyes rolled back in her head. He should've been illegal.

"Hmm, I'm not sure." He nipped at her ear. "Maybe you should show me how you really like it."

"I really like it like this."

"I would like it better if you helped me."

Lizzie's eyes flew open when he caught her hand and pushed it inside of her shorts. His arm tightened around her and she went to pieces when she felt how slick and hot she was. She was so close and he was ramping her up hotter.

"That's better."

"You like making me do this."

"Oh, you have no idea what I like, Lizzie." He was growling again and carrying her through to the bedroom. He urged her onto her hands and knees, surrounding her and shoving her shorts down her hips.

Boneless and liquid, she shivered when his jeans hit the floor and the condom wrapper ripped. "I did miss you, Lizzie." He groaned against the back of her neck, his mouth hot on her skin. "Don't leave me again."

"I won't." She meant it. Whatever happened, they'd figure it out.

"I'll find you." He eased into her when she expected him to go quickly. This time she was groaning as he drew out the pleasure of possession as long as possible. "I'll hunt you down."

"Where would I go?" She gasped the words out, looking over her shoulder at him smiling back at the deadly serious expression on his face. "Well?" she teased, pushing up slightly so she could kiss him, and nip at his lower lip. "Show me what you like."

He kissed her back and started to move. Her arms collapsed beneath her and she turned her face until her cheek pressed into the mattress. She watched his hand digging into the mattress next to hers. She smiled to herself then eased her trembling fingers over. She hooked her pinky over his thumb, and held on while Nic drove them both wild.

CHAPTER SIXTEEN

Nic shifted in surprise when Lizzie covered his hand with hers to stop him from tapping the wooden armrest with his fingers. She gave him a reassuring smile which startled him more than her unexpected touch had. He turned his hand palm up and she slid her fingers between his and squeezed.

Nic couldn't remember the last time anyone had tried to reassure him about anything. The warmth of her touch and her smile chased the churning sickness pumping through him and he relaxed. He was coming to terms with the way Lizzie affected him on such a visceral level.

"You don't have to do this," she whispered, turning her face away from the receptionist darting nervous glances at them. "I don't care what they say about me."

"I do," Nic clipped out, squeezing her hand back when his voice came out sharper than he intended. He'd lost count of how many times Lizzie had told him he didn't have to do what he was planning. It made him more determined to do it. He'd wanted to sever this tie for a long time. Lizzie gave him the perfect excuse. Nic shifted again in the uncomfortable chair, catching the brown envelope before it fell to the floor. "He's not getting away with this. Not when I bailed him out of bankruptcy."

"Bankruptcy?"

Nic nodded. "He's only good at one thing and it's not business."

"It's not decorating either." Lizzie leaned in with one of her conspiratorial whispers. "This place is a total renaissance fail."

His laugh drew the receptionist's attention again. "Are you sure I can't get you coffee? He shouldn't be much longer."

"If I asked you stay out here, would you do it?"

"Maybe." She gave him a playful smile that made him want to forget the whole thing and make off with her. "Since you're defending my honor and all."

She stood when he did and wrapped her arms around him. He rested his forehead on hers. "Don't disappear."

He suppressed the sigh of pleasure as her hands brushed imaginary dust off his shoulders, then smoothed down his chest. She straightened his tie. "Don't worry, Mr. Darcy. You're stuck with me now that I've seen your penthouse apartment."

He grinned, waiting patiently while she made sure he was presentable. His eyes closed when her fingers stroked along his jaw. He was starting to feel like a cat who wanted to be stroked all the time. He breathed deeply enjoying the lightness of his chest. When he opened his eyes he found her smiling up at him, all sorts of things shining through her eyes. Things he had never considered letting into his life.

"Go get him," she whispered, then turned toward the nervous receptionist. "You know, coffee sounds like a great idea. Can you show me where it is?"

Thankful for something to do, the girl jumped to her feet and led Lizzie around the corner. Nic reached under the desk and pressed the door release. The double doors slid open, and Nic slipped into the person he never wanted to be again once he left this place for good.

"Nicolas, you can't burst in here. I'm in a meeting."

A meeting? Nic's gaze swept the room, sizing it up in less than a second.

Red Baker rose to his feet. Baker had been Andreas' attorney for years. He'd referred him to Winston Robicheaux when Andreas had decided to sue the De Santis Trust after Claudia took Nic out of boarding school. Nic ignored the older man's attempted greeting. He had nothing for Baker.

He hadn't expected to find Angie. The way she avoided his eyes told him Lizzie had been right. Angie had sent those roses and bracelet. It gutted him but he was too furious to feel it.

"You want to tell me what this is about?" Nic slid the envelope across Andreas' desk like a shot of whiskey down a saloon bar.

Andreas stopped it before it careened off the slick desktop. "It's an insurance policy." Andreas straightened to his full height, but Nic could sense the defensiveness in the stance. He lifted the envelope and dropped it on the desk. "Now the swamp rat your sister made the mistake of marrying will stop contesting the divorce and give her full custody."

"Except it's a pack of lies," Nic shot back at him. "If you think I'm going to let you drag Lizzie's name through the mud like this—"

"What do you mean it's not true?" Angie's voice shook. "She's in Orange Beach with him. What more proof do you need?"

"She's with me, Angie," Nic said impatiently. "How many times do I have to tell you he is not cheating on you with Lizzie?"

"How do you know?" Her hands clenched into fists and Nic realized she wanted to believe him. It was the first glimmer of hope.

"Trust me. I know."

"Nic, you should read the file before…" Red Baker trailed off when Nic's attention focused on him. Baker shrugged, sat down and got busy on his phone.

"It's too late. Rogan's agreed to give me full custody if I'll agree to stay in New Orleans."

"We're going to fight that too," Andreas inserted.

Nic ignored him, keeping his focus on Angie. "You should move to New Orleans." As soon as the words left him he knew it was what he wanted. The plan formed in his head as he spoke. "I'm moving my headquarters—"

"What?" Andreas' tone rose with indignation. "Houston is your home."

Nic stopped ignoring him. Incredulous rage made it hard to speak as he turned on the other man. "My home?" He tasted the word, then spit it back out. "Home? You have some nerve tossing that word at me. Houston has never been my home."

"What is? Florence?" Derision twisted Andreas' too handsome features.

"No, you made sure Italy wasn't my home either." An eerie calm settled over him.

Andreas stepped back. "Well it won't be in some backwoods Louisiana swamp."

"You have no say in anything I do." Nic kept his words calm, while Andreas' temper grew with each syllable. "You never did. As soon as I leave here, we're done."

"You ungrateful…" He choked on righteous indignation when Nic's expression cut him off. Then Andreas turned nasty. "Fine, Nicolas. I'm not surprised. You are just like your mother. You think you're so superior, but you still like to chase after trash."

The response blew out of Nic without warning. "I'm nothing like my mother but—" he paused for effect. He wanted to say it for so long, "—I'm very much like my father."

Andreas went white. Then gray. The painstakingly preserved handsome features dissolved into a fury Nic had seen on him only once before but this time, Andreas' fist came down hard on the desk and not on Nic. "Nicolas Maretti, you are my son. I raised you. Me!"

Nic's head snapped back, almost laughing out loud at the other man's gall. "You raised me? Seriously? Is that what you call it?"

"You sign my name when you put pen to paper. I'm your father and you'd better—"

"You are not my father." Nic exploded without warning, oblivious to Angie's shocked cry. The words ripped out of him, cutting his final tie to the lie this man and his mother's family had forced him to live. "My uncle told me everything and if you continue using Lizzie to destroy your daughter's marriage, I'll make sure the whole world knows it."

"You won't. You don't want to air your mother's dirty laundry in public."

Nic shook his head in disbelief. "My mother has been dead more than twenty-five years. I don't think the scandal will hurt her but it will hurt you, Andreas. Claudia will see you for what you are."

"You wouldn't."

"I absolutely would. Leave Lizzie and her family alone or I will take you down piece by piece. Maretti may be your company but only because I bailed you out. Don't forget who holds the paper on all your assets. Keep it up and I'll sell every scrap of it to Mac Sellers for pennies on the dollar and I will make sure the whole world knows who you are."

"You would risk everything for some no-name piece of white trash one generation out of a trailer park?"

Rage slammed hard into Nic. "You want to test your theory? Insult her again."

Lizzie stood outside the office doors, listening to Nic and Andreas shouting at each other. She flinched at each harsh word. Oddly enough, hearing Andreas Maretti call her white trash didn't bother her nearly as much as the raw fury straining Nic's voice. Her stomach turned inside out as his anger set fire to her rare temper.

Her fingers tightened into fists at her side and she turned towards the receptionist who pushed the button under her desk without having to be asked. When the doors opened, Lizzie didn't hesitate. She walked into the office then stopped short. Nic was pale and shaking with anger. His jaw was clenched so hard his teeth would shatter any minute. She looked from Nic to the pompous old man screaming back at him. They didn't notice her.

Yeah, she was putting an end to this. No one talked to Nic like that. Not with her around. A strange wave of protectiveness swelled up inside her and Lizzie rode it all the way into the room. She caught Nic's trembling hand, lacing her fingers with his and trying not to let go when he jumped.

He looked down at her, astonishment stopping him midsentence. His mouth gaped, his eyes widened. He couldn't believe she was standing in front of him. She tried to smile, but the horror in his eyes was so intense instinct told her there was no way to soothe him. No way to make this better. There was nothing she could say to make up for the abuse he'd suffered from Andreas Maretti and it wasn't helping his ego that she'd caught him at a weak moment.

Not knowing what else to do, she took a deep breath and decided to be the party girl one more time. The last thing she wanted to do was add to the melodrama in the room. She kept her face blank and her tone exasperated as she released a long sigh. "I'm bored, Nic. Can we go?"

He closed his mouth, then opened it again. Then Andreas exploded. "You brought the whore responsible for destroying your sister's marriage here?"

Lizzie flinched then slapped both hands over her mouth so she wouldn't burst into laughter. It was like a bad B-movie. All Andreas Maretti needed was a white cat and a tank of sharks with laser beams on their heads. He was absurd.

She stepped in front of Nic, turning toward the sputtering blowhard. Andreas stared at her, disgust rampant in his artificially smooth face.

"Are you for real?" She choked back more laughter. She glanced over her shoulder. "That's the big bad?" She turned back to Andreas. The murderous expression on the old man's face making her even more determined to get Nic out the room. "Gotta say, I'm not impressed."

"Get your whore out of my sight," Andreas exploded and this time

Lizzie giggled.

"Me?" She sputtered with laughter. "I'm not the one wearing guy-liner!"

"What?" Nic rasped.

She turned, grabbed Nic's hand, and laced their fingers together. "He's wearing guy-liner."

Nic stared at her, then looked past her to Andreas.

"Bor...ing," she sing-songed, dragging his attention back. She smiled up at him, resisting the urge to sob in relief as the painful edge of fury melted away from him.

His expression softened into wonder. "Guy-liner?" he whispered to himself.

"I know, right? That's so over."

Nic looked down and found Lizzie rolling her eyes and patting her mouth with her fingers to suppress a fake yawn. For a second, Nic had no idea who she was.

Andreas went ballistic behind her but she ignored it. She smiled up at him and Nic saw her. The real her. Mac Sellers' daughter. An easy-going, light-hearted public persona concealed an exceptional intelligence and fierce loyalty. She was solid steel under her candy coating. She was ready to shred Andreas Maretti in his own office. She could do it too. Nic had no doubt.

He'd been so completely wrong about her, despite what he'd been telling himself and her. She'd been an amusing change of pace. An indulgence. An asset. An extension of himself.

He'd been a complete fool. The depth of his stupidity was extraordinary.

A future Nic had never considered played out in front of him. A shared life with this amazing, intelligent woman he didn't deserve. She filled in all his gaps. She softened the edges of his world, creating a shelter around them that reduced the bane of his existence to background noise.

He couldn't believe he hadn't seen it until now. She was absolutely everything.

Emotion and a strange kind of joy exploded in his chest. Despite the world war going on around them, he felt it bubbling out of his chest. There was no way to stop it from happening. It was inevitable and he was so grateful he hadn't completely blown his chance.

"I love you." The words slipped out without the slightest hesitation. "I'm in love with you."

The false indifference and boredom on her face melted into disbelief. "What?"

Another heartbeat passed. Asteroids did not hit the earth. The moon did not explode. No earthquakes or tidal waves or the end of the world.

"I'm in love with you, Lizzie. I think I have been for a long time. I just realized what it was and it's amazing."

Her head tilted and her lips parted but no sound came out.

He watched her struggle with the revelation and fell a little more in love with her because she really hadn't expected him to ever say it. Joy exploded inside him at the same time the world crashed back in on them. Andreas was screaming for someone to call security. Angie was on her feet trying to calm him down. Red Baker was shouting into a cell phone.

Lizzie paused then suddenly spun away from him, and in a voice Nic hadn't believed her capable of she blew back at Andreas. "Will you please give it a rest?"

Everyone froze and the room went eerily silent.

"Don't bother with security. I'm leaving and I'm taking Nic with me. Get a good look because he's mine now and I'm never letting you near him again. You don't deserve him. You say you're his father, but when did you ever act like one. He might have your name, but that's the only thing he got from you. He's one of the good guys, in spite of you."

"Who do you think you are? You can't talk to me like that."

"I'm sorry, I thought I just did," Lizzie shot back. "You have no idea what a father is. You're supposed to protect your children. Not manipulate their happiness for your own financial gain. You're disgusting. No wonder my father thinks you're a joke. You're not even a funny joke. You're just lame."

Andreas went from indignant shock to outright fury. "Get her out of my sight."

Lizzie huffed, then turned back to Nic. "Seriously. Bored now. Can we go before I get stabby?"

"Don't you dare walk out of here!" Andreas blasted.

Lizzie laughed with a lot more bravado than she felt. She wanted Nic out of the room and as far away from this monster as possible but she couldn't resist one last shot. "Make up your mind. He can't get me out of your sight without walking out of here."

The confusion on Andreas' face was priceless as he struggled to respond.

Nic slid his arm around Lizzie. "You are trouble, Lizzie Sellers. With a capital T."

"Yeah, but I'm your trouble."

"All mine."

Lizzie's knees went weak and she was glad his arm was around her otherwise she'd be a puddle at his feet. He leaned to kiss her. Then he stopped, straightened and turned back toward the man Lizzie was never letting near him again. "One more thing, I didn't bail you out so you could bankroll Winston Robicheaux. Do not give him one more penny."

"I can't cut him off. He won't—"

"I don't care. You either cut him off or Mac Sellers will be sitting on the board of Maretti Oil as soon as I can arrange it."

Andreas gasped and staggered back.

"Help him," Nic said to Red Baker who was on his feet moving Andreas back to his chair.

"My pills." Andreas wheezed.

Angie found a medicine bottle in the top drawer of his desk and handed him one of the pills.

"Is he okay?" Lizzie whispered.

"Yes, he has these attacks when he doesn't get his way. Let's go."

They stopped when Angie interrupted them. "What did you mean about him not being your real father?"

"It's a long story," Nic said.

"You're not my brother?" Angie's voice broke.

Lizzie felt the shudder of emotion ripple through him. Before she could stop herself, she let go of him and took a couple of steps closer to the other girl. She'd never seen someone in so much pain before and as much as she didn't like Angie, it still hurt to see her suffer. "Angie," she said carefully, afraid to get too close. "Blood doesn't always make family."

Angie gasped. "You're helping me? Why?"

Lizzie's smile was tentative. "Because I love Rogan. Not the way you think I do, 'cause that's just gross. You should come with us now."

"He agreed to the divorce." Angie choked on tears so genuine any doubts Lizzie ever had about the girl loving Rogan dissolved.

"Oh, please." Lizzie shook her head. "He's playing you. He agreed so you'd go back to New Orleans. He'll have you right where he wants you. You know him. Do you really think he's going to let you divorce him?"

Angie relaxed, new tears starting for a different reason. "No."

"He's waiting downstairs," Nic said. "I had Tag keep him occupied until we got finished."

"He's not very cooperative." Lizzie smirked.

Angie beat them to the elevator despite her father's protests and threats. She kept her finger on the door-open button until Lizzie and Nic stepped into the elevator with her.

"I've been horrible to you," Angie said as the doors shut. "I lied to you about Xia and I sent those roses...I don't know who I am anymore."

"Yeah, jealous rage will do that to you," Lizzie teased her.

Angie laughed and cried at the same time. "Where do I start with an apology?"

"Can we start over? I'll tell you all of Rogan's embarrassing stories if you'll tell me Nic's."

"Uh, no." Nic interrupted their reconciliation before they got carried away. "There'll be none of that."

"Oh." Lizzie beamed. "Nic must have some good ones."

Rogan froze when they rounded the corner in the parking garage. He'd been talking to Tag and stopped midsentence. Angie froze and they stared at each other.

"This could take a while," Lizzie whispered to Nic.

Angie was in Rogan's arms before Lizzie finished her prediction.

"Or not." She flinched, slightly nauseated at the way they were kissing each other. "Ew."

Nic smirked as she turned away, shivering in revulsion. "It never occurred to you to tell Angie I wasn't her biological brother, did it? Even when she lied to you about Xia. You could have hurt her but you didn't."

Lizzie shrugged. "You're still her brother and they're going to get arrested." Lizzie dropped her forehead onto Nic's chest before she had to bleach her eyes. She was glad they were happy to see each other but if they continued, she and Nic would be seeing way more of their reunion than either wanted. He must have signaled Tag because a few minutes later Tag was hustling the kissing pair into the back of an SUV.

His fingers sifted through her hair as the SUV screeched out of the parking garage. "I can't believe you did that."

"Did what?"

"Upstairs. I've never seen him so angry."

"Am I in trouble?" she asked, only half kidding because she couldn't read his expression.

"He does wear guy-liner."

Startled, she met his eyes. "What?"

"I never noticed it before. He's not much of a big bad, is he? He was when I was a kid. I left Texas when I turned eighteen. He gave me a black eye the day before."

"Oh, Nic," she whispered, reaching for him. He caught her hand, rubbing her fingers.

"I went to Italy, thinking I was going home but it wasn't home. Nothing was familiar. Everything felt empty. Then my uncle told me why Andreas resented me so much and all that emptiness filled with guilt and anger. I left Italy, then realized I didn't have anywhere to go."

She could see how difficult it was for him to talk about these things. So she listened, winding her arms around his middle. "What did you do?"

He shrugged, wrapping his arms around her. "I was eighteen, had unlimited funds, so I got a map and a dart and went wherever the dart hit. Europe at first, then Africa, spent a lot of time in New Zealand. It's so beautiful. We should go. I ended up in Hong Kong, but I've been pretty much everywhere."

"You haven't stopped moving have you?" She pressed her cheek against his chest.

"Not until now." The response was low and gruff. "I've never had a reason to stay in one place for long. I think I've been running from him all this time. Then you come in and take one look at the monster from my childhood, roll your eyes and announce you're bored and I...I think you slayed my dragon."

She swallowed hard, turned her forehead into his chest and whispered. "He wasn't much of a dragon. More of a lizard."

Nic laughed. "For years, I've felt so guilty for what my mother's family did to him. I've put up with his passive aggressive bullshit for years but today you made me see him for what he is. A sad aging bully. I almost feel sorry for him. He did get a raw deal from the De Santis family."

"It was his own fault, Nic. He got greedy."

"I don't owe him anything, do I?"

"No." Her hands moved to smooth the worry off his beautiful face. "He owes you."

Her cell phone dinged with a familiar but unwelcome tone. Her shoulders sagged as she swiped the screen open. "Busted," she whispered, cringing as she read the text message.

Your mother and I expect you for dinner at 7:30. Bring Nic. Not a request.

"What is it?" Nic opened her car door and waited for her to climb in.

"We've been summoned."

"We?"

"Yes, my parents. Can you get us to New Orleans by 7:30 p.m.? I don't want to explain why I'm in Houston."

"Do you have to explain it to them? You're an adult."

"Yeah," she scoffed. "Try telling them."

Nic smiled, not looking nearly as concerned as he should. "I think I can get us there in time. Don't look so worried." He leaned in and dropped a kiss on her forehead. "Your dad likes me. I don't know why you think he doesn't."

"Something about dismemberment," she grumbled.

Then he was kissing her again. Long and lingering it sizzled straight through her. He raised his face a fraction from hers. "Whatever happens, we'll deal with it. I'm not letting you go, Lizzie. I meant what I said."

She smiled. "I forgot something," she whispered, holding him to her when he started to move.

"What?" Now he looked concerned.

"I love you too."

His eyes closed and his forehead touched hers. "You've messed up now. I'm never letting you go. I don't care if we're uncountable or irrational. We're a set, Lizzie. I love you. Don't ever doubt it."

"I did the math," she whispered.

"Did you solve us?"

She shook her head. "No, but I'd like to spend the rest of my life trying."

He kissed her and her cell phone dinged again. "Right." He half laughed and stepped away from her. "Dinner."

"I'm sorry."

He shook his head. "Wear something boring. I like all my limbs where they are."

He shut her door and Lizzie watched him walk around the front of the SUV. Her chest squeezed and she didn't think she'd ever take another breath. He loved her. Nic Maretti was in love with her.

Tears blinded her as the belief settled deep in her chest. He caught her hand when he slid behind the wheel and brought her fingers to his lips but instead of kissing her, he bit her fingertips lightly.

"Ow." She tried to pull her hand back but he kept it against his mouth.

"See. You're not dreaming, Lizzie."

"I know." Her voice was barely audible. "This is the good part."

"Your dress is not boring." Nic's eyes devoured her when she joined him in the suite's living room later that evening.

She glanced down at the simple floral crepe dress. The high boat neck covered everything and the full circle skirt went past her knees. There was nothing remotely sexy about the dress, except for the trashy underwear she wore underneath it but Nic hadn't seen it yet.

"It's not boring," she informed him. "It's demure."

"It's criminal." He snorted, his arm stretching along the back of the sofa he was lounging on. He stood then and she took a step back.

"You're one to talk," she accused. He was lethal in the charcoal suit and power tie he wore. She knew her father wouldn't be wearing a tie, but he would like that Nic was.

"Here, I have something for you."

He turned her away from him and Lizzie looked up at the mirror over the fireplace so she could see what he was doing. Her breath caught in her throat, but not because of the white gold chain he was fastening around her neck, or the sparkling emerald pendant dangling from the end.

All Lizzie could see was the two of them together. The muted colors of her crepe dress blended with the gunmetal gray suit he wore. Her heels and intricate updo had her brushing just under his chin. He was tall and dark behind her, his face fierce with concentration as he adjusted the drop in place. He looked up and met her eyes. "Perfect."

And they were. They looked great together. She did not look a bit out of place. Heat prickled at the back of her eyes as she realized she was not out of her league with Nic at all. They had their own league. She definitely belonged right next to him and she knew in her heart there was no place he'd rather be.

He slid his arms through hers and rested his chin on her shoulder. "What's that look for? Don't you like your necklace?"

She glanced down at the gorgeous stone. "Yes, of course, I'm sorry. It's lovely. Thank you."

"It almost matches your eyes. The next one will."

"You don't have to buy me jewelry."

He grinned, pressing a quick kiss to her cheek. "That's why I like doing it."

She turned and wound her arms around his neck. "Thank you," she said again. "Are you sure you're ready for dinner with the parents?"

"As long as we're together, Lizzie, I'm ready for anything."

EPIL☺GUE

Nic managed to slip into the lecture hall unnoticed. He'd tried to do it before but Lizzie had seen him walk in. She'd stopped mid-sentence and ended the class early. This time she had no idea he was even in town. He'd come back two days early so he could surprise her by flying her to Hawaii in time to see Stefan run the Ironman.

Since they would be in Hawaii, Nic had another surprise for her but he wasn't sure if he could wait until they landed.

He sat down in the back row and watched her in action. He'd thought he'd been prepared for this. He thought he could handle it but he almost didn't recognize the woman standing at the base of the lecture hall, scribbling on her tablet without looking up at the number and equations that appeared on the overhead.

Nic had never considered himself a slouch, but the things Lizzie talked about on rare occasions made no sense to him at all. Now the words flying out of her sounded like Greek. Most of the class was having a hard time keeping up but they were as riveted as he was.

She was graphing something called imaginary time. Nic became fascinated by strange things called Wick rotations, Minkowski space vs Euclidean, special relativity, and all sorts of thing she couldn't keep up with without his head exploding.

He'd thought he'd understood how smart she was.

He hadn't had the first clue. They were light years apart. They didn't even function in the same reality. Lizzie was special, brilliant in a way that redefined brilliance. Gifted.

Amazing.

She was his.

Lizzie was the center of his universe. He wanted to spend the rest of his life orbiting all that dazzling fire and light.

She turned to ask for questions, then spotted him.

Lizzie turned, caught her breath and found Nic Maretti right in her line of sight. That slow sexy smile was impossible to look away from. He was always so sure of himself and once again, he owned the room.

Now warm brown eyes stared back at her, completely engaged in her world. All those beautiful hollows and angles now had an easy going side to them. He was relaxed and happy and he was hers.

"Class dismissed," she said without looking away from him. Her eyes never left his as the students filed out of the room. She folded her arms across her chest and waited until the last student was gone. "If only I had a ruler." She sighed.

Even from the distance she could see him tense up. His bottom lip dropped and she knew his heart rate had increased. He wanted her. In the worst way. But knowing him like she did now, it wasn't enough. She wanted him more.

She pushed the wire-rimmed glasses up her nose. "I hope you got your homework finished."

"I may need some help with it."

"Oh, really?"

He stretched one long arm across the back of the desk next to him then opened his hand.

Lizzie faltered and for a moment she thought she saw a small black box in his upturned palm.

"It's a test," he said simply.

"Nic…"

"It's yes or no, not a discussion question."

"But…"

He tossed the box in the air and caught it as he stood up.

"No." She took a quick step back, panic slicking through her.

"No?" His head snapped back. A heartbeat later he was coming down the stairs as quickly as she was backing up. "No?"

She shook her head. "You can't do that here. It's all wrong. There's supposed to be candles and violins and…"

He opened the box and a pair of gorgeous diamond earrings winked up at her. Lizzie's heart stopped and fire roasted across her face as she realized her mistake. Nic snapped the box shut.

"Oops, wrong box." He grinned.

"Not funny." She pushed against his chest. He didn't move, just grinned at her. This sense of humor was a new thing for him. So far it was a complete fail for Lizzie.

"It was a little funny." He dropped the box back in his pocket and pulled out a long slim box that obviously held a bracelet. "Try this one."

"Stop it with the jewelry already."

"Okay, then close your eyes."

"What?" She looked up in confusion.

"You really have a problem with following directions, don't you?"

"You didn't think so a few nights ago." She smiled sweetly at him.

"Close your eyes," he grumbled.

"Fine." She huffed and shut her eyes.

"We're on the fly bridge." His voice was raspy and he had to clear his throat to continue. "Drinking some ridiculously sweet champagne and I'm feeding you strawberries."

"Mmmm." She smiled at the images unfolding in her mind and snuggled against his chest. "Chocolate covered strawberries?"

"Yes, with the tuxedos," he added impatiently.

"What am I wearing?" She tilted her head back but didn't open her eyes.

His frustrated sigh made her smile. "Nothing. You're naked."

Her eyes flew open. "That's not true. I would be wearing something fabulous and my crystal Jimmy Choos."

"You were wearing a fabulous dress but I ripped it off you a few minutes ago. You still have on the shoes. Now can I finish?"

Lizzie nodded, she would ask for details on the dress later. "Yes, please."

She closed her eyes without having to be told. She bit her lip to keep from laughing when he muttered something in Italian she had no need to translate.

"Then what?"

He took her hand and it was hard to keep her eyes closed because she wanted to throw her arms around him and kiss him.

"I give you my grandmother's ring. The diamond has been in my family over two hundred years."

"I'm not going to wear it."

"Yes, you are. I slide it onto your finger and say, 'Elizabeth Hope Sellers, will you marry me?'"

She opened her mouth but he cut her off. "And you say yes."

She pouted and her shoulders slumped but she kept her eyes closed.

He definitely didn't sound irritated when he said, "I promise to love you for the rest of my life."

She had to squeeze her eyes tight to keep the tears from escaping. They did anyway.

"Is that what you want?"

She nodded. "Eventually."

She opened her eyes long enough to kiss him, then her eyelids were fluttering shut. The kiss was lazy and sweet and she never wanted it to end. When he raised his head, she smiled at him. "You're not giving me a two hundred year old ring. I'll be terrified I'd lose it."

"This is not up for discussion."

"I won't wear it."

"You will," he promised her. "It's expected. You're marrying the De Santis heir, remember?"

She huffed and folded her arms across her chest, and fought off a smile. "You can't have everything."

He shook his head in defeat, kissed her quickly. "I already have everything, Lizzie."

He pulled a small gray box out of his other pocket. "I was going to wait until after the race, but I can't…" He opened the box and Lizzie's heart stopped again. For real this time.

"Are you sure I'm not dreaming?"

"If you are, please, don't wake up."

Too stunned to move, she couldn't take her eyes off the stone as he took it from the box and slid it on her fingers.

"It feels a little loose," he said and started to slip it back off.

Lizzie made a fist and jerked it back.

Nic grinned. "So you do like it."

"Shut up," she whispered, looking at the ring again. The brilliant cut diamond in the square setting was flanked by smaller round diamonds. It was a classic engagement ring from the 1950s and it was everything she could have ever wanted in a ring. "It's gorgeous, but it's not two hundred years old."

"No, the diamond is millions of years old, but it has only belonged to the De Santis family for the last two hundred. My grandfather had it made into an engagement ring for my grandmother. I know you like everything midcentury modern and—"

"I love it, but—"

"I know it's too soon, Lizzie, but I want our relationship to be clear to our families."

"You mean my father?"

"Yes, but also Andreas. All of them. I'm tired of the drama. I don't want you distracted. I know how important your work is, Lizzie, and we can have a long engagement, wait until after you've finished school to get…" he paused as he heard himself. Lizzie bit back a laugh.

"Married?" she finished for him.

"Yeah." He grinned. "There's no rush."

"Nic." She slid her arms around his middle. He sounded nervous and Nic Maretti nervous was wrong on so many levels. "You do know you're just as important to me, right? If I had to choose between you and my work I would—"

"I would never ask you to choose," he inserted quickly.

She nodded, her vision blurring. "That's the reason I choose you."

Nic did take Lizzie to Italy. They went at Christmas and stayed through the New Year. Lizzie loved it so much she decided she wanted to get married in the village church where generations of the De Santis family had been wed.

On the first Sunday after Advent the following year, on an unseasonably warm day, Lizzie walked with Nic to the old church and they were married in a quiet ceremony with family and a few friends.

Lizzie's mom, Jen, Pam and Nic's aunt planned the reception to end all receptions. There were Christmas trees, fresh flowers, and ribbons everywhere. Even a new crèche had been constructed with live animals from De Santis Farms to entertain all the children. There was a huge reception at the De Santis Estate. Jen had made a traditional Italian Wedding cake so tall they almost needed a ladder. There was food and wine and family and friends.

The Bride and Groom didn't notice a single detail. All they could see was each other. After their first dance as man and wife, Nic reluctantly released her so she could dance with her father.

"One dance," Nic warned Mac.

"Boy," Mac warned Nic, but he was smiling, "do not start with me—"

"One dance."

"I sure like my new son-in-law, Lizzie," Mac said as Nic walked away and she danced with her father. "Thank you, baby girl. Best Christmas present ever."

"Because he gave you a seat on the board?"

"Yep," Mac shamelessly admitted. Andreas Maretti had retired days before the first board meeting Mac had decided to attend. They hadn't heard much from him, but Lizzie was pleased Claudia had flown over with Angie and Rogan for the wedding.

"What did your father say?" Nic asked her later when they boarded the helicopter waiting to take them to Lake Como.

"He liked his Christmas present."

"What did we give him this year?"

"A trip to Italy."

He didn't believe her but he let the subject drop. Lizzie had learned the difference between Nic's fishing trawler and Nic's yacht on a previous trip. She'd wanted to spend their honeymoon night on the yacht despite the wintery cold. Lake Como and Bellagio were as beautiful in December as they were in summer. She was starting to get used to the way Nic lived but she promised herself she would never take Nic or his lifestyle for granted.

They cuddled on the deck under warm faux furs and watched the stars come out. They drank champagne, ate strawberries and pretended they were in Key Largo when he kissed her.

"Did we really—"

"Get married?" He lifted his head to see her expression.

She nodded.

He held up his hand so she could see the platinum ring on his finger. "Yes. Why? Are you panicking?"

"Maybe," she admitted. She leaned into him, winding her arms around his chest and pressing her face to his chest. "But only because I'm worried you might be upset I'm not a virgin."

Nic's laughter echoed through the cool night air. She drank up the sound, although she was used to it by now since it was a daily occurrence. It was another thing about Nic she would never take for granted.

His arms tightened around her. "I didn't know I could feel like this, Lizzie."

"Loved?" She hadn't known she could love anyone so much. She loved him more every day.

He shook his head, his voice tight with emotion. "No, *bella*, I feel like I'm home."

She snuggled in tighter, holding him close. "Always."

He kissed the top of her head. "I love you, you know. Don't ever doubt it. Not for a second."

She smiled at him and took a deep breath, saying the words Angie had patiently taught her. "Nic, *ti amerò per sempre.*"

I will love you forever.

She got that slow sexy smile despite her horrible accent. "Do you make love in Italian too?" he asked.

Lizzie laughed as he pulled her on top of him. She braced her hands on his shoulders and leaned down to trace the line of his jaw with her tongue. "I don't know. Let's find out."

Thank you for reading Solving for Nic. I sincerely hope you enjoyed it. Reviews are critical for self-published writers, so if you enjoyed this book, please consider leaving a review somewhere, Amazon, Barnes and Noble, Goodreads, etc. It really does make a difference on getting a book noticed. So your input and help will be very much appreciated.

Find me Online:

http://www.twitter.com/callahanlexxie
http://www.facebook.com/lexie.callahan
http://www.pinterest.com/lexcallahan
http://www.lexxicallahan.com
http://www.goodreads.com/LexxiCallahan

Jared's book is coming in 2015

Southern Style Series Cast of Characters

The Sellers Family

Mac and Nadine Sellers: Stefan and Lizzie's parents. Raised Jen after her parents died.

Stefan Sellers: Long-distance athlete, control freak, so in love with his wife Jen Taylor Sellers it's embarrassing.

Lizzie Sellers: Brilliant mathematician but doesn't like for people to know it. She's had a crush on Nic Maretti since she met him at Angie and Rogan's wedding.

Ben Rogan: His mother and Nadine Sellers' mother are distantly related. One of eleven siblings, Rogan won a football scholarship to the private school Stefan attended. The Sellers pretty much raised Rogan too. He and Stefan have been best friends since they beat each other up in fifth grade.

The Taylor Family

Rob and Michelle Taylor: Killed in a car accident 10 years earlier.

Robert Taylor, Jr.: Also killed in a car accident. Was engaged to Madlyn Robicheaux.

Jen Taylor Sellers: Daughter and only survivor of Taylor Family. Heir to Taylor Family Trust and half of Sellers Taylor International, Jen has loved Stefan all her life. She does crazy things with sugar and opens a bakery in the French Quarter with Jared Marshall when they get back from pastry school in Paris.

The Robicheaux Family

Judge Winston Robicheaux: The notorious hanging judge of Louisiana. Lots of powerful friends, rumors of ties to Gulf Coast organized crime. Also has ties to Oil Tycoon Andreas Maretti.

Madlyn Robicheaux: Judge's granddaughter. She was engaged to Robert Taylor, Jr. when he died in a car accident.

Robbie Robicheaux: Madlyn and Robert Taylor Jr's son.

The Marshall Family

Jared Marshall: Rock god, baker, reluctant attorney. He and Jen met in cooking school, went to pastry school together in Paris and returned to New Orleans to open a bakery. He and his best friend Adam Granger have a band called Sugar Coma. He went to law school to make his parents happy but that turned out to be more complicated than he expected.

Grant Marshall: Jared's other brother. Head of the family law firm now. Used to work for Judge Robicheaux. The exact opposite of Jared, he's conservative, cautious and has no idea how to have a good time.

The Maretti Family

Andreas Maretti: Andreas is business rival of Mac Sellers. Friends with Judge Robicheaux.

Claudia Maretti: Andreas' second wife.

Angie Maretti Rogan: Andreas and Claudia's daughter. Married to Ben Rogan.

Nic Maretti: Andreas' son from a previous marriage. Heir to the Italian De Santis fortune. He is a silent partner in Stefan and Rogan's Real Estate Development Company. Madlyn introduced Nic to Stefan and Rogan shortly after Hurricane Katrina. Rogan also met Angie that same night.

Pam: Nic's executive assistant. They've been best friends since they met in the principal's office in middle school. She runs his company, consoles his exes and generally gives him a hard time. She's in a long-term relationship with Stacey and they have two children.

Stefan's fraternity brothers

Elliot Carter: Local chef/owner of Bistro Lagniappe.

Jackson Napier: Former LSU football player, now NOPD about to make detective. He and Elliot Carter have been in a long-term relationship since college.

Other characters

Adam Granger: Other founding member of Jared's band Sugar Coma. Brilliant musician and well respected in the New Orleans music scene. When he's not playing with Sugar Coma at Trick's, he can likely be found playing in local clubs in the Marigny or Treme.

Alexander Volikov: Crazy Russian trying to drill for oil off the coast of Cuba. He contracts with Sellers Taylor International for construction materials for his deep water wells.

Trick: Owner of Trick's, a biker bar slash dance club on the edge of the French Quarter and member of Legion MC. Oh, wait, you haven't met Trick yet...

EXCERPT FROM THE FALL OF THE RED QUEEN

"Have you lost your mind?"

Jared Marshall pushed up from the chair he was draped across in Grant's office. There was no way he could've heard his older brother right. Maybe his hearing really was going after too many too loud gigs at Trick's.

"We need her." Grant said calmly as he tapped a pen absently against the small notebook that he always kept handy.

"Yeah." Jared snorted. "In jail."

If Grant kept tapping that pen, Jared was going to snap. He forced himself to slump back in the chair and ignore the uneven tapping. Grant had no rhythm.

"Do you want to take down Judge Robicheaux or not?" Grant asked.

"You know I do." Anger curled up in his gut again, and angry wasn't a natural state for Jared. He resented the hell out of the fury that'd been eating away since the old man had threatened Jen Taylor...no, make that Jen Sellers. Mrs. Stefan Sellers.

Jared wanted to puke.

"Madlyn was a partner in her grandfather's law firm. She has access to all of their files and we need those before he posts bond."

"What makes you think she'll even consider letting me...oh, hell no!"

"C'mon, Jared, you can sweet talk a woman into anything. It's your superpower. Put it to good use for a change."

"Fuck. You."

Grant ignored him, and continued on with that patient, lawyer tone that drove Jared up the wall. "You don't think you can charm her?"

"What? Like a snake?"

"Bake her a cheesecake."

He folded his arm across his chest and huffed. "Do cobras like cheesecake?"

"She's not that bad."

"I'm not going anywhere near that venomous bitch."

"Not even for Jen?"

Jared flew out of his seat like someone had electrified it. "Cheap shot, big brother. That's a fucking cheap shot."

"Yeah, well, I didn't want to play that card either but this is serious. We probably have seventy two hours before Judge Robicheaux is out on bail and if Madlyn is not on board with us, I'm not sure there's much we can do."

"Fine." Jared dragged his hands through his hair. "But this is the one and only time you pimp me out like this."

"I'm not asking you to sleep with her."

"As if." Jared shivered in revulsion. "My dick would go on strike."

"Look, we need her. I don't like it either but there it is. Convincing her solves several problems. She has high profile clients that will come with her. Nic Maretti for one and I can't begin to explain what that would mean for this firm. She can help us with the case against her grandfather. And we can find out what the hell is going on."

"As long as we overlook the fact that she's psycho?"

"Madlyn Robicheaux is a lot of things, but psycho is not one of them. Stefan and I are convinced she's playing a long game, and we want to know what it is. I'm sure it has to do with Robbie."

"Robbie? She didn't even want him. She signed custody over to that old bastard within hours of having Robbie then went back to college like nothing had happened."

"I don't think it's that simple. Nothing with that family is ever cut and dried." Grant sighed. "Ok, look, you get her to come on board and I'll take on some pro bono cases."

Jared perked up immediately. "Any that I want? Not just the ones you think will help your future political career?"

Grant's normal bland expression went dark. There were very few buttons to push on his older brother but their parents' obsession with Grant running for office was one of them. "Ok. Fuck you."

"What?" Jared relaxed back in his seat, jumping up and down on that button as hard as he could. "You're getting close to forty. You need to start thinking about your future in politics."

That stopped the pen tapping. "I am not close to forty."

Jared shrugged, and brushed some nonexistent lent off his shoulder. "Closer than me."

"Well, smartass, if you want to make it to thirty, I suggest you get to snake charming."

***